A Price for Everything

POETRY ALSO BY THIS AUTHOR

Patterns in the Dark 1990
Thinning Grapes 1992

Mary Sheepshanks

A PRICE FOR EVERYTHING

St. Martin's Press
New York

To my daughters and daughter-in-law
Belinda, Susannah, and Alice
with love

This novel is a work of fiction. Names and characters are the product of the author's imagination and any resemblance to actual persons, living or dead, is entirely coincidental.

The organizations *The Brothers of Love* and *Heritage at Risk* are fictional and bear no resemblance to any organizations with similar briefs.

A THOMAS DUNNE BOOK.
An imprint of St. Martin's Press.

Library of Congress Cataloging-in-Publication Data

Sheepshanks, Mary.
A price for everything / by Mary Sheepshanks.
p. cm.
"A Thomas Dunne book."
ISBN 0-312-14394-X
1. Country homes—England—Conservation and restoration—Fiction.
2. Married women—England—Fiction. I. Title.
PR6069.H399P75 1996
823'.914—dc20 96-1736 CIP

First published simultaneously in the United Kingdom, Australia, New Zealand, and South Africa by Random House.

First U.S. Edition: May 1996

10 9 8 7 6 5 4 3 2 1

ACKNOWLEDGMENTS

I would like to thank Hilary Johnson and Elizabeth Buchan for great help and encouragement. Special thanks to Sarah Molloy my agent, and Kate Parkin my editor, for all their kindness, patience and wonderful support, and also to Nicola Sands and everyone in the editorial department of Century who have taken so much trouble over the book.

Grateful thanks to Nigel Forbes Adam, Kitty Tempest (North), John Sutton and various other kind friends for helpful advice – any mistakes will be my own – and special love and thanks to my wonderful family for having faith in me.

Chapter 1

Visitors to Duntan, unless they knew the house well enough to take the little road through the village that wandered down to the church and led to the back drive, turned in at the main entrance off the top road. The gates themselves had long since gone, melted down to help the war effort. After the war there had been so many difficulties keeping the house and estate running that no one had even contemplated replacing them. The stone griffins that sat on top of the pillars from which the gates had hung were still there. They had the look of two pugilists pausing between rounds. One had lost a claw and the other sustained serious injury to its beak, and they gave the impression that hostilities were by no means over.

'Have they been fighting this morning?' asked Birdie, christened Henrietta but seldom called by that name, bouncing about in the back of the car. She always asked the same question at exactly the same place.

'I don't think so, not today.'

'How can you tell?'

Sonia slowed down and changed gear before rattling over the cattle-grid.

'Well they're not out of breath today, and then you see they had such a big battle last week. They're probably tired.' Sonia was not in the mood for storytelling. Tom tried to look aloof and uninterested. He would have died rather than admit that he did not really like the saga of the griffins' battles; that at night, if the wind was howling round the house, the idea that some of the mysterious clangings and bangings might be made by the clash of wings from the two great beasts fighting overhead was a far from comfortable one. It was odd, because it was Birdie who was the nervous one of the family.

From the main road there was no hint that the land fell away so sharply. It came as a surprise, after rounding the first corner in the drive, to see the whole park sloping away on either side. The sight of the great beeches standing so tall and straight that they might have been lowered from the sky to act as plumblines only served to emphasise the steepness of the hill. Halfway down, on a sort of platform above the river, lay the house; then the ground fell away again and the countryside could be seen for miles beyond, stretching into the blue distance.

The house itself was beautiful to look at, but sick within, its perfect proportions and mellow stone showing no signs of the disease that threatened its survival. The stones changed colour with the changing light, so that on wet days it seemed grey as the sky itself, but in brighter weather, when the sun was shining, it took on a yellow colour, as though the light emanated from the stones themselves.

Every time Sonia saw Duntan, the beauty of it struck her anew. She thought she would never get used to it, would never cease to see it with a fresh eye, as she had on her first visit.

The drive curved down to the front door but today Sonia drove through the archway in the wall at the left-hand side of the house, which led into the stable yard. This was partly because it gave the easiest access to the kitchen, but partly because she knew that if she went in at the front she would be faced by two letters which had arrived by that morning's post. They would be lying on the round hall table where she had left them earlier, not feeling strong enough to open them at the time. One she knew contained her bank statement, and though she had a rough idea of what it would reveal she was certainly not anxious for any confirmation. The other letter, equally unwelcome but more of an unknown quantity, was addressed in the spiky, flamboyant writing of her mother-in-law. Sonia had noticed with a sinking heart that it bore a London postmark, though she had thought her to be at a safe distance in New York; this raised ominous possibilities of an impending visit. In any case, any communication from that quarter always heralded trouble and she decided that she was still not ready to face reading it. The thought of unloading the shopping from the back of the car seemed an unusually inviting prospect as a delaying tactic.

On this particular morning, Sonia staggered along the passage, her arms full of precariously balanced objects. Birdie ran behind her, fielding oranges that had burst from their bag and were rolling over the uneven stone flags, but Tom had vanished, as he was apt to do when help was required.

'I'm sorry we've been so long,' said Sonia, dumping her first load on the scrubbed wooden table in the middle of the kitchen, 'but the supermarket was ghastly this morning and the trolleys had a conspiracy and would only go round and round, and they'd altered all the shelves again so everything was in a different place.'

Minnie, flour to the elbows, sniffed disparagingly. 'I never did hold with those places. Now in the old days, Mr Moss used to call on your granny regular in his white overall, take an order and deliver it on Wednesdays, and then he used to come into the kitchen, get a nice cup of tea from Mrs Barrett and she'd tell his fortune, after, in the leaves. Proper tea it was then, too, not like all this sawdust in silly little bags.' And she looked scornfully at the super-economy box of tea bags Sonia had just unpacked.

'But Min, she couldn't have told his fortune *every* Wednesday. It wouldn't have changed often enough.' Birdie loved to hear about the old days when Minnie had started in service.

'Every Wednesday.' Minnie was firm. 'A lot can happen in a week. Why, one day she saw *great changes* in Mr Moss's cup, and the following Friday Mr Moss went home and found Mrs Moss dead as a doornail on the rag rug by the fire. You'd never learn that from a tea bag.'

'Just as well perhaps.' Sonia staggered in with a last carboard box of groceries. 'If you've got the kettle on, Min darling, I'd love a nice safe mug of Nes, and don't you go peering in it for impending disasters. There's a letter from Lady Rosamund in the hall, and that's more than enough to be going on with.'

'That one,' said Minnie darkly, 'she spells trouble like an east wind causes liver chills. You head her off, Sonia, or we'll none of us have a minute's peace.'

'Don't you like Granny then?' asked Birdie, helping herself to a dollop of raw pastry.

'I wouldn't presume to air my views,' said Minnie mendaciously, her voice grown suddenly refined. 'Now take your fingers out of the bowl, Birdie, or by shots you'll have a lead-lined stomach as'll give you a pain before lunch. Shall I put these things away, Sonia, or will you? I thought you wanted to paint this morning.'

'No, I'll do them. I'll just go and read the post first. I'll paint when I've cleared up in here.'

Even as she said it, she asked herself why she should so often allow the jobs that she did not want to do to stand in the way of the one job she really did want to do. Minnie would have been quite happy to put everything away on her own, would probably have quite enjoyed doing it, whereas to Sonia it was just a chore, and an unwelcome one at that. In her heart she knew it was largely a fear of failing that held her back. 'Sonia's so gifted, you know. She was a promising artist before she married Archie.' It was pleasant to hear people say that and to rest on this half-earned reputation with no further effort. 'Isn't she marvellous? So talented herself and yet she copes with all those children and that huge great house and all Archie's demands as well, but of course you know it's a wonderful marriage.' Sonia wondered how soon it would be before the cracks that were starting to appear in her marriage would become as obvious as the cracks in the house.

There were in fact three letters on the hall table. The bank statement Sonia decided to ignore, to put off opening it until she felt stronger, but the letter from her mother-in-law might require action and could not be left, so she thrust her finger into the gap in the envelope and tore it open. Archie opened all his letters with an ivory paperknife, slitting them open neatly at the top. He infuriated the children at Christmas by untying the knots on string and ribbon instead of pulling the wrappings off anyhow and diving straight in. It was always possible to tell whether he or Sonia had opened a letter. Sonia read the one before her with a sinking heart:

Darling Sonia,

I have been thinking so much about the difficulties which you and Archie are facing, with all the decisions that must soon be taken about the future of the house. As you know, I can't help feeling involved in any troubles that concern you both, and it seems that I may really be able to be of great help in this matter – you might say I have received Guidance! I had intended to stay in the States with Martha this summer, but I have no intention of being selfish when you may need me, and have therefore decided to come over to England. Later on I may rent a flat in London – at the moment we are staying with dear Mimi – but I think Martha could do with some good country air after the long New York winter, and I have much to tell you, *so I thought perhaps we would come down to Duntan for a little visit – perhaps even base ourselves with you for the summer??! I long to see the darling children, and it will be a joy to be of* real *use to you both. Do ring me, darling, at this number and we can have a cosy chat about plans. Dearest love – R.*

What can the old bitch be up to? wondered Sonia. Guidance – unselfish – country air? Oh no. This is all I need.

The third letter was from the Heritage at Risk association, which offered an advisory service to the owners of historic houses. Sonia had written to ask for their expert help, though Archie had been against it, convinced of the pointlessness of pouring money they would have to borrow into a building he felt could never be anything but a liability. The letter thanked her for her enquiry and proposed that a Simon Hadleigh should pay a visit to Duntan as soon as possible to assess the state of the house, the potential of the property and alternative schemes for its future. She supposed she would have to show this letter to Archie. It was, after all, his house, though already she felt a fierce possessiveness about it, and knew in her heart that she would only be prepared to accept advice about its future that tallied with her own existing ideas, and which somehow made possible her passionate desire that they should go on living there.

It was strange to her that Archie should not feel this way too, but his interest lay in the land, in the estate rather than the house, although it was his forebears who had built and lived in it for more than two hundred years. He was by nature so much more conventional than she was that she had expected him to wish to cling on to the house above all else, and it had come as a surprise to her that he would be so easily prepared to let it go. It was nothing to do with pride in the idea of living in so grand a building that made her wish to remain in possession. It was rather that the house itself seemed to possess her. It was a love affair, and like many love affairs, it was inconvenient.

Just to keep the house watertight would be impossible without spending enormous sums of money on the roof, and they were only just beginning to be aware of the extent of other problems. They had known, of course, during his grandmother's lifetime that the house was growing increasingly shabby, but as with the old lady herself, the air of fading elegance had been part of the charm. After her death, however, it seemed as if some new evidence of damp rot, dry rot or mould was always coming to light, as though the battle of the griffins, a product of her own imagination, was becoming a menacing reality. It was as if some awful guerrilla warfare were going on inside the house, and it was not possible to anticipate from which direction the next offensive would appear. It was not a pleasant thought.

She stuffed the letters into the pocket of her jeans so that she could show them to Archie herself, choosing her moment rather than leaving them open on the table for him to discover when he came in for lunch. She wanted to stop him from hardening his opinions before she had any chance to influence him, though she was uneasily aware that her power to influence him was not what it had once been, that nowadays his admiration for her was too often eroded by dissatisfaction.

Chapter 2

When Sonia returned, Cassie, the youngest of their four children, was under the kitchen table in a cardboard box, reclining on a pile of tea towels taken from Minnie's washing basket while Birdie crawled round on all fours alternately mooing, baaing and making a noise like the bray of a donkey. Cassie wore her white sunhat but was otherwise stark-naked. She looked very comfortable and rather grand, and from time to time waved graciously out of the box like the Queen in the Ascot procession.

'Come along then, Cassie,' said Minnie. 'Time for rest.'

'No rest,' said Cassie uncompromisingly, her small figure stiffening with resistance and her feet, which were hanging over the side of the box, beginning to drum warningly.

'She's Little Lord Jesus in the manger,' explained Birdie, 'and I'm the Ox and the Ass and the Sheep, and I'm worshipping her.'

'Whatever next?' asked Minnie. 'Well she'll just have to go and be Jesus in her bed,' and she pulled the manger from under the table and held out the discarded clothes invitingly. Cassie, clutching her hat as if it represented the last remnants of decency in a naughty world, started to scream.

'She wants me to go on worshipping her,' said Birdie, who often acted as Cassie's interpreter and despite being three years older always had to play the supporting role in their games. 'And her hat's a halo like in the window in church. Do let her stay a bit longer, Min. She loves being worshipped.'

'I dare say she does – it must be very pleasant – but some of us haven't time for this sort of fool carry-on. Now come along young lady, up to Bedfordshire.' Minnie scooped up the loudly protesting Jesus and bore her bellowing out of the kitchen.

'It's all spoilt now. It won't ever be the same again. It was a lovely game,' said Birdie tragically.

'Oh darling, I am sorry. I do understand, but she gets so grumpy if she doesn't have a rest. Let me shove these things away, and then how would you like to come with me and do some painting?' Sonia looked at Birdie's disconsolate figure, her foot gently kicking the leg of the kitchen table. Not given to the robust rages of her brother and sisters, Birdie was sometimes the more difficult to deal with.

'Really paint, in your studio?'

Sonia nodded. This was a real olive branch, a special treat, because the studio was the one private place in the house where even her children were only welcome by express invitation. Birdie brightened up at once.

Sonia had her studio upstairs in what had once been the sewing room. The deep fitted drawers with open shelves above them where linen requiring mending had once been piled made ideal storage space. Archie's grandmother had installed a double sink there for Sonia so that she could wash her brushes and generally clean up, although it seldom looked as if much cleaning went on. It always amazed Archie, himself so meticulous, that out of the chaos of Sonia's studio such immaculate finished pictures could be produced. He considered her untidy and disorganised in the rest of her life too, and could never understand how she could leave such a trail of chaos behind her and yet manage to achieve a degree of perfection in much that she undertook. Half-finished canvases leant against the walls and pots of paint sat about on the floor, making it hazardous to walk about without getting paint on your clothes. Door handles and light switches were always coated with different colours where Sonia had too hastily opened a door or turned on the light with a painty hand. Along the shelves were vases and jars, useful for keeping fresh any flowers or leaves she was using for the paintings of plants and foliage that were her speciality. What set her pictures apart from an artistic point of view were the strange, surrealist backgrounds in which she set the precisely painted botanical material. It lifted them above the ordinary and merely decorative, and had very much excited a few critics in her early days, especially at her degree exhibition. But somehow her promise had not been quite fulfilled, and she was miserably aware that her contemporaries at the Slade, no more gifted than she herself was, had gone on to make names for themselves while she had let her first advantage slip. She knew that talent alone is not enough, and that so far she had lacked the drive and determination that were also necessary if she was to reach her potential as an artist. She also knew that had she been perfectly content to find fulfilment as a wife and mother the other would not have mattered, but this split within herself often caused her to be restless and unsatisfied so that she felt herself deficient in both roles.

To begin with, she had kept the studio strictly as a place for work when she was at Duntan, but as the dissatisfactions of her marriage loomed larger she was aware that it was becoming something more, and that she was beginning to bring much-loved books and objects in there, as a dog will take a bone to its basket. She had started to spend more of her time in the studio, doing things she would once have done elsewhere in the house, while actually painting less and less. Once in there with the door closed, it was as if, along with the rest of the household, she could also shut off a part of herself.

It was this feeling that there was a part of Sonia he couldn't reach, which shut him out, that so tantalised Archie. In their early married days she had sometimes tried to let him in, to share her deepest feelings and longings with him, but he had been unable to enter her private world and had shied off like a frightened horse. He very rarely came into the studio now, for nothing was more calculated to set them on edge with each other. Too often she had made him feel an unwelcome intruder. Lately he had made her feel like a spoilt child who spent too much time selfishly playing alone with a private toy. A telephone had now been installed in the studio, the painty marks on the receiver in their bedroom having become more than Archie could bear. Telephone bills were a cause of friction between them.

'You shoot – I telephone,' Sonia would tell him crossly when she had just had a long gossip with a friend in the middle of the morning and been interrupted by him. Now that he was no longer in the army and was self-employed farming and running the estate, he was too often under her feet and she felt a victim of the old adage 'For better, for worse – but not for lunch'.

The children adored the studio for precisely the reasons that Archie disliked it. Because they were so sure of Sonia, knew that she loved them, it represented no kind of threat, and had the irresistible appeal of all things not easily available. Polly, in fact, drew quite well and showed genuine promise, but because by nature she required a response, whether of praise or criticism, Sonia could never really get on well with her own work when Polly was with her. Tom, who was no artist, would buzz around his mother like a mosquito, constantly picking things up and putting them down, so that in the end she would find herself weakly agreeing to go and play ping-pong or tennis, or to accompany him on some armed expedition, for Tom was a man of action. Of all the children, he needed to be occupied the most, lacking the ability of the girls to withdraw into a totally imaginary world.

Birdie was the most peaceful, and was soon happily occupied with drawing paper and crayons. She did not at the moment show any great artistic promise, but could happily create for herself an alternative to the sometimes rather threatening world in which she lived. In Birdie's private world mothers were totally occupied with their children's welfare. Fathers led unadventurous existences and never went hang-gliding or hunting or raced boats as her own father did. Nobody ever quarrelled. In particular the fathers and mothers never quarrelled with each other. Her drawings were mostly of stiff ladies wearing curious triangular skirts, to the bottom of which their stout legs appeared to be pinned. These rigid ladies, sporting overdecorated floral hats on their round heads, invariably pushed prams or carried vegetable-marrow babies in their arms. Looking at these strip cartoons of uneventful family life, Sonia was always guiltily aware of how far Birdie's real family must fall short of her ideal. She had written a poem at school, currently stuck on the fridge, that reproached Sonia every time she read it:

Mother mother meek and mild
Love thee thou thy tiny child.
Comfort it in every way
And LOVE IT LOVE IT ALL THE DAY.

'You can't say "thee thou thy",' Polly had said scornfully. 'It's not grammar.' But grammar or not, Birdie had obstinately refused to change it, even though Polly could make her cry by mouthing it at her silently as though speaking to someone who could lip-read. Sonia had had to ban a satirical version of the poem produced by Tom, which went:

Birdie Birdie wet and weepy
Love thee thou thy crawly creepy
Keep it in a bed of slime
To slither slither all the time.

As Birdie was known to have a horror of worms, slugs, snakes and all things that go upon their bellies, this was considered the acme of schoolroom wit. Sonia thought it pretty funny herself, but the torrent of hurt tears produced by the author of the original poem was too much to be allowed. Poor Birdie had been born with several skins too few.

For about an hour they worked away in silence. Sonia was trying to get enough paintings together for a small exhibition in the late summer at a local gallery that had recently opened, and found the discipline of having a date to work for helpful in combating her own talent for procrastination.

Because she did not feel in the right mood for creating dream worlds on paper, which required time, it being all too easy to lose the spark of inspiration if the creative process were interrupted, she decided to concentrate instead on finishing a delicate watercolour of 'Angel's Tears' narcissi that she had begun the day before. If she left it any longer the flowers might have opened up too much. Perhaps later their name would give her inspiration for the surroundings in which to place them. As her eye was more involved than her imagination in this occupation, it gave her a chance to think.

Why had she married Archie? Certainly she had always been enslaved by the magic of the house, its feeling of permanence so different from the army quarters that had been home throughout her own itinerant childhood, but she could honestly say that the knowledge that Archie would one day inherit it had not entered into her calculations. She had been very attracted to him at the time, but marriage had also seemed a way out of her self-doubts, a postponing of the decision to go all out for her career. Archie had been a subaltern in her father's regiment. As the General's daughter she had met a lot of young officers, many of whom had been attracted by her vivacity and wit and intrigued by her talent and lack of convention, and Archie had been no exception. She had mistaken his ready social laughter for a sense of the ridiculous similar to her own, and because he had seemed so delighted by everything she said, had thought they shared a point of view. His grandmother, who was fond of him in a clear but not uncritical way, had tried to warn her about their possible incompatibility but she had not listened.

Archie was not really without a sense of humour, but it was as though his rather bleak childhood had suppressed it and he needed her to activate it for him. It was her ability to make him laugh and look at the world through a change of spectacles that had so captivated him in the first place. She had opened a door into a whole new part of himself he had not known existed, and he had been entranced. But now, having left the army and come to live at Duntan, the spell no longer seemed to be working so well. As she painted, and the small flowers sprang to life on the paper in front of her, Sonia agonised over her marriage, but could reach no conclusions.

When Archie came in for lunch Sonia could tell immediately that he was not in the right frame of mind to be amenable.

At forty he looked in his prime, sleek, energetic and, except with his wife, outwardly very assured; if the leather belt he wore today caused the flesh around the top of his trousers to bulge very slightly, still nobody could possibly call him fat. His fresh-coloured face might one day become florid, but that day had not yet arrived. He smelt a shade too strongly of expensive aftershave from Trumper's, but gave the impression of someone who was in no way above tough manual work. It could be assumed that when he did it, it would be because he would not ask a subordinate to do anything of which he himself was not capable.

He had acquired a set of beliefs early in life that until he met Sonia he had never seriously questioned, and he still felt very much safer if keeping them in a locked drawer. He liked fair play, honest dealings, and a God who was available by appointment at eleven o'clock on Sunday mornings in the Church of England. He was kind, competent, and capable of great devotion, though Sonia was uneasily beginning to be aware that there might be a limit as to how much cold water he was prepared to put up with, either poured over him by his wife or leaking through the roof of his ancestral home.

'Your mother,' said Sonia, 'is coming to stay.'

'Oh, jolly good,' said Archie. Loyalty to family was part of his creed, no matter how deeply the thorns of their presence might penetrate the flesh.

'Your mother,' said Sonia, 'wants to come and live with us for the summer to help us with our difficulties with the house. Your mother has had Guidance.'

'Guidance from who?'

'Presumably from Above. She doesn't specify. Could be the Pope or the Archangel Gabriel. More likely to be Lucifer or some new man.'

Archie looked a little disconcerted.

'Oh well, if she wants to come, of course she must. This is her home, too, in a way.'

'Like hell! If she comes, then it's as a guest. I'm not having her coming the hostess over me in my own house. But I suppose we'll have to have her for a bit. Better to know what she's up to, anyhow, scheming old devil. At least she's good for a laugh if one's feeling tough enough.'

In fact, Sonia enjoyed her mother-in-law's company a good deal more than Archie did. She couldn't quite resist her when she was actually there, whereas Archie, who always defended her in her absence, frequently found her presence trying in the extreme. Minnie always said that Cassie took after her, which boded an eventful future.

Archie had been brought up mostly by his grandmother. His mother, Lady Rosamund, ever a tiger for new experiences, had quickly become bored by her solid tweedy husband and the heir she had provided, and when Archie was two had left them both for the first time to join an ashram in India. The rigours of the spiritual quest, however, had not been to her taste for very long, and she had been sidetracked by a rajah who owned strings of polo ponies and ropes of pearls. Eventually she had returned to Archie's father, plus the pearls, but minus the ponies and the lover, to take up the reins of her life in English Society, occasionally dazzling her young son with her presence but mostly leaving his upbringing to her mother-in-law and a succession of nannies.

An affair with a rich Italian count had finally proved too much for her bemused husband to accept and had steered her through the divorce courts towards a spell in a castello near Florence. During this interlude she had become very Italian and more Catholic than the Pope. Her first marriage had not counted, she said, since it had only taken place in the Church of England, while the Rajah had been just a small sin of the flesh, on a par, it was to be presumed, with an overdose of Charbonnel and Walker chocolates. Conveniently enough, her second marriage later turned out not to have counted either: because of her divorce it had not been conducted with the full rights of Mother Church and was not therefore a true spiritual union, leaving her splendidly free to embark on her next alliance with an American banker, by whom she had had a child, Archie's half-sister Martha. This marriage had lasted surprisingly well until a couple of years ago when, perhaps unable to stand the pace of life with Lady Rosamund, despite a diet of bran and polyunsaturated oils, the banker had died.

There could be no doubt that the state of widowhood suited her. The little fleshly sins could now be regarded more in the light of a keep-fit regime, a sort of workout in the gymnasium for the purpose of keeping herself in trim. She also had control of the dollars, which was certainly an advantage. Since Archie's father had been killed in a riding accident during her Italian marriage, she was able to regard herself, if not quite accurately, as twice widowed, a tragic figure. Though she had never actually owned Duntan, she chose, when it suited her, to behave as a sort of Queen Mother, with a right to be consulted about its future.

Through all these storms and flittings, old Lady Duntan had remained, infuriated but amused by her daughter-in-law's career. She had been a not unaffectionate, if somewhat alarming, figure, so determined had she been to instil into him the moral fibre his mother so conspicuously lacked, but she had provided a measure of continuity, and Duntan was the base to which Archie, in truth a lonely little boy, had returned from school or from visits to his mother in various parts of the world.

Since Archie had appeared to take the news of his mother's impending arrival with equanimity, Sonia took the plunge.

'Here's another letter perhaps you should look at.' She flicked the one from Heritage at Risk across the table, backhanded, as the children threw Frisbees. It landed neatly on Archie's side plate. It was an irritating talent of which she was proud.

'Who the hell?'

He read the letter with a look of growing annoyance.

'Look, darling. I'm sorry.' Archie had on his patiently-explaining-for-the-twentieth-time voice. 'We cannot afford to go on living in this house. The fact that you've got hold of some lily-fingered queer who's good at advising people how to spend money they haven't got is not going to make any difference.'

'That's not fair,' said Sonia. 'You haven't even met him. It's free advice. We're not committed.'

'What's lily-fingered queer?' asked Birdie.

'Shirley Gillespie's mother,' said Polly, shovelling macaroni cheese into her mouth and using her parents' argument as a shield to cover her second Coca-Cola, 'says queers are men who like sleeping together.'

The advantage of having Shirley Gillespie as a best friend was that her mother, who lectured in feminine psychology at the university, believed in having *frank open discussions* about the *truth*. There had to be some advantage. Shirley Gillespie was rather a dull little girl, but some of the things her mother told her were absolutely thrilling.

'The art beak at school's a queer,' said Tom. 'We call him Sponge Fingers. Sponge because he drinks, and Fingers because –'

'Yes, well.' Archie gave his children a dissatisfied look. 'If you children got on with your lunch and shut up, your mother and I might be able to have a decent conversation.'

Sonia tried not to laugh, and put on her most wheedling voice.

'Archie, darling, please think about it – just for me. You don't know anything about this chap. He might have a really bright idea.'

'That's what I'm afraid of,' said Archie gloomily. 'Too many god-damn bright ideas. But have it your own way. You usually do. Let him come if you must, but let me make one thing clear: I am not, repeat *not*, selling any land to finance the upkeep of this house. Enough of that has gone on already. You don't begin to realise what the income required just to live here would be, let alone what we'd have to spend to make it all sound in the first place.'

Sound was a favourite word of Archie's, and could be applied alike to houses and horses, politicians and parsons. She wondered if Archie tapped his fellow members on the county council, to which he had just been elected, to see if they rang hollow. She supposed it must be awful for him to have both his wife and his mother so thoroughly unsound.

'And another thing. I do wish you'd realise what a much better lifestyle we could have if we were in the Dial House. What is the point of living in this house and spending the whole time in the kitchen while water pours in everywhere else and ruins the furniture?'

'You don't mean a better lifestyle, you mean a grander one. Fewer rooms but more butlers.'

Birdie started to scrape her bottom lip with her top teeth, and crossed her fingers for safety. The argument was becoming horribly familiar to her, and the macaroni cheese, so lovely and liquid in the dish, seemed to have formed itself into a solid lump somewhere between her ribs.

'Nothing wrong with butlers. Jolly good if you can get 'em.' Archie might have been talking about fruit out of season. 'And while we're on the subject, you might like to get a proper cook lined up before the shooting season starts. If I manage to get all the guns, there'll be endless shooting lunches to be provided. Far too much for you and Minnie to do, and I know you want a bit more time to yourself to get your little exhibition going,' he added kindly.

Sonia started to clear the table.

'Why do you always have to call it my "little exhibition"?' she asked, though she always called it that herself. 'It sounds so patronising.'

'I'm sorry,' said Archie stiffly. 'I was just trying to be helpful. You always say I don't take any interest in your painting. When I do, you bite my head off.'

'Oh well, I'm sorry,' said Sonia, feeling that she had gained her point about the Heritage at Risk appointment. 'No need to get all hot and bothered about it.'

'I am not hot or bothered.'

'Well, you're sweating under your left armpit.' A small dark stain disfigured the broad blue and white stripes of Archie's New and Lingwood shirt. It was a warm April day and he had thrown his regimental blazer over the back of a chair. Furiously he put it on again and glared at Sonia. She shot him a mocking look, which was a mistake because it caused her to catch her toe in a hole in the worn linoleum so that she stumbled and the top two plates from the pile she was carrying to the sink shot off and smashed on the floor.

Inanimate objects sometimes behaved badly with Sonia. The small-boned hands that could wield a paintbrush with such delicacy could have a disastrous effect on china and glass. It seemed unfair that Archie's much larger frame never seemed to collide with occasional tables, and he seldom snapped the stems off wineglasses, or caught his sleeve on doorknobs while carrying cups of coffee.

'Oh bad luck,' said Archie. 'It's a pity we haven't got many of those plates left now.'

'Shirley Gillespie's mother,' said Polly, 'says all aggression has a territorial or sexual root.'

Tom wondered if this was or was not a good moment to ask his father to take him pigeon shooting. Cassie had the kind of enthralled glitter in her eyes that Minnie got when she was watching the all-in wrestling on television.

'Bugger Shirley Gillespie's mother,' said Sonia.

'I think I'm going to be sick,' said Birdie.

Chapter 3

It was a year now since Archie had left the army and six months since his grandmother's death. They had always spent a lot of time at Duntan, had stayed there during his various leaves, and actually lived there when Archie had been stationed at Catterick for two years. They had always known that one day they would live here permanently, and in fact the decision for Archie to leave the army and come to Yorkshire to run the estate and farm had been taken some time ago. When The Dial House, a small and charming house on the estate, had become vacant, old Lady Duntan had offered to retire there, but her doctor had advised that the upheaval might be too great, so Archie would not hear of it. He and Sonia had been trying to decide whether to go and live in it themselves for the time being, though they would need to build on to it, or to go on sharing the Big House with her, when the old lady had suddenly caused the whole situation to be viewed differently by dying.

She was a good age, so it should not have been such a shock, but she had seemed to be as indestructible as they had once thought the house to be. She had been in full possession of her faculties, still walked in the upright fashion of her generation, still supervised the garden and retained an interest in all that went on. She read widely and Sonia had loved discussing books and music with her, and was often surprised by her views, which were by no means always those that might have been expected. The children had adored her, feeling none of the anxiety in her presence that their father had done as a child. She treated them as equals, expected and usually got good behaviour from them, and appeared to pay as much attention to their opinions as she would have done to far more important people. She had no doubt mellowed with the years, and though there were those who feared her sometimes sharp tongue and acerbic wit, she was much loved locally.

She had never sought to change the house as some of her predecessors had done, and yet she had left her mark on it more surely just by living in it than if she had altered the whole house. Her portrait by Lavery, painted when she was a young woman, hung at the top of the stairs; the fine soft leather gloves in which she had expertly pruned the roses still lived in the drawer of the library table in the hall. The pot-pourri that filled the two big *famille verte* vases in the drawing room had been dried and spiced by her, and many of the soft cushions in fine needlepoint scattered about sofas and chairs owed their faded charm to her skilful fingers. Part of the charm of Duntan, to those that fell victim to it, lay in the overflowing clutter that spanned so many generations. A piece of embroidery or an open book left lying on a window seat might just as easily have been put down ten minutes before or abandoned fifty years ago.

Neither Sonia nor Archie had been at Duntan when she died. Archie had gone down to Hampshire to shoot with Bill Bruce, a long-standing and particular friend, and Sonia had seized the chance of a few days in London on her own, doing some of the things she enjoyed so much more without his resigned and restless presence. He had been hurt and disappointed that she had not wanted to go with him, but had reluctantly rung the Bruces and explained that Sonia had to see her mother and that it was her one chance to do some Christmas shopping before the rush started.

'They were very sad but awfully decent about it,' he had said. 'It does rather put their numbers out, you know.'

Sonia had been unrepentant. 'Oh well, I expect Caroline will dredge up some lovely horsy local lady to pair with you. You go and have a lovely time in your way, and I'll have one in mine.'

But she couldn't help secretly wishing that she had a lovely male companion with whom to share her lovely time; someone who had the same interests and who understood her tastes without the need for explanations.

Before they left, Birdie had been unaccountably upset, begging them both not to go away.

'But darling, you're always so happy with Great-Grandmama and Min, and it isn't as if we were taking any of the others,' Sonia had reasoned.

'What's up, Bird?' Archie had asked, putting his arms round her.

'Something awful might happen while you're gone.'

'Oh darling, what could possibly happen?' But Birdie didn't know and refused to be reassured.

There had been an exhibition of Chinese porcelain on at the Blount Gallery. Sonia went to it twice. It was a small collection, so the exhibition was completely digestible, a delicious light meal, as it were, that did not leave her sated and exhausted or feeling that she had tasted nothing properly. There had been a pair of plates of the Yung-cheng period at which she gazed for a long time. The only decoration on the pearl-white porcelain of each plate was a single spray of fruiting peach in *famille rose* enamels. There was a feeling of space and serenity about them that had given her great pleasure and a rare sense of peace. The feeling of peace had remained with her after she had left the little gallery, giving her sufficient detachment to ignore all the expensive luxuries in the shop windows that usually drew her as she walked up Bond Street.

It was one of those clear early November days that seem to hang between summer and winter. There was still warmth in the sun, but the air had a bite to it that menaced colder times ahead. The leaves falling from the plane trees were whirling about in the wind, piling up against the pavement at one moment, and then dispersing again as though they were playing some complicated game and had to go back to base every so often.

When she got off the bus and started to walk down the King's Road, she was still lit by the mood of contentment that had been triggered by the porcelain. She had a feeling of being outside time, of having a breathing space, of being an onlooker at herself, while remaining acutely aware of her own body and of all that was going on around her. She was conscious of the rare physical pleasure of feeling exactly the right temperature. The sun warmed her back, and the wind blowing through her pale hair was exhilarating. She walked briskly, her skirt flaring out from her elegant legs, and felt quite sorry when she reached Radnor Walk, where her mother lived. I will hang on to this moment, she thought; I will do better with my life – be nicer.

She let herself into her mother's house with the spare key, and the whole day, which was to remain so clearly impressed on her memory because of the news that followed, changed.

Her mother was out, but there was a note on the table in the narrow passage that served as a hall. *The children are* all right, she read, and this was heavily underlined, *but will you ring Duntan as soon as you get in? Oh darling, I'm so sorry – I'm afraid it may be bad news. Archie's grandmother has had a fall.*

'Please don't let her die,' she had prayed. 'Don't let her go before I can even say goodbye,' and this had seemed of the utmost importance.

Afterwards, her happy morning had remained vividly in her mind as a sort of benediction, a lull before the storm, but of her long drive north up the motorway, she had very little recollection.

When she arrived home, her prayers had not been answered. Old Lady Duntan was dead.

'I told you and Daddy not to go away. I begged you. I said something awful would happen,' said Birdie, white-faced and reproachful.

Sonia had been overcome with misery. She had not realised how much she had depended on the old lady, how much she would miss her companionship or how much of a buffer she had been between herself and Archie. It might have been her own beloved grandmother who had died, so deeply did she mourn for her, and she became very depressed. After a few months Archie, who had been very sympathetic for a bit, started to find it irritating that she seemed so preoccupied with the past and so unwilling to face the future, or to start planning all the changes he considered inevitable.

For Archie, the six months following his grandmother's death were full of discoveries. He found he had a tremendous feeling for and interest in the land. It went further than pride of possession, though that was certainly there; and it was more than just affection for his home and its surroundings. He became as wrapped up in running the estate as a successful tycoon is involved with his business. He was fascinated by the farm; in the idea of using the land to its fullest potential so that the stock would thrive, fruit would be fruitful, vegetables grown to the maximum advantage and crops cultivated to produce the best possible yield. All the government rules and restrictions were a challenge and he became absorbed in new marketing ideas.

Everything had been allowed to follow a pattern set years before, and though nothing had been exactly neglected, there was still tremendous scope for combining new technology with the best of the traditional ways. The prospect was an inviting one and Archie threw his considerable energy and efficiency into modernising the whole enterprise with huge enthusiasm. The life of a country landowner fitted him like a Savile Row suit. In no time at all he was sitting on endless county committees at the very centre of Yorkshire life.

The discoveries about the house had been less pleasant. It soon became apparent that in this respect things had been very seriously neglected for years. Any money from the farm was immediately swallowed up just keeping the house running, and over the years, several of the let farms and cottages on the estate had been sold to try to keep things afloat. Archie was determined that this should not go on happening. He still thought it could be made into a going concern – but not while the house gobbled up the proceeds.

As the weeks went by it became clear that the whole structure of the house was outworn. The lead on the roof had become porous, and though to the naked eye it looked all right, it seemed to absorb water rather than repel it so that in heavy rain the oak beams became saturated, whilst the lead conduits running through the attics like a network of canals to carry water from the circle surrounding the dome became water-logged and overflowed. There was dry rot and wet rot. Much of the beautiful plasterwork in the rooms was damaged, and the mouldings were in need of repair. Pictures needed cleaning and restoring, carpets and curtains were threadbare, and furniture required expert attention. On top of this, there were death duties to pay. Not enough had been made over.

Sonia discovered in herself a fierce, protective and highly personal love for the house. The more flaws that came to light, the more defensive she felt about it. She was amazed at how often they had stayed in it without noticing how increasingly dilapidated it was becoming. Then she had been aware only of its special atmosphere, and had not noticed all the defects – the flaking paintwork and dark patches on carpets where drips from the ceiling had fallen too often. Now, as she saw them more and more clearly, she became even more conscious of the beauty of the whole. It had always been for her both a place where she felt at home, and the home where she felt most truly herself – a happy house full of flowers and piles of books, where you might meet unexpected people and encounter unusual points of view. The old lady had had a talent for unlikely friendships that had extended far beyond the immediate county neighbours, and Sonia hoped desperately that she could keep this feeling alive and add her own special flavour to it too.

The contents of the house were delightful and, taken together, valuable. But there was no single item of extreme value that could be sacrificed to save the whole. Had there been one very rare picture that could realise a sensational saleroom price, or a unique piece of furniture or porcelain, then it would have been easy, if sad, for them to decide to sell it and put the money towards restoring everything else. There was no such outstanding treasure: just a collection of English country-house possessions, spanning the centuries, that fitted their setting to perfection. A sale of the whole contents of the house would probably fetch a large sum of money, but it would be a pointless exercise, for of what use is a large, empty shell?

Archie was quite certain what they should do: move to the

Dial House and enlarge it, fill it with their favourite pieces, sell the rest and make the smaller house really comfortable and pretty. Duntan itself could then be sold, if a buyer could be found to take on such a large, decaying white elephant. Its size was another difficulty. It was far too big to be lived in as a private house, but possibly not quite big enough to be turned into a hotel, now that the economic climate demanded a minimum number of bedrooms for such a venture to be profitable. It was simply uneconomic for the present times.

Sonia knew that Archie was right; knew they were unbelievably lucky to have another house available, but the saving of the Big House was becoming an obsession with her. Sometimes she could think of nothing else.

The disagreement over the house was becoming the peg on which they both hung the other dissatisfactions and differences between them. It was as though they had found a reason for the warfare that already existed, and having found it, they used it as a cover for everything else.

There was another area in which married life was proving difficult, an arca about which Archie refused to have any sort of discussion, and which undermined their self-confidence and aggravated their aggression. They both blamed themselves, while paradoxically resenting the other for being the cause of the problem. Since leaving the army, Archie had suddenly become impotent, at any rate as far as Sonia was concerned. He had been so appalled when it first occurred that he was unwilling to risk further humiliation, and Sonia, aware that she had often overdone the cold shoulder in the past, but now in need of comfort as well as sex, had felt increasingly isolated and undervalued. Shirley Gillespie's mother may possibly have had a point.

Chapter 4

It was perhaps a good thing that they were going out for the day, since Minnie was taking a few days off and being without help always made Archie feel irritable. It was partly to please him, and partly because she was daunted at the thought of a long spell with Lady Rosamund in the house, that Sonia wrote out an advertisement to put in *The Lady* for a temporary cook for the summer months, stipulating that she was looking for a non-smoker of cordon bleu standards who also loved children and dogs. Not everyone would be prepared to cook over the top of three shih-tzus and two labradors.

Minnie had sniffed in a very expressive way when Sonia had shown her what she was going to put, but had made no other comment. Sonia's heart had sunk.

Minnie's comforting presence, cackling laugh and caustic wit had been part of the children's lives as long as they could remember. She had started work at Duntan when she was fifteen, having spent all her childhood on the estate, where her father had been head keeper, and attended the village school to which Birdie now went. She had married from Duntan – a 'foreigner' who came from the other side of the county – but after her husband's untimely death in his fifties their son had taken on the running of the farm, and though he and his wife pressed her to make her home with them, she had wished to preserve her independence and also to have an occupation to take her mind off her grief. She had gone to work at a hotel in Scarborough, where she had been vastly amused by the customers, and certainly became the life and soul of the place, but her heart had not really been in it.

At this state in her life she had come over to Duntan to visit one of her many relations and had met Archie's grandmother in the post office. Sonia, or young Lady D. as she was called in the village, had just given birth to Polly, and was far from well. It had been a difficult labour, and Sonia had followed this up with a severe attack of pneumonia that had left her exhausted and delayed her from taking the baby out to join Archie, whose regiment was stationed in Germany. It had been old Lady Duntan's bright idea that Minnie might like to accompany Sonia and the baby on the flight to Germany, and perhaps stay for a little to get them settled. She had been with the family, on and off, ever since. They had given her a small cottage on the estate as a place of her own, which she loved, but being of an energetic and gregarious nature she soon got bored if she was there too long. When her own family required her ministrations she was free to go and help them, but for most of the year she stayed with Sonia, a much-loved and vital part of the family. There was not much Minnie did not know about joy or sorrow.

Sonia had always thought Minnie looked as if she had been assembled out of a collection of spare parts, as though her Creator had not wanted to waste anything and had had a lot of perfectly usable limbs left over from other projects that needed using up. Her legs were so bowed that they formed an almost complete circle and might have been moulded to fit round a giant pumpkin, but again, they were not really a perfect match since one was shorter than the other so that she had to have the heel of one shoe built up. It in no way impeded her progress, however, and she scuttled about at great speed with a rolling gait such as sailors are supposed to have. Also, the top joints of her thumbs bent right backwards, which was nothing to do with the rheumatism that made her other fingers knobbly, and was a drawback only when shelling peas, she said.

'Why do they do that?' Tom used to ask, leaning against her knee and waggling her thumbs to and fro.

'It's how the Good Lord made them,' Minnie would answer. 'They've always been like that.'

Her face had a lopsided look, as though it had been taken out of the mould before it had set properly and had slipped sideways, but her blue eyes, soft white hair, clear skin and rosy cheeks came straight from a Frans Hals portrait. The children thought she was beautiful.

Sonia had written two other letters that morning. One was to Simon Hadleigh asking him to come to lunch and give advice as to how they might achieve their joint ambition of continuing to live at Duntan while somehow making it pay for itself. Any suggestions would be welcomed. She had not shown this letter to Archie, only told him casually that she had written it. She had then written what she hoped was a masterly letter to her mother-in-law, asking her to come down for 'as long as is convenient to you and us', but making it clear that Lady Rosamund should feel free to go and visit other friends as they would quite understand that she would want to be independent. She had not commented on the offer of help, but added that they would be delighted for Martha to make her home with them until her return to America. Sonia and her mother-in-law always understood each other perfectly, even if neither acknowledged the fact. The prospect of having Martha around was a cheering one. Martha made Sonia laugh.

Having finished her letters, Sonia remembered that she was supposed to do the church flowers that weekend. When she put her name down on the list of volunteers in the church porch, it always seemed as though it would be convenient, but somehow, when Saturday morning came round, it never was.

Sonia went down the long passage that led to the gunroom and the flower room. An army could have been kitted out from the curious assortment of coats and hats that had gathered there over the generations. It seemed as though nothing had ever been thrown away, but they came in handy if people came to stay unprepared for cold northern winds and weather, and the hats in particular were useful for charades. She collected some flat baskets and hunted through various coat pockets for a pair of clippers before going out.

The park ended about thirty yards short of the front of the house, where a ha-ha prevented stock from getting over. The drop was a big one as it had originally been designed to keep deer out, but these had now been replaced by sheep and cattle, and sometimes the children's ponies. The grass on top of the ha-ha was thick with daffodils. People came from miles to see them at this time of year, when they always opened the gardens for one day for the National Trust gardens scheme. It was possible to pick great armfuls without making the slightest impression. Sonia set to work while Cassie helped her, plucking off the heads and filling her doll's pram with them. The three shih-tzus accompanied them, Lotus delicately picking her way along the edge of the grass like Agag, while Folly and Shambles, her two silly daughters whom Sonia had intended to sell but had then been unable to bear parting with, crashed about breaking stems and getting their long coats very wet in the process.

When Sonia had filled the baskets, she set off with the dogs and Cassie for the church. As you looked down from the middle of the park, the little church of St Stephen could be seen to the right of the house, almost adjoining it, but higher than the gardens proper which were at the back and ran down to the river. A track ran from the church along the garden wall and came out in the village further down, where the bridge was. Anyone walking along it could see into the garden, but this had never bothered generations of Duntans, filled with the confidence of their upbringing and not being used to total privacy. The iron kissing-gate that led to the church squeaked and was tricky to negotiate with a doll's pram and two flower baskets. It was only possible to go through one at a time and any impedimenta had to be lifted over the top; then there were six stone steps to be climbed, by which time a good many daffodils had fallen out. Sonia, having got her little party to the top, had to go down and retrieve them. As usual she realised too late that it would have been easier to make two journeys in the first place and not have attempted to carry up the flower baskets on one arm and the overcrowded pram on the other.

She pushed open the heavy oak door of the church, and turned on the lights. Last week's flowers were dead, so she fetched a canvas sheet from the vestry and started to dismantle the arrangements in the two pedestals on either side of the chancel. It was very peaceful. The sunlight, catching the fine dust that always seems to be in the air of old churches, turned it to gold and made beams across the aisle. Cassie dragged hassocks out of the pews and laid them end to end in a long line for her dolls. Apart from her self-contained muttering, there was no sound except for the rooks busying themselves with building projects in the big limes outside.

Having topped them up with fresh water, Sonia started to redo the pedestals. She put branches of white cherry blossom at the back and sides and drooping over the front, and then started to fill in with daffodils. She was rather pleased with the effect. Easter had been early this year, when few flowers were out; now that it was over, they were at their best.

She heard the door from the vestry creak and the Vicar came in.

'Good morning, Terry,' said Sonia, wishing he hadn't come. He was an earnest young man, whose round face glistened with good intentions. He had fine, straight hair that hung from a centre parting in a sort of bob, not unlike Birdie's, and which looked as if Millicent, his wife, had trimmed it round a pudding basin. She probably had. Of late he had sprouted an unlikely-looking moustache that perched uncertainly on his top lip like a pale brown moth. If he went out in the dark and got too close to a lantern, or had the misfortune to pass a tree coated with beer and honey, it might flutter away, one felt, leaving his lip as pink and virginal as before. Sonia supposed he had grown it to disprove the supposition that he did not need to shave, but thought that four children under the age of six should have contented him as proof of his virility.

'Good morning, good morning,' said the Vicar. 'What beautiful flowers, Sonia. Together you and the Almighty have produced a work of art for us all to look at tomorrow morning.'

It was on the tip of Sonia's tongue to say she hadn't noticed the Almighty being much help, but she bit it back. Terry had many excellent qualities, but a sense of humour was not among them.

'Hullo then, Cassie,' said the Vicar. 'Why, what a big family you have. What are they all doing?' The dolls, all six of them, were lying face down in a row along the aisle. They had no clothes on. Minnie and Birdie were always making clothes for Cassie's dolls, but they seldom wore them. Nudity and religion were Cassie's current preoccupations. Last time Lady Rosamund had come to stay she had said to Sonia, 'That child will either be a nun or a stripper,' and Martha, looking hard at her mother, had said, 'Oh well, blood will out! It must run in the family.'

'All dollies are very naughty,' said Cassie, looking severely at the Vicar through her fringe. 'They must lie on the cold floor till Cassie says up.' She was a great disciplinarian.

'Well, well,' said Terry, beaming through his rimless spectacles. 'Well, well.' There didn't seem to be much else to say.

'I hope Millicent is well,' said Sonia, 'and the children? I must get her to bring them all round to tea again soon.' She liked Millicent.

'Yes, thank you, all flourishing – touch our green bay tree!' answered Terry playfully. 'I have been wanting to have a word with you, Sonia. Millicent and I have been having little experiments with meditation.' He might have been talking about making jam. 'And we thought we might try and get a little group together to meet sometimes. I have sounded a few people out. Mrs Forsyth is very keen.'

Sonia was surprised. Marcia Forsyth was a tremendous organiser, but she hadn't imagined her as the contemplative type. She and Colonel Forsyth lived in Duntan Grange, a pretty house on the edge of the village, and were greatly involved in all local activities, and fought a continuous rearguard action against Terry over the form of service and choice of hymns.

'Well, I'll try and come of course,' she said a little doubtfully, and then with a flash of inspiration added, 'You know my mother-in-law's coming to us for a long visit soon. Perhaps I could bring her too. It could be right up her street.' Lady Rosamund and Marcia Forsyth loathed each other.

'Lovely, lovely. I'll be in touch, then. See you in the morning?'

'I expect so.' Sonia had been planning to give church a miss with Minnie being away. 'Come on then, Cass. Pick up the dolls and we'll be getting back.' Cassie started to look mutinous, but Sonia quickly stuffed her mouth with several of the Smarties she kept for just such emergencies, and swept the naked penitents into the pram.

Sonia sometimes felt that she had brought up her eldest three children reasonably well, but reason didn't seem to work too well with her youngest daughter, and it was much less trouble to use bribery.

The road to Cassie's heart was paved with Smarties.

After lunch they all piled into Archie's car. There was a lot of traffic on the road and it was market day in Winterbridge, which always caused a good deal of congestion, the narrow main street not really being wide enough for the stalls down each side as well as through traffic. The market square, where it was normally possible to park, was also full of stalls, and was thronged with people.

'I must just go to the lovely cheese man while we're here,' said Sonia. 'Do stop a minute, darling.'

'I can't possibly park,' said Archie, 'and anyhow, we haven't time.'

'Oh yes we have. You needn't park. Just lurk and I won't be a mo.' As the car was stationary at the time, Sonia got out, to be followed quickly by all four children, so Archie was left with no option but to drive crossly round the block.

There were stalls for everything imaginable: fruit, vegetables, fish, toffee, linen, sheets of polystyrene foam, jeans, flowered overalls and home-made produce. Over the cheap shoe stand, a large placard read: *Jesus sandals greatly reduced.*

'He must have had a lot of pairs,' said Tom.

Sonia fought her way to the lovely cheese man, who did indeed have an enormous selection.

' 'Ullo, soonshine,' said the cheese man, ' 'ow's tricks?'

'Tricks are just fine,' said Sonia, and bought a delicious chunk of blue Wensleydale and half a creamy-looking vignotte. She always bought the wrong amount, so that there was either not enough or so much that it would turn into rubber and sit about the larder for days. While she was paying for the cheese, the children had found the ice-cream van and were clutching choc-bars in their hot hands. The clean T-shirts they had started out with seemed unlikely to remain that way for long.

When they eventually linked up with Archie again he was on his fourth circuit of the town and a farmer in an old Land-Rover behind him hooted angrily while he stopped to pick them up. Archie looked distinctly cross.

'I wonder who else will be there this afternoon?' Sonia hoped to divert his mind into other channels. 'The Forsyths perhaps?'

'Well I know that Roger and Rosie Bartlett will be there, anyway,' said Archie.

Sonia looked surprised. 'How d'you know that? We haven't seen them for ages.'

There was a slight pause before Archie answered, a shade too casually, 'Oh I just happened to bump into Rosie in Harrogate the other day.' Archie hardly ever went to Harrogate. A red flush crept up the back of his neck.

Afterwards, Sonia realised that this was the first time she really felt the pricking of her thumbs.

'Well, that will be a treat,' she said. 'I suppose Rosie will play tennis with a carnation between her teeth.'

'Why will she?' Birdie was interested.

'She has a Spanish grandmother, so she has Spanish genes. She thinks she's Carmen.'

'What are Spanish jeans like?'

'Oh Birdie, you are silly! Not those kind of jeans.' Polly was impatient. 'We did all about genes in human bilge,' she said. She and Shirley Gillespie loved it. It was their favourite subject.

'We had human bilge last term, too,' announced Tom. 'Phallic got this old trout from some planning department to come and talk to us.' Phallic was Tom's prep-school headmaster. 'She told us all about genes. She had this tray of condoms, which stop people having babies and getting Aids. We put them on the taps and tried to burst them.'

'Well really! Whatever do they teach these children, I'd like to know.' Archie was glad to get off the subject of Rosie Bartlett, but Sonia remained thoughtful for the rest of the way.

Sally and John Brown-Goring lived in an old rectory near the village of Crossthwaites. John was a lawyer, primarily a bloodstock solicitor, but he also acted as agent for various enterprises connected with sport. He was a great authority on racing and an outstanding shot. Sally, his cheerful, pretty wife, was an easygoing woman who seemed able to cope with a busy social life, children and ponies without any apparent stress or strain. Archie thought John a thoroughly sound chap, and Sonia found Sally undemanding and fun, though they didn't really have many tastes in common.

They pulled up at the front door and tooted the horn. John and Sally came out to greet them.

'How's Yorkshire's most beautiful lady then?' asked John, giving Sonia a safe, sexless bear-hug.

'Blooming, thank you.' Sonia returned the hug and gave one to Sally too. She knew she wasn't beautiful, though a good many people were deceived into thinking that she was. Charm is perhaps an even better christening gift than beauty, and doesn't fade as easily.

'The others have started a set, so come down to the court and we'll join them. The children are all out there too. We almost filled the pool but thought that would be bound to make it rain. Isn't it heaven to have it so hot like this already? Last year we never played till June.'

They all went round the side of the house. Energetic sounds of a tennis ball being whacked to and fro could be heard, as could the sound of cricket bat and ball. Birdie slipped her hand into Archie's, and he gave it a reassuring squeeze. Birdie's anxieties brought out the very best in Archie. She dreaded cricket. She could just bear bowling – at least one was sending the ball in the opposite direction – but batting and fielding were torture to her, a terrible combination of periods of suspense interspersed with terror, like sitting through a Hitchcock film. She need not have worried. Kind Sally had produced a huge mound of assorted wooden building bricks comfortably close to the grown-ups' chairs, and she and Cassie were soon immersed in designing prisons. Cassie never wanted to build houses like other children did. Polly and Tom immediately disappeared with the Brown-Goring children and the Bartlett offspring, whose Spanish genes were far from evident. They were two pale, docile little boys who were destined to spend the rest of the afternoon being bossed about by Polly.

The set of tennis was just finishing, and George and Marcia Forsyth and the Bartletts came off the court. Rose Bartlett greeted Sonia with particular effusion but she hardly looked at Archie.

'Heaven to see you, darling,' she said.

'Lovely to see you, too,' lied Sonia.

There really was something gypsy-like about Rosie, who, though she was wearing a tennis dress, the brevity of which was probably a mistake given her not very slender thighs, had a scarlet cotton handkerchief tied round her abundant dark hair, and large gold hoop earrings.

Roger Bartlett was tall and thin and pale. He had been in the diplomatic service before giving it up to concentrate on making obscure medieval and Elizabethan musical instruments. A fondness for lacing his conversation with little snippets of French – the language of grace and diplomacy – had earned him the not very kind nickname of Joli Roger.

'Now, then,' Sally organised her guests. 'I think we'll have Bartletts and Duntans on the court, and George and Marcia can sit this one out. I know John wants to pick George's brains about some of the young hopefuls for the May meeting at York, and Marcia and I can have a cosy gossip.' The Colonel, who was a great racing man, instantly put on a knowledgeable face, but Marcia looked less pleased. Nice gossips were not her line.

'Will you play families or split up?' Sally shepherded them through the wire door.

'Oh, Roger and I can't possibly play together again. We've

just been slaughtered by the Forsyths. Let's split up,' Rosie suggested quickly.

'*Enchanté*,' murmured Roger, giving Sonia one of his gallant little bows. She wondered what the French for 'Rough or smooth?' was, but perhaps Roger's French wasn't quite up to that either.

All four were good players. Tom, who hated partnering his mother because he complained that she had 'no killer instinct', might have been surprised that afternoon, had he been watching, to see in her an unusual determination to win. Rosie Bartlett's gasps of admiration and cries of 'Clever Archie!' seemed to produce an unexpected resolution in Sonia, while Roger's tendency to remain rooted to the spot saying '*A vous, chère Madame*,' sent her flying up to the net, the adrenaline of irritation lending wings to her tennis shoes.

At ten all, a tie-break was suggested, but no one felt quite capable of remembering how it worked.

'How about sudden death?' suggested Rosie. It was Sonia's serve.

'Sudden death it is.' The light of battle was in Sonia's eyes.

At deuce, Sonia served an ace to Rosie that met with applause from the spectators.

'Oh silly, silly me! It's up to you to save us now, Archie,' cried Rosie.

The next serve was a good one too, but was firmly returned by Archie, and the two women then exchanged a series of forehand drives, to cries of admiration and encouragement from their partners, until Roger intercepted one of Rosie's shots and slammed the ball into the net.

'Oh, *bien joué*, pard,' said Sonia crossly, needled by Rosie's exaggeratedly girlish gasps of relief.

Deuce again, and again and again.

It seemed the battle might go on all afternoon.

'Damn well matched, those two girls,' said the Colonel to his hostess. 'Wouldn't like to lay a bet either way.' But at that moment, Rosie Bartlett, earrings swinging, bosoms bouncing, stormed the net and cut off Sonia's drive with a winning volley.

'Well played, Rosie!' Archie threw his racquet in the air and embraced his partner enthusiastically.

'*Quel dommage!*' said Joli Roger.

Sonia gave Rosie, flushed with success, a long, speculative look. 'Oh that's just the first round,' she said lightly. 'We'll have our revenge another time.'

The next set, between the Colonel and Sally, John and Rosie, somehow lacked excitement. Archie and Roger, who had very little common ground on which to stroll with any conversational comfort, made desultory remarks to each other while pretending to watch the tennis, though Sonia could see that Archie's eyes were concentrating on one side of the net only.

'I've been wanting to get hold of you, Sonia, about this new scheme of the vicar's for starting a prayer group,' said Marcia. 'I think it's a jolly good idea. Get something new going. Bring the village together. I think we should give him full support.'

Sonia lay back in her chair and closed her eyes. It was usually easier to let Marcia's words go over one like a steam-roller. Outright opposition required a lot of energy.

Marcia was firm of flesh, firm of jaw and firm of opinion. If she suffered from doubts on any subject whatever, she disguised it well. Even her hair was firm. It reminded Sonia of a sponge cake: 'done when firm and springy to the touch'. She wondered if Marcia's hairdresser tested it this way to see if it was dry, and pictured him running a skewer into her head to see if it came out clear. Her solid but not ungraceful form filled her well-cut tweed skirts to the limit – not a sag, not a bag, not a fold, not a wrinkle. If in her youth she might have been 'a great big mountainous sports girl', now, in her fifties, she still whacked a useful backhand drive across the tennis court, her well-upholstered legs managing to convey her from one place to another with surprising agility and speed.

'I have absolutely no time for slackers,' she was fond of saying, 'no time at all,' though Sonia suspected that by slackers Marcia simply meant anyone who was not prepared to do things her way, because in fact she loved doing things for helpless people, organising their lives, saving them trouble. She was endlessly, exhaustingly kind, but for those who preferred to muddle along in their own way she had no understanding and very little tolerance.

'So, we'll count on you to beat up a bit of support from some of our drifters then,' said Marcia. 'The whole parish needs waking up in my opinion, and Terry may be the man to do it.' But only so long as he went along with her ideas.

'And how's your painting coming along?' she continued. 'Must get the arrangements going for your exhibition, you know. That Zara Bennet who's taken on the gallery is very inefficient if you ask me. I'd be delighted to help you, you know – only got to ask. Get the whole thing organised in no time.'

'How very kind.' The idea of being organised by Marcia made Sonia feel like an anaemic with a haemorrhage. Marcia leaned across to Archie.

'You must be jolly proud of your little wife. George and I said so only the other day. I said, "Archie must be jolly proud of Sonia's painting", and George said, "Jolly proud of Sonia altogether. Jolly attractive girl." ' She pronounced it 'gairl'. 'Aren't you proud of her, then?' she prodded.

'Yes. Rather. 'Course I am.' Archie's eyes were glued to Rosie's mobile bust.

'There,' said Marcia triumphantly, as though she'd produced a rabbit out of a hat. 'What did I tell you? He's jolly proud of you.'

'He likes to wear me in his buttonhole sometimes,' said Sonia drily.

When the next set finished, Sonia offered to help Sally get tea and they walked back to the house. There wasn't really much to do, since competent Sally had put most things ready in two large baskets, so Sonia sat on the kitchen table while they waited for the kettles to boil and Sally put dollops of ice-cream into a large jug of iced coffee.

'My old man,' said Sonia, 'rather fancies Gypsy Rose Bartlett. Had you noticed?'

Sally laughed. 'Oh you don't want to worry about her. She bowls all the men over with those great big knockers of hers and they fall like ninepins. But it doesn't mean a thing in the long run. They get overwhelmed by all that open admiration, but it doesn't last. John carried a torch for her for a bit, too, but he soon got tired. All that eagerness is very wearing.'

'Mmm,' said Sonia. 'All that ripe flesh too. Makes me feel like a desiccated monkey.'

Sally laughed. 'You don't have to worry! You're about the sexiest stick insect that ever walked. Besides, I think poor old Rosie has troubles of her own.'

'Not with Joli Roger surely? Not my idea of Don Giovanni.'

'Not quite what you think. *Je crois que Joli* Roger *aime les garçons beaucoup plus que les filles*.'

'*Non!*' said Sonia.

'*Oui*,' said Sally.

'How on earth do you know?'

'Little bit of trouble at the choir school where he teaches the lute. John's a governor. He'd kill me if he knew I'd told you.'

'Goodness. So *pauvre* Rosie.'

'Yes,' said Sally. '*Pauvre* both of them, really, under the circs. Miracle they achieved those weedy little boys. But I'll tell you what, Lady Duntan,' and she looked at Sonia severely, 'that husband of yours is a very attractive man, and he's been licking your little Gucci shoes for years while you've just trampled over him in hobnailed boots.'

'Sounds a bit complicated.'

'You know quite well what I mean. So I think if he's swooning over our Rosie, you'd better take a good pull on yourself. More soft soap and less cold water. That's what Aunt Sally says, anyway, or hungry Gypsy Rose will eat him up for tea.'

'I know you're right really. I am foul to him sometimes, but lately he's been pretty bloody too. It's just he can be so boring, so conventional, so dreadfully hearty and *sensible*. Makes me want to do something wild.'

'But it's you that wants to hang on to Duntan. That's not exactly breaking with tradition, is it?'

'Yes, I want to stay there more than anything. But that's just what I mean, Sal. Archie would like to stay there too, but he's worked it all out, sees it's not the practical thing to do. Oh, I don't know. He won't ever throw his hat over the windmill, won't do that at life,' and Sonia stuck two fingers in the air.

'Perhaps he's throwing his hat over Mrs Bartlett?'

'Perhaps. And there are other things.' Sonia started to draw a very complicated pattern on the kitchen table with one finger. 'If Rosie got him for her tea, she just might find he's not much cop.'

Sally gave Sonia a shrewd look.

'Don't tell me, darling,' she advised. 'You'd only regret it afterwards, and I can't keep a thing to myself. You just think about my little pearl of wisdom, that's all.'

They walked back through the garden, laden with tea things.

The tennis had finished, and the children, sensing food, had turned up and were lying about on the grass while the grown-ups sat in deck chairs and talked. In spite of the wonderful sunshine it was beginning to be chilly; a hot April is so unexpected in Yorkshire that everyone had rather forgotten how early in the year it was. Marcia had already put on her green Husky, and Rosie had zipped herself into a scarlet track suit. Sonia made up her mind to be very nice to her, and even nicer to Archie, but it was difficult to begin since they were deep in conversation and neither of them noticed her arrival.

Roger was telling Marcia how to string a theorbo, not a piece of information she was likely to find very useful.

'You should get more fresh air,' she told him disapprovingly, which was very unfair considering he had just played as many sets of tennis as she had. 'Get those boys of yours out more too. They're far too pale. Why not bring them beagling some time?'

Roger looked appalled. '*Hélas! Pas possible*,' he said, giving a Gallic little shrug. 'I have to go to the Auvergne for some weeks to run a course on regional instruments.' You could see him thanking his stars.

'Lucky you,' said Sonia. 'Rosie going with you?'

'Er, no.' Roger pulled his long top lip, an irritating habit of his. Perhaps he had to keep it flexible for blowing down reeds. 'No, sadly I have to go before the boys go back to school. Naturally', he added, as though to dispel doubts on the question, 'I shall be very disappointed not to have her with me.'

'Yes, poor little me! I shall be on my ownio once the boys go back.' Rosie parted her full lips and she and Archie exchanged a veiled look.

Sonia's thumbs pricked. She decided not to be very nice to Rosie after all, and, despite Sally's little pearl of wisdom, not to be nice to Archie either. She threw the little pearl away from her as far as it would go.

Sally unpacked the tea. 'Oh do let me help you,' cried Rosie just as she had finished. Marcia, who was already manning the large jug of orange and organising the children into a queue, threw her a scornful look. She had no time for the Bartletts.

'How are your grouse prospects, Archie?' asked John.

'If this weather goes on into May and we have a good breeding season, we should have a few, I think. We shot fairly heavily last year, so there shouldn't be a problem with disease, but I shall have to try and let the moor. My grandmother never did you know, but the estate just couldn't carry the expense now. Matter of fact, I wanted to talk to you about that.'

'I think I could help you. I have one or two other clients who want to let for a few weeks, including the Vanalleyns on Wathergill, and I have a possible American syndicate lined up, but I also have an Arab who's interested. If I could find him two or three weeks on neighbouring moors it might really be the big money. He simply doesn't know how to use up his shekels, but we'd have to produce the goods. He wouldn't be amused by a little rough day – probably shoot the beaters out of hand. But I thought if you and old Dukie Vanalleyn got together we might produce quite a profitable little scheme.'

'Sounds interesting.' Archie accepted a long glass of iced coffee from Sally.

'Well, why not give me a ring at the office and we'll make a date to talk, either here or in London. I could give you lunch at the club if you're going up at all.'

'Fine,' said Archie. 'I'll do that.'

'What have you decided to do about the house?' asked the Colonel.

'Oh, nothing definite yet – all still in the melting pot,' said Archie, who tried to play fair.

'But we're definitely staying in the house. Probably opening to the public, but definitely not moving out,' said Sonia, who didn't.

Chapter 5

Everyone was quiet on the way home. The children were tired and their parents preoccupied. Cassie went to sleep on Sonia's lap.

Archie was thinking mainly about grouse prospects, about what it would be like to have Arabs shooting on the moor. Would they turn up properly kitted out or in outlandish flowing white robes that would put down every bird within miles? Would they be safe? Know the drill? He was afraid they might be a trigger-happy lot. But what if the moor could be made to pay for itself, perhaps even be profitable? The farm badly needed a new combine harvester, and some new machines for picking blackcurrants. He had a daydream about an expensive new pig unit. He also had a daydream about the weeks when Roger Bartlett would be away in France.

Sonia had a daydream about the house. She saw herself taking parties round, showing them all the lovely things in it, sharing it with the public while retaining it as a family home. She would tell them about its legends and history: about the small child who could be heard singing to itself in the nursery passage (she herself had heard it several times and had been fooled into thinking it was one of her own children until she discovered there was no one there) and the footsteps that were sometimes heard tramping about in the attics where the servants had slept under the great roof beams until a servants' wing had been built in 1900. She would tell them how Archie's grandmother had always slept with a lead cosh by her bed, not because she was afraid of burglars but because she had once had a butler with a frightful temper who drank too much, but who was so good at his job that this precaution had seemed preferable to sacking him.

In her imagination, she was a wonderful guide, and the

people who came were deeply appreciative not only of the house and its charms, but of herself and hers. Somewhere on the edge of her dream Archie stood, admitting to himself that she had been right all along and listening appreciatively to all the complimentary things the tourists said about her, marvelling that he, so insensitive to the artistic temperament, should have the luck to win such an amazingly talented and attractive wife. Rather annoyingly, Rosie Bartlett kept hanging about near Archie. She had no right to be there and Sonia decided to banish her, then changed her mind and decided to let her stay and witness Sonia's triumph, see how deeply (though hopelessly, of course, that went without saying) Archie was still in love with his wife.

She also thought about the weeks when Roger would be away in France.

Archie cut down through the village, over the bridge and up the back drive that led into the yard on the east side of the house. Cassie had to be woken up and she started to grizzle while Archie unlocked the heavy side door, first with the enormous iron key that looked as if it might open a medieval fortress, and then with the smaller, more modern one that was supposed to be the more burglarproof of the two.

As they got inside, they could hear the persistent clanging of a bell. 'It's the front door,' announced Tom, who had rushed down the passage to look.

'Oh damn,' said Sonia. 'Who on earth can it be? What a ghastly time for anyone to turn up. Run and see who it is,' she told the children, 'but don't let anyone see you.' In a minute they were back, jostling to get through the door first, eyes popping, all talking at once.

'You'll never guess who it is!' said Tom dramatically. 'It's Granny Rosamund and Martha and a funny man with no hair and a dress on!'

'And piles and piles of luggage,' said Birdie. 'They're just sitting on it and waiting and Granny has her eyes shut.'

Archie and Sonia looked at each other in horror, their differences temporarily forgotten.

'What the hell? I didn't think she was coming yet. I thought you hadn't fixed a date.'

'I hadn't,' said Sonia. 'I'd hoped not to have them till the holidays were over. She can't even have got my letter. I only got hers yesterday and she hasn't telephoned or anything. Oh Archie! It's too bad of her. The rooms aren't ready and Minnie's away till Monday, and you know how demanding she is. What shall we do? Could we pretend we're away? Did she see you, children?'

'She didn't,' said Birdie, 'because she had her eyes shut, but the funny man did. He was peering through the window with his nose all squashed up on the glass, and Tom squashed his nose up on our side and made a face at him. He didn't seem to like it much.'

Archie groaned and Tom looked pleased with himself. He knew his parents were too preoccupied to be cross about this rudeness. He and Polly exchanged conspiratorial looks. The rest of the holidays should be exciting. Granny Rosamund always caused upsets.

'Who on earth is this man?' Sonia wondered. It was inevitable that her mother-in-law should have a man in her life, but it didn't sound as if this one was her usual type.

'What did you say he was like?'

'With no hair and in a nightie,' explained Birdie patiently.

'He looks awfully cross and dirty,' said Polly. 'And Martha stood behind him and sort of rolled her eyes. You know how funny she is. You can tell she think's he's a real grot, and she signed at us to let them in, but we came back to tell you first, because that's what you told us to do,' she added virtuously.

'Oh God!' said Archie. 'Well it's no good if you've been seen. You'd be hopeless on a recce in a war – give the whole show away at once. What useless children you are. We'll have to let them in.'

The children rushed headlong back to the hall, Cassie by now thoroughly wide awake and shouting, 'See the funny man in a nightie!' at the top of her voice while Archie strode after them. Sonia followed slowly, suddenly feeling very tired.

The front door took a bit of unlocking, since one of the bolts was stiff, but eventually Archie pulled it open; the children fell out, followed by five dogs, all barking hysterically.

Archie's mother, quite unmoved by the drama and looking more as if she were dressed for Ascot than a visit to the country, was indeed seated among an enormous pile of suitcases and boxes.

'Darlings,' she said reproachfully, 'where have you been? We've been waiting here for quite an hour and we couldn't raise a soul. Too irresponsible of you both to leave this precious house quite empty like this. You don't know who might turn up!'

She had long ago learnt that when in the wrong – a condition with which she was well acquainted – it is wise to launch an attack immediately. As always, her effrontery took Sonia's breath away and most of her indignation with it. It was so absurd. Rosamund extended her arms to them all in a huge gesture of welcome and forgiveness, and her magnificent eyes flashed, darted and dazzled like a pair of dragonflies.

Sonia suddenly caught Martha's eye and began to laugh.

'Oh Roz,' she said, accepting the exchanged pressure of cheeks that made up one of Lady Rosamund's long, scented kisses, 'you are impossible. You didn't let us know. How could we have guessed you were coming today?'

'We tried to ring this afternoon before we left London but there was no reply.' Lady Rosamund managed to imply it had been all their own fault. 'So we just had to pile into dear Brother Ambrose's car and set out into the unknown.' She made it sound like an expedition into the rain forests of New Guinea.

'Now you must all meet Brother Ambrose. Ambrose adores children, don't you, Ambrose?' The man she addressed didn't look as if he was exactly bowled over by the selection in front of him, all of whom were gazing at him with unabashed curiosity.

He was a thickset man, whose neck appeared to start at his ears and end at the outside edge of his shoulders, but it was hard to tell if the rest of him was muscular or merely fat since his figure was enveloped in a long flowing garment that looked as though it was not only homespun, but spun in a rather grubby home. His hairstyle, if that was the right word, was that of Yul Brynner in *The King and I*, only much less attractive. It looked as though having taken the decision to shave his head, he was not very conscientious about doing it, so that rather than looking polished and virile, a sort of six o'clock shadow of the scalp gave his bald pate the appearance of a dusty kitchen shelf. He wore purple nylon socks and sandals. He could have been any age between thirty and sixty. Sonia thought he was the most unattractive man she had ever seen.

'How do you do?' she said, putting out her hand, but Brother Ambrose ignored it and, placing his palms together, made a little Indian bow, though he was clearly not of Indian origin himself. He did not speak.

Martha began hugging everyone. She adored being at Duntan.

Archie looked gloomily at the mound of luggage. It certainly looked as if his mother was intending a long visit.

'How much of this stuff do you want up?' he asked.

'Why all of it, darling, naturally. Those two cases are Martha's, and the rest are mine – except for the rucksack, which is Brother Ambrose's.' No one could imagine that a backpack would belong to Rosamund – all her luggage came from Hermès – and this announcement confirmed Sonia's worst fears. It was clear that Brother Ambrose was not intending to return to London. She felt she must have more information, and Martha seemed the best source.

'Perhaps, er, Brother Ambrose would like a bed for the night?' she suggested, hoping that this offer would make it clear that hospitality could not last indefinitely. 'Archie, take Rosamund to the Blue Room. I know the beds are made up there. And show Brother Ambrose to the Bachelor Room, so he can have a wash and unpack. Polly and Tom, you help take up the smaller cases, and Birdie darling, if you and Cassie are very good and don't argue, you can have your bath together in my bathroom and use my bubble bath. Run it carefully and don't put your hand under the hot tap. Martha, you come with me and get some sheets and we'll do a bit of bedmaking together.'

Having disposed of everyone in this masterly fashion, she gave Martha a nudge and led her upstairs to the linen cupboard. They leant against the shelves and eyed each other.

Martha had the look of a fledgling bird, her feathers not yet fully grown, the gracefulness of flight not quite within her capabilities so that she still hopped and flapped, but for those with a discerning eye, the signs that she would one day soar smoothly away on wings of beauty were there. Her fluffy hair had been cut short on top and stuck out from the centre, 'Like a chicken's bottom,' said Polly later, while the longer strands that hung down at the back might have been newly grown feathers. She stood there, her skinny legs twining round each other as if they had been hung on the wrong sides and were frantically trying to right themselves, and her arms hugging her thin body as though an alien wind was blowing. For all this, Martha had a presence. Even if she was curled up absorbed in a book, you knew she was in a room, and there were those who found her half-derisive, half-defensive blue glance more than a little disconcerting.

Sonia was very fond of her.

'So come on, Martha,' she said, 'give. What is your mother up to and who is that revolting man?'

'Isn't he frighters? He belongs to some weird organisation that Ma's got mixed up with called the Brothers of Love. They're all totally bogus. Actually,' said Martha casually, 'this one's a defrocked priest.'

'What does your ma see in them? Surely she's not sleeping with that creep? What are they after?'

'Oh, they're after her money, no doubt about that. But they don't know what a tough nut they've got to crack.' Martha had always been very clear-eyed about her parent. 'She's well aware what they want and they won't get a dime more than she wants them to have. She's certainly not sleeping with old Ambrose. Not sure about the boss one, though. Could be.'

'Why bring one here? What does she want from them?'

'Well, this one's got a car and he was free to drive us. Also, he can run errands for her, and you know how she likes to have someone at her beck and call. I'm not really sure what she *wants* in the long run, except, perhaps, a new ploy and a bit of power possibly – and Duntan of course. She'd love that.'

'Duntan!' shrieked Sonia. 'How can she have Duntan?'

Martha wrinkled her nose, considering the question.

'Well, I think she's always fancied it, you know – that was her only regret at leaving Archie's dad – and she's loaded with money since Pa died. But she'd never let Archie touch it unless she controlled Duntan. The Brothers are big in the States but they want a base in England that looks good so that they can lure poor innocents there and bag their money. She thinks you might be prepared to let some organisation rent it if you could go on living in part of it, and then she'd have control of them – and you – and Duntan. Simple really.' And Martha laughed at Sonia's horrified face.

'I'm not letting anyone have Duntan, least of all your mother and her unsavoury friends. I don't know what I shall do,' said Sonia, 'but I shall think of something. Just you see.'

Chapter 6

Sunday morning started badly. Sonia woke to a horribly familiar zigzag flickering across her left eye like the pattern on a radar screen. She reckoned she had a short time in which to get breakfast ready before the pain in one side of her head became impossible and drove her back to bed in a darkened room.

She reached for the bottle of migraine pills on her bedside table and gobbled down a double dose. Archie, an early riser, was already up and would be out exercising his horse, and Polly would probably have gone with him. She groped for her dressing-gown, pressing her fingers into the bone above her left eye, and then carefully pulled back the curtains. All the windows at Duntan were enormous, and to replace the now faded and extremely fragile ones in her bedroom would take hundreds of yards of material, so they had to be treated with respect. Too violent a tug and they might disintegrate altogether. Outside, the wonderful weather of the preceding day was gone, and in its place a grey cloudiness hung like a damp shroud, taking the colour out of everything, so that the daffodils looked as though they were controlled by a dimmer switch. The air felt raw and the temperature had fallen ten degrees.

She went downstairs, walking cautiously so as not to aggravate her throbbing temple. Archie had already opened the shutters and the front door, and Keeper and Poacher, his two labradors, had obviously gone out with him, but the shih-tzus burst from their baskets like animated hearthrugs, seizing the hem of her dressing-gown and giving her a frantic welcome, so that she felt it would be churlish not to respond with her usual enthusiasm. She put the big kettle on the Aga and ground the coffee beans, though the noise made her wince. She wished she had laid breakfast the night before, but by the time she had cooked dinner, got the children to bed and dealt with her uninvited guests, she had been exhausted. The kitchen table looked crumby and uninviting now, and on the sink there was a pile of unwashed knives that could not be put in the dishwasher and had been forgotten. She wished she was the sort of person who automatically finished the job in hand and was not given to leaving things that bored her for a later and possibly more favourable moment. It certainly wasn't a better moment now. She mopped the table, got out the old blue and white china and laid eight places, putting out a tray for her mother-in-law. Archie could take her breakfast up to her in bed, which would at least mean that she was unlikely to appear before lunch. What Brother Ambrose's plans were they had been unable to discover, but presumably he would want breakfast.

The kettle, which she had filled too full, suddenly boiled over with a sizzling noise that made her jump, and the pounding in her head worsened. She made a large jug of coffee and put more water on for boiled eggs before making herself a mug of tea and sitting down in the old rocking chair. She thought that if she could stagger back to bed and be left alone for a couple of hours, she might, with luck and one of the injections she kept for real emergencies, be in a better state to cope with life by lunch time. At that moment, the banging of the back door and some rather off-key whistling announced the arrival of Archie and Polly, both looking radiantly well and energetic. Polly's hair hung in wet rat's tails round her pink face.

'Hullo, Mum.' She banged her riding hat down on the table and a wet pool started to form on the floor from her dripping Husky. 'We've had a super time. Dad and me've been practising the jumps for the Pony Club gymkhana, and Dusty's going really well – right up to her bit. It's started to rain like stink. What's for breakfast?'

'How lovely, darling. Boiled eggs, and please don't leave your wet things in here.'

'You don't look too good.' Archie cast a look at Sonia. 'Should you be up?'

'Well, I do feel awful. I'm so sorry, Archie, I'm not sure I'll make it. Could you cope till lunch time? I might be better then.'

'Yes, of course.' Archie might not have very sensitive antennae for some things, but he was extremely kind and had always been protective of Sonia when she wasn't well. 'I'll take the children to church. That'll fill the morning in for them. You go back to bed and when you're feeling a bit more the thing we'll talk about getting rid of this bloody monk, or whatever he is. I'm not having him loafing round here helping himself to all my drink – or anything else, come to that.'

'Thank you, darling. You really are good,' said Sonia, meaning it.

The night before, Brother Ambrose had outraged Archie by asking for 'a Cointreau and lemonade'. It was the first time he had spoken, and he had revealed a thick Liverpudlian accent with Damon Runyan Chicago-gangster overtones. What he must have sounded like taking a service, if he really was a defrocked priest, Sonia could not imagine. Archie had been incensed at the idea of polluting his Cointreau with lemonade, but had paid for the lie he told pretending he hadn't got any by Brother Ambrose's enormous consumption of whisky, about which he waxed quite loquacious without giving away any information as to his plans for departure. Eventually they had sat down to scrambled eggs in the kitchen. Sonia, knowing that her mother-in-law greatly disliked this kind of informality, was determined not to pander to her by making the effort to open up the dining room in Minnie's absence. But Lady Rosamund, having achieved her own way, had been at her sunniest. 'I adore a picnic! What fun!' she had said, and Sonia had given her a sour look.

Everyone had forgotten about Cassie till Birdie appeared for supper in her dressing-gown with the information that Cassie wouldn't get out of the bath. For the sake of peace, Sonia had decided to leave her there to play until she had fed everyone. She regretted this decision later, when Cassie suddenly burst in, very wet and smelling strangely potent, but at her most beguiling.

'Done you lickle favour in your barfroom,' she had announced. 'I cleaned it *all* up for you,' and she had smiled seraphically. A hasty inspection had revealed a flooded carpet, soaked towels, and an amazing mixture of Vim, talcum powder, Dettol and Floris bath essence smeared over everything. It had been the last straw.

'But she was trying to *help* you,' wailed Birdie reproachfully. She couldn't bear anyone to be cross with Cassie.

All in all, it had not been a good evening, and it had also proved very difficult to get Brother Ambrose to go to bed, Archie's repeated and pointed shooting-out of his left arm to study his watch and his hopeful exclamations of 'By Jove! Getting a bit late! Time to turn in, d'you think?' having no effect whatsoever. He had been loath to leave his strange guest alone downstairs, not sure which would be the worse fate – to find he had departed in the night and taken the silver with him, or to find him still there in the morning. In the end everyone else had gone to bed, leaving Archie and Ambrose to sit it out in a state of complete incompatibility, the one determined not to leave his visitor the freedom of the house and the whisky decanter, and the other in an alcoholic haze that did nothing to improve his charms.

'Right,' said Archie now. 'Polly, you go and wake everyone up and get them down here sharpish, and let your mother go up to bed. Church parade at eleven and no one is to be late.' He sometimes forgot that he was no longer in the army, though it could not be said that his children exactly jumped to his commands.

'Pol, be an angel and get the little ones up. And darling, be a little bit tactful?' Sonia gave her eldest daughter a pleading look. Given the licence to boss, Polly was apt to cause a good deal of trouble.

'Shall I wake Granny and the monk man too?' asked Polly hopefully.

'No, I think I'd leave them, but wake Martha and she'll give you a hand. And Polly, no water-pouring when you wake Tom. I had enough mess last night. I really couldn't take any more.'

Sonia crept thankfully upstairs again, her headache having reached the stage when she no longer cared what any of them did.

It could not be said that the congregation at St Stephen's was a very large one. The Duntan party sat in the front pew on the left, so that the whisperings and giggling of the children were in full view. Archie held the living in his gift, a little talk from the Bishop on the undesirability of the system of private patronage having failed to persuade him to hand it back to the diocese. In this stand he was much encouraged by Colonel Forsyth, his fellow church warden.

'I accept we don't have much choice anyway, but at least it gives us the power of veto. Let the clergy have a free rein and you don't know how it might end. Must keep some control over the fellahs. You stand firm, Archie, dear boy. We're all behind you.'

In fact, Terry Miller had been the Bishop's own candidate for the joint livings of Duntan and South Swale. There had not exactly been a flood of applications, but the PCC felt stronger for the knowledge that technically Archie could have refused to accept the appointment. The last incumbent had been much loved by everyone but his increasing absent-mindedness, and the length and tediousness of his rambling sermons, had hardly swelled the congregation. Terry, a new broom ready to do some energetic clean-sweeping, had thought that the pews would fill up in no time, given some swinging new ideas and the advantages of the Alternative Service Book, but somehow this new awakening among his parishioners had not been as dramatic as he had expected.

The latest idea, about to be put into practice this morning, was that Millicent should hold 'A Children's Special Time' (Sunday school sounded too old-fashioned) and take the children into the vestry during the sermon. He had zoomed round the village on his Honda moped, trying to enlist support from the young mothers, and was much encouraged to see the three little Slaters, offspring of Archie's cowman, sniffling and scuffling in the back pew. He might not have been quite so pleased had he realised that it presented their feckless mother, who was supposed to help Minnie in the house but frequently failed to turn up, with a literally heaven-sent opportunity to go off to the pub. Poor Millicent, with four small children of her own to cope with, had not been quite so enthusiastic about the idea as her husband had hoped, and he had let her know (kindly, of course) that her reaction had been a disappointment to him.

The service seldom started on time. The Vicar, who had to come on from his other church at South Swale, was apt to arrive a little late, and since the St Stephen's congregation knew this, they allowed for it and arrived late too. It would not have mattered if Terry had cracked off smartly the moment he got there, but he liked his congregation to settle into reverence before he began, so he would bob in and out of the vestry like one of those little figures presaging wet weather on gift-shop barometers. Movement and shuffling in the pews, latecomers in the aisle, and he would bob back in again. It could have gone on indefinitely.

Whilst this was going on, Colonel Forsyth, his grandfather's half-hunter watch held ostentatiously in his hand, would be in a state of seething irritation. For years he had selected the hymns each Sunday, and Terry's propensity to change them at the very last moment was another potential source of ill-will, upsetting not only the Colonel, but Mrs Dickinson, the headmistress of the village school who played the organ, and Joe, who acted as verger and climbed up a stepladder to put the numbers up. With unusual generosity (blessed are the peacemakers), the Colonel had offered to let the Vicar choose them himself in future, but Terry, anxious not to throw his weight about too soon (blessed are the humble), had declined, and so the irritation festered each Sunday.

Lady Rosamund, a drift of black lace thrown becomingly over her blue-rinsed hair, had surprisingly decided to attend church too, armed with her rosary so that no one should be in any doubt about what a splendidly ecumenical gesture she was making. Brother Ambrose was presumably sleeping it off, and Martha, the inside of her boiled egg scooped out on to a large piece of toast, was finishing her breakfast as they arrived at the church door. She looked as if she was about to attend a fancy-dress party as a tramp. Her clothes always tended to be of the parent-teasing variety, and that morning she had on hot pants and a baggy old football jersey that accentuated her skinny frame, but all the same she had a kind of elegance that was deeply irritating to her mother. The effect was rather spoiled at the moment by the old mackintosh she had seized from the large collection down the passage and her canvas baseball boots, which were sopping wet and making dark marks on the stone floor.

'Is it Matts or Holy Commers?' asked Martha as they trooped up the aisle.

'Matts,' said Polly. 'Second Sunday.'

'Pity.' Martha gulped down the last crumbs of eggy toast and licked her fingers. 'I could have done with a nice swig of vino to wash that down.'

After a good deal of bobbing in and out and waiting for the Duntan pew to settle, the Vicar finally came in and Mrs Dickinson struck up the opening bars of 'Crown him with many crowns'.

'It's the dentist's hymn!' whispered Tom to Polly.

'Bloody little man's changed the hymns again!' said the Colonel, not in a whisper at all.

Archie and the Colonel each read a lesson. They had so far resisted the Vicar's efforts to get them to read from the 'Good News Bible'.

'Bloody bad news if you ask me,' said the Colonel, a remark Terry considered in very poor taste.

The Colonel barked out his lesson as though he were giving the commands at the Queen's Birthday Parade, and Archie read his in a series of clipped jerks through clenched teeth, managing to be quite audible without moving his mouth. It was quite difficult to do. The children knew, because after much practice they could all do it perfectly. After the Christmas carol service, Martha had made them rehearse saying 'Seeking diligently for the young child' without any movement of their lips. 'Let's be Daddy reading the lesson,' they would say, and sometimes spent whole days talking to each other like this. Archie found it very trying, particularly since Sonia sometimes forgot about parents showing a united front and did it too.

After the second hymn, Millicent led her not very happy band of pilgrims away to the vestry. Apart from her own four children, there were only the three Slaters, Birdie and Cassie. The two youngest Slaters were crying, but this was more because Jem, the eldest, had just pinched them than because they had any particular objection to Sunday school. It seemed that Terry's idea for 'pulling the young people into the Church' had got off to a slow start.

It took some time to get everyone settled. Jem Slater pushed Reg Slater off his chair as a matter of routine, and Reg stuck out his leg and tripped up Marlene. Millicent did not at all like the look of Marlene's runny nose, and hoped she wouldn't pass on anything nasty to Elizabeth, Ruth, Daniel and Benjamin; then she reminded herself about Jesus touching all those lepers and thrust the thought away as unworthy.

'Now children,' she started, hoping the Slater boys would not detect the nervous tremor in her voice, 'I think we'll have a story in a minute, but first shall we say a little prayer together? I expect you all know "Gentle Jesus" don't you?'

'Naughty, noisy, bad Jesus,' said Cassie. Millicent looked horrified.

'Oh no, Cassie dear. Jesus is loving and gentle and good. We all love Jesus, don't we, children?'

'Don't think ought to 'im,' said Jem Slater with magnificent indifference.

'Naughty, noisy, rough Jesus,' insisted Cassie. 'Naughty Jesus and naughty thunder.'

Millicent was mystified, and looked helplessly to Birdie for clarification.

'She doesn't like the noise of thunder,' explained Birdie, 'and Polly told her it was Jesus fighting in the sky.'

Millicent made a mental note to have a quiet word with Sonia. She sometimes thought the Duntan children got the weeniest bit out of hand. She supposed it was because Sonia, whom she much admired, was artistic. She hoped desperately that her own little family were not going to get hold of any unsuitable ideas. It seemed that Marlene's runny nose was not the only thing they might pick up.

'Me dad says "Cor Jesus, gi' oos a break," when me mum natters 'im,' announced Reg Slater.

'I still don't like Jesus,' said Cassie.

'She doesn't like Father Christmas either,' volunteered Birdie helpfully, softening the blow for Millicent.

Cassie, not at all unaware of the effect she was having, went on in a whiny voice, 'And I don't want Jesus coming down my chimney.'

'Could he, Mummy? Could he?' Elizabeth wanted to know.

'No, of course not.' Millicent felt thoroughly rattled. The Children's Special Time was not going according to plan.

After leaving theological college, Terry had set his heart on becoming a missionary. He had seen himself carrying a bright light into dark continents and had been deeply disappointed that his principal had not seen him in this role too. Millicent felt she could truly tell him that there was much torch-bearing to be done in Duntan and South Swale, and amongst some unexpected people too.

'Jesus doesn't need to come down chimneys, Elizabeth,' she said. 'He is right here in our hearts now. He is inside each one of us.'

Jem Slater gave her a pitying look. He knew a great deal about the facts of life from observing the performance of the prizewinning Charollais bull that was his father's particular pride, and he also knew about the less exciting advantages of artificial insemination. The idea of this bloke coming down chimneys and fetching up in their hearts seemed a load of old codswallop. He thought Millicent might be soft in the head.

At this point Reg Slater created a not unwelcome diversion

by pulling Marlene's hair so hard that she screamed and broke into roars loud enough to drown the organ.

'That's very unkind and naughty, Reg.' Millicent felt on firmer ground. 'Whatever would your mummy say if she saw you do that?'

'Leave t'little booger alone,' said Reg truthfully.

One way and another Millicent was relieved to shepherd her little flock – goats rather than sheep perhaps – back into the church to join in the last hymn in time for the collection. She would have been appalled had she known that the Slater children not only had no intention of putting anything into the offertory bag, but actually managed to extract coins from it. Jem thought church might well prove to be a useful future source of revenue, but made a mental note that there would be no point in turning up before twelve. He had every intention of frisking Reg and Marlene and taking their ill-gotten gains off them for his personal use, though he decided it would be wise to get well shot of 'parson's wife' before putting this plan into practice.

After giving the blessing, the Vicar, surplice flapping, galloped down the aisle in order to shake hands with the departing congregation. 'A kind word and smile for everyone' was how he thought of this laudible activity, and that morning his best smile and kindest word were reserved for Lady Rosamund. He had met her briefly at Christmas when he was new to the parish, and had been fascinated by her. Her predatory eyes and something slightly sinister about her teeth had been an alarming reminder that cannibalism was said to be by no means extinct. She certainly looked capable of gobbling him up alive, and as he took her elegantly gloved hand in both of his for a warm Christian handclasp, he thrust away the absurd fancy that she might suddenly bite him to the bone. He told himself that her influence might be useful in the parish, but like many another ardent egalitarian, he was really a sucker for a title, and in his eyes Lady Rosamund walked about with an illuminated scroll over her head bearing the exciting legend 'Daughter of an

Earl'. He was not, in fact, quite sure how to address her, but thought that 'Dear lady' perhaps struck the right note.

'Dear lady,' he said, daringly prolonging the handclasp, 'what a privilege to have you with us again. Sonia tells me she thinks you may be able to assist us with our newly formed group experimenting with the adventure of contemplative worship.'

Lady Rosamund extracted her hand skilfully. The gloves were new and she had no intention of allowing the nap to be rubbed from the suede for the advancement of Christian love.

'Any help I can give – so delighted to be of use – we must have a little talk,' she murmured graciously, giving Terry the full treatment of a blazing look. She seldom drove with dipped headlights. 'You must come along and meet my dear friend Brother Ambrose who is staying with us at present. A member of the Brothers of Love. We have great plans. You have perhaps heard of the Brotherhood?'

'Indeed!' said Terry untruthfully, deciding to look them up in his *Encyclopaedia of Comparative Religion* the moment he got home. It struck Lady Rosamund that the Vicar might be a useful if unwitting accomplice.

Martha gave Polly a nudge. 'Watch Mum getting to work on your parson,' she whispered. 'He doesn't know what's hit him.'

The Forsyths were also greeting Lady Rosamund, though not with quite the same enthusiasm.

'Hullo, Roz.' Marcia stuck a weather-beaten cheek in her direction and they exchanged a ritual kiss in the air, expressive of their mutual dislike.

'Keeping fit I hope?' enquired the Colonel. It was not an adjective that seemed suitable for Rosamund, carrying as it did visions of singlets and shorts, of lithe lean bodies, bulging muscles and cold plunges rather than her particular brand of velvety voluptuousness. She was certainly possessed of wonderfully good health, though she hated to acknowledge the fact, and always kept a limp available for enlisting help and sympathy. She had a collection of glass walking-sticks that she used as fashion accessories rather than for support; had she really needed to put any weight on one of them, it would almost certainly have snapped in half.

Colonel Forsyth, who had an eye for a lady, considered her to be a damn fine woman, but despite his MC and reputation for courage in the face of the enemy, he would not have been so foolhardy as to express this sentiment in front of his wife, and had to agree with her that Rosamund could be rather tiresome.

'I keep going.' Rosamund put on what Martha called her 'brave widow's smile'. 'One mustn't give way. And of course one's faith is such a support.' Terry looked awfully excited.

Perhaps, he thought, St Stephen's might become the nursery of a new charismatic movement. One should not despise the influential if they could be used for God's purposes, he continued, justifying his secret snobbery to himself. He felt sure that God must have a purpose for Lady Rosamund. The thought that Rosamund might have a purpose for God in mind, and one entirely for the furtherance of her own ends, would have shocked him profoundly.

A date, conditional on Sonia's ability to attend, was fixed with Marcia and Lady Rosamund for the meeting of the new prayer group. The two church wardens, the whites of their eyes clearly visible, both declined to be involved. The Forsyths then drove off in their battered estate car, and Archie shepherded his family back through the little wicket-gate to Duntan.

Chapter 7

The following week several things became clear. Brother Ambrose had no intention of departing and Lady Rosamund no intention of letting him go. Minnie and Ambrose had taken an instant aversion to each other, and it remained to be seen who would prove the more powerful adversary. Both had some useful weapons in their armoury.

Brother Ambrose was a guest, albeit uninvited, which gave him a sort of diplomatic immunity according to the traditions of Duntan hospitality. Minnie, on the other hand, as a gamekeeper's daughter, had been brought up with firm views on the necessity for exterminating vermin.

Minnie had a sharp tongue, a quick wit and a burning loyalty to what she considered to be the best interests of the family. She also had a certain amount of control over the running of the house and the kitchen, and it soon became clear that Brother Ambrose was extremely greedy and comfort-loving. This seemed his only vulnerable point; his skin otherwise was remarkably thick. He also enjoyed the patronage and protection of Lady Rosamund, a powerful ally. Minnie, however, could call on the wholehearted support of the children, and they not only constituted a highly efficient espionage network, but were also quite ruthless in carrying out the commissions of their commandant, in the best traditions of an underground movement.

The bad weather continued and the torrential rain found all the weak spots in the fabric of the house. The stairs and landings looked as if they had been got ready for a gymkhana, with buckets and bowls set out at frequent intervals to catch the worst drips. Towels had to be placed in these overnight to deaden the infuriating ker-plunk, ker-plunk that went on incessantly. A great chunk of the beautiful plasterwork round the dome fell on to the stairs, leaving a bald patch quite out of reach of anything except full scaffolding.

As Archie's face grew longer, Sonia grew more determinedly cheerful and optimistic. Positions were becoming entrenched. The truce that had existed on Sunday while Sonia had felt too ill to care and had been grateful for Archie's cooperation, had not lasted. The discovery of her mother-in-law taking Ambrose for a tour of the house and actually discussing with him how it might all be arranged to accommodate his sinister sect, give the best rooms to herself and squeeze a flat in the old servants' wing for Archie and Sonia, had sent her into such a rage that she could hardly get her words out when she reported the incident to Archie. His reply that his mother was welcome to deal with the leaking roof, dry rot and uncertain electrical wiring, and that since they themselves would be snugly installed in the Dial House, it would be a matter of complete indifference to him which rooms his mother or the Brothers occupied, had left her with a feeling of such cold fury that it even surprised herself.

'Might be a jolly good solution,' said Archie. 'Better than letting it rot away. I think there's a lot to be said for the idea.'

'You can't be serious! That slob of a monk! And the whole organisation sounds evil – really evil. Besides, think of having your mother queening it here in my place, when she chucked it all up years ago. And think of having her at such close quarters all the year round. Think of that, Archie.'

'Oh, it wouldn't last long. Nothing with her ever does. She'll probably find some new millionaire or think she's had a call to darn the holes in the ozone layer or something.' Archie usually kept up a fiction that his mother was really a pillar of respectability, but it didn't suit him to do so at the moment. 'I shall consider their proposition seriously, I can tell you that.'

'And I can tell you that nothing would induce me to agree to it. *Nothing*.'

'Fortunately, your agreement itsn't legally necessary,' said Archie nastily. 'And what other suggestions have you got in mind? We're in debt as it is with those Lloyd's losses. I suppose you think you can conjure hundreds of thousands out of thin air, just like that?'

'I don't know yet, but I'll think of something. Something will turn up, you'll see. If you want a thing badly enough you can *make* it happen – and I shall make this happen.' Sonia sounded very certain, but she hadn't the faintest idea how she was going to achieve it. 'You don't seem to give a hoot about Tom's future,' she went on. 'I should have thought you would have wanted your son to be able to inherit a house that's been in your family for so many generations.'

'Oddly enough,' said Archie, 'it's Tom and his future that I'm most concerned with. He might not thank us for trying to hang a huge white elephant round his neck, even if we could manage it – and I'm telling you flatly that we can't. He certainly won't be able to. Do stop being such a blind romantic, Sonia, and face a few facts.'

'And do stop being such a pusillanimous old pessimist and try looking at a few new ideas,' she flashed, and went off to telephone Simon Hadleigh to make an appointment for him to come down and see the house, banging the door as hard as she could and dislodging a few more bits of plaster.

Archie went off to the estate office to attend to farm business and telephone Rosie Bartlett.

Sonia managed to fix a date for the following week for Mr Hadleigh to come to lunch. His secretary said he would want a detailed tour of the house, though he already knew something about it. Sonia felt well satisfied with the result of the conversation, but did not know whether to be pleased or sorry when Archie announced that he would not be able to be present as he was going up to London for a couple of days to meet John Brown-Goring and go into the question of letting the shooting. She felt furious with Archie because she suspected that he was deliberately sabotaging her plans; on the other hand, there could be no denying the fact that the meeting would be a great deal easier and more relaxed without his potentially disruptive presence. On the whole she decided that it was probably a good thing, and would give her a freer hand if he was not there.

'All the same, it seems ridiculous to go all the way up to London to see Johnnie when you could quite well see him in the York office.'

Archie went rather red, and fidgeted with the change in his pocket.

'Oh well, it's the London end where all the main business is done, and besides, he might want me to meet a potential taker. Anyhow, I have several other things to do in London.'

'Like what?'

'Like a meeting with Grandmother's solicitors.' Archie had the look of someone who suddenly discovers an unexpected trump in his hand, but Sonia was convinced he had not yet made the appointment.

Sonia made another telephone call. She rang Rosie Barlett to ask her to bring the children over next week.

'Sonia darling! Heavenly idea. We'd have adored it but I'm afraid the boys are going over to Roger's mother for a few days, so they won't be here. How sad.'

'Why don't you come yourself, then, and we could have a cosy girls' chat? I know you're on your own with Roger being in France,' suggested Sonia, thumbs pricking madly. Rosie gave a little yelp of dismay.

'Oh darling, I'd have loved it. Sweet of you to think of it, but I feel I must seize the chance and pay a duty visit to my poor old mum.' Rosie's very glamorous mother was in her mid-fifties, married to a Swede and spent most of her time cruising on his yacht.

'Oh poor you. How noble. Hope you manage to have some fun too. See you sometime, then.' Sonia rang off looking very thoughtful, and went to her studio, where she painted furiously for the rest of the day.

The advertisement for a temporary cook brought forth one answer that seemed a possibility. The lady in question was a widow called Hilda Bean. She had, she said, a lot of experience of cooking; she and the late Mr Bean had run a hotel together in Yorkshire, though she was now living in retirement in Norfolk. She liked children and dogs; had, in fact, a small poodle of her own, very good-tempered, very obedient, which she would have to bring with her. Sonia decided to keep this bit of information from Archie until the poodle arrived. Mrs Bean was doubtful about an interview, though she would be prepared to come if Lady Duntan really thought it necessary, and was prepared to pay her fare and accommodation for the night, it being a long way to come just for the day. 'But I know we shall get on, dear,' said Mrs Bean. 'I can tell by your voice. Mr Bean always said I was funny like that – quite psychic.'

'Oh well, then,' said Sonia weakly. 'That will be lovely. Why don't you come for a few weeks' trial to see if you really like us?' She felt Archie deserved to pay the exorbitant wage that had been mentioned. There was the little score about Rosie Bartlett to be paid off.

She went to tell Minnie and the children the news. Minnie was making steak-and-kidney pie for lunch and the children were sitting on the breakfast table absorbed in the saga of Martha's latest romance. The kitchen was the hub of the house, a place that invited confidences, where the Aga provided welcome warmth at all times, even when the rest of the house was freezing. Polly was apt to use its bar for ballet practice, which had loosened it considerably and was inconvenient for the cook.

'Martha's dying, absolutely dying for an Italian man called Tomato, Mum,' announced Birdie, round-eyed.

'Tomaso, stupid. You're too much of a baby to understand anyway.' Polly gave her sister a woman-of-the-world look calculated to cause maximum aggravation.

'Show Mum the Sellotape,' said Tom. 'That's really soppy.'

'Bags I tell,' said Polly, forgetting to be worldly and reverting to nursery pecking order. 'I'm the eldest so I can tell. Look, Mum, isn't it romantic? Tomaso plucked the first hair out of his chest and gave it to Martha as a keepsake, and they've sworn undying love. She keeps it on a bit of Selly in her bag. Do look.'

Sonia inspected this unusual talisman of love. It looked as if Tomaso's hair was not the only thing adhering to the Sellotape – a sojourn at the bottom of Martha's bag had caused several bits of fluff and dust to join the sacred offering on the sticky twist of tape.

'I thought Arch might let me have one of those darling little snuffboxes from the drawing room to keep it in,' said Martha.

'Sooch a carry on!' said Minnie, rolling out the pastry. 'I never did! You are a bad lass, Martha.'

'Doubt if you could have a snuffbox.' Sonia perched on the table too. 'A matchbox would be quite good enough for that. What did you give him, Martha? A tuft of your henna hairdo?'

'Oh nothing so old-fashioned. Much more intimate. I tweaked out a pubic hair with Ma's eyebrow tweezers. It was absolute *ag*. I really suffered for him. Like old Philip Sid. "My true love hath my hair and I have his, by just exchange one for the other giv'n",' she misquoted.

'You are frightful.' Sonia felt she ought to look disapproving in front of Polly but was unable to resist the lure of Martha's gossip. 'What does your mum think about him?'

'Oh Ma doesn't know. She wouldn't approve at all – not for me, that is. Might fancy him for herself. He works in Harry's Bar.'

'You mean he's a *waiter*?' Polly looked very disappointed. 'I thought you'd have met him at a grand dance, swirling away in your ball dress, melting in his arms.'

'I don't go much for swirling. The chaps at those kind of dances are all ghastly anyway. Grots and wimps with acne and sweaty palms. Gross. Wouldn't want to melt with any of them.'

'But you'd melt with old Tomato?' asked Tom.

'Oh absolute melters. He's a real dish.'

'Talking of dishes,' said Sonia, 'I think I've got us a cook for the summer. Won't that be a help to you and me, Min darling?'

'Maybe. Maybe not.' Minnie was noncommittal. 'Did you ask if she was a Roman or one of those Methodees?' Anyone not labelled C of E was immediately suspect in Minnie's eyes.

'No of course I didn't. She likes cooking for lots of people and she's coming next week. She sounded so nice. She's lost her husband poor thing.' Sonia started to enthuse nervously to try and bypass Minnie's hostility.

'What her name?'

'Mrs Bean.'

The children shrieked.

'Bet she's a broad bean,' said Tom.

'Or a dwarf bean,' giggled Polly.

'Or an old bean,' Birdie was pleased to contribute.

'Anyway, the husband's a has-been, and she's probably *been* around,' said Martha. They were all convulsed at their own wit. Sonia foresaw trouble.

'Well anyway, she can help us feed that greedy monk, and leave us a bit freer for other things. You're not to be naughty to her. I won't have it.'

Birdie flung her arms round Minnie's ample waist. 'I like Min's cooking best – or Mum's. No one else ever makes things as nice. Other people always put *flavour* in. I hate flavour.' Birdie was not one for life's gastronomic adventures.

'Well if this Mrs Has-been starts producing nasty foreign food full of wine and garlic and all that fool carry-on, you and me and Cassie will still have our own nice meals together made by me,' said Minnie.

'Oh Min! She's a Yorkshire body like you, and you're making her out to be a scarlet woman,' said Sonia, trying not to laugh as Tom muttered 'Scarlet runner'. 'I'm sure she's going to be awfully cosy. What is the point of me trying to get help with the cooking if you're going to go on doing it too? You talk as if she was going to poison us all.'

Minnie sniffed. 'She can cook for that Brother What's-it and welcome. Drop of poison's just what he needs. Now get shot off that table the lot of you. I want to lay lunch for me and the little ones in here and Polly and Martha can start laying it in the dining room for the rest of you.'

'Why not Tom? Why doesn't he lay lunch?' But Tom had vanished, safe in the knowledge that Minnie encouraged male chauvinism.

It took Sonia some time to locate Mrs Bean when she went to meet the train at York. The picture she had conjured up in her mind was of a homely, rosy-cheeked country dumpling, Yorkshire as Ribston Pippin, and smelling of home-baked bread. There was no such paragon to be seen. Instead she was being approached by a woman who had been standing by the first-class carriage from which she had stepped when the train arrived, and whom Sonia had immediately discarded as being a possibility. With a sinking heart she saw that this lady was accompanied by an extremely bald, fat poodle that was being dragged along the station in a sitting position, rubbing its bottom on the platform in a very unattractive fashion.

'I am Hilda Bean,' announced the woman, 'and this is Croompet.' The image of the rosy countrywoman faded and in its place Sonia saw a large, florid lady whose hair was a rich and unlikely shade of cinnamon that did not blend well with her shocking-pink suit and matching complexion. It was impossible to tell her age since her face was so heavily encrusted with pancake make-up that it might have been necessary to sink a borehole to reach her skin. Her eyebrows had long since been plucked bare, but two strong lines in burnt sienna had been drawn in by a firm hand over her beady eyes. She wore very high-heeled shoes, over which her ankles bulged alarmingly, and she breathed as wheezily as a harmonium with several leaks in its bellows.

'How do you do? I hope you had a good journey?' Sonia imagined she would soon be called upon to pay for the first-class ticket.

Grabbing a trolley, she hauled Mrs Bean's enormous suitcase on to it and they progressed slowly to the car park. It was clear that neither dog nor owner could move with any speed. Sonia's heart took a further downward dive when they were settled in the car and Mrs Bean removed her rather grubby crochet gloves, revealing gnarled fingers stained orange by nicotine, and lit up a cigarette. There was certainly no whiff of home-made bread; instead the car was filled with a strong smell of cheap scent, reminiscent of hyacinths much past their prime, which together with an unpleasant odour emanating from Crumpet was far from pleasing. It was pouring with rain, but Sonia opened the window wide to let in the raw Yorkshire air. The thought of introducing her passenger to Minnie filled her with foreboding.

Perhaps it would be wise to start at once to make the job sound less attractive than she had tried to suggest on the telephone.

'I'm afraid you will find us rather a large party, and my husband is going to have to do much more entertaining than I had expected. I may not have made it quite clear how much work is involved. Having met you, I am just wondering if you may not find the job a little bit much for you, but if so we would quite understand . . .' Her voice trailed away. Mrs Bean shot her a shrewd look and inhaled deeply on her cigarette.

'I am lucky in being so yoong for my age. My late husband marvelled at my energy. "Hilda," he used to say, "you are a bloody marvel." I have all my own hair and all my own teeth,' she added.

They drove the rest of the way to Duntan in silence.

The introduction on arrival went no better than expected. Minnie's face was a study of disapproval. Sonia took Mrs Bean to her room to unpack, and came down to face the verdict.

'Oh dear, Minnie darling! What do you think?'

'I know her sort. All top dressing. Red hats and no knickers.'

'*No knickers?*' Birdie looked terribly shocked. 'How do you know?'

Minnie continued: 'And that smelly poodle – that's not setting foot in this kitchen. Where's it going to sleep? Riddled with worms, I should think. Don't you go touching it, children. There's no knowing what you might pick up.'

'I shouldn't think it's got worms,' said Tom judiciously. 'It's too fat for worms. Keeper got awfully thin and scrawny when he had them. Could be good if it has, though, because Brother Ambrose might catch them.'

Minnie ignored him.

'And is she cooking dinner tonight?' she demanded.

'Well, yes. I suppose so. Perhaps I'll give her a hand, though, just for tonight, and we'll see how it goes.'

'Well, don't you take on.' Minnie took pity on the hunted look on Sonia's face. 'You leave her to me. I'll sort her. You go and do a nice bit of painting. You've got enough to be going on with without Madam there upsetting you as well.' Some of Archie's recent telephone calls had not been lost on Minnie, who considered eavesdropping perfectly justified in a good cause.

Sonia gave her a grateful hug and went off to her studio, but once there she did not really get on with the water-colour of wild flowers set against a tangled wood that she had intended to finish. Her mind was too full of problems.

Mrs Bean was certainly a new one, though comparatively minor when set against her own disagreements with Archie and the sinister intentions of the Brothers of Love. She had very little doubt that the organisation was at best unpleasant, at worst possibly evil. Her mother-in-law was neither – but was certainly not to be trusted. It seemed to Sonia that since the death of old Lady Duntan, the pattern of their lives had shattered and she was beginning to doubt her own ability to bind the fragments together in any acceptable shape or form. Her wish to remain at Duntan was assuming a far greater significance than just the protection of a much-loved inheritance. It was becoming a crusade, and by focusing her fight on one issue she felt as though she was tackling a great many other problems too. She could not have explained it to herself, let alone to anyone else.

She felt the presence of the house all round her, pounding at her consciousness, invading her thoughts and undermining her will to work. It was like having a very demanding lover. She thought about Archie and Rosie Bartlett, and was shocked to discover herself thinking that if she allowed Rosie to get too firm a hold over Archie, then Rosie might succeed in taking over not only her husband but her house as well, and it was this last idea that was the most unwelcome. Perhaps Sally had been right and she ought to make a conscious effort to win him back. She knew she had snubbed him too often over the years, slapping him down like an over-enthusiastic spaniel that needed to be taught not to jump up, while at the same time taking for granted his support in times of crisis. She had hinted to Sally that Rosie might not find Archie a very satisfactory lover if she got him, but she did not for a moment think this would be so. If Archie had a problem, it was with her alone.

The flowers in the pot in front of her were beginning to droop, especially the fragile wood anemones. She enjoyed the challenge of painting white flowers, using the palest shades of grey and green and pink that could be blended to give an impression of translucent whiteness. She also remembered from a book she had once had as a child on 'the language of flowers' that anemone meant forsaken.

She had never thought of herself as a forsaken wife, though in imagination she had sometimes forsaken Archie, dreamt of an ideal lover who could not only ignite her body with fire but her mind as well. Luckily the paragon had not so far materialised, and though she had indulged in some light and enjoyable flirtations, and there had certainly been several more serious lures cast before her, she had so far remained physically faithful to her marriage vows, even if unfaithful in thought. If she herself had been having a passionate affair she knew she would not have minded Archie's pursuit of Rosie half as much, might even have welcomed it, but at the moment it presented a serious threat to her influence over him just when a conflict of interests made it important.

She felt pulled in too many directions for comfort, her artistic ambitions pulling one way, her maternal instinct another, and her obsession with the house threatening to prove the strongest pull of all.

She picked the wilting wood anemones out of the vase, threw them in the bin and went to the window. The grey rain-clouds were lifting, and in the park the great beeches, whose trunks had appeared black in the wet weather, were once more silver in the April sunshine and their young leaves a brilliant green. She laid her hand on the wall of the room as one might touch the arm of a friend, in love and reassurance, and a great determination hardened inside her.

Chapter 8

'Shirley Gillespie's mother,' announced Polly at breakfast, 'says multiple orgasms are every woman's right. Shirley's mother's a Ms.'

'What's a muzz?' asked Birdie.

'It's a lady who's married but doesn't want anyone to know, or one who *isn't* married and doesn't want anyone to know that either.'

Birdie looked rather puzzled.

'And a norgasm, what's that?'

'Well,' Polly looked very knowledgeable, 'it's *sex*, and it's like a sneeze, only in your bottom. Shirley's mum says it's lovely, and multiple ones are like lots and lots of sneezes.'

'Sort of like hay fever?' Birdie suffered from this herself, and couldn't see why it should be every woman's right.

'Do you have them, Mum?'

'Mmm, no, I shouldn't think so.' Sonia wasn't really listening and had switched on the automatic pilot that steered her through the children's breakfast conversation while she read her letters.

'Probably Archie's faulty technique then,' suggested Martha naughtily. 'You ought to go to some clinic you know, Arch, and get advice. Mrs Gillespie'd be bound to know of somewhere, or I bet Ma could tell you a tip or two. She's had loads of experience. I expect it explains why you're both so snappy nowadays. Sonia's probably *unfulfilled*, and –'

'Oh for God's sake!' Archie flung down *The Times* and got up. 'I never heard such a load of tripe, and as for this Gillespie woman, she sounds thoroughly unsuitable. I don't know why you let Polly go there, Sonia. All she does is pick up silly ideas. Their whole set-up must be most unsound. I'm catching the ten o'clock train to London and I won't be back till Friday. At least

I may get some decent food at the club. That breakfast was absolutely disgusting.'

He banged out of the dining room, but not before he heard Martha's light, mocking voice say, 'Well poor old Arch, then! Must have touched him on the raw!'

It had certainly not been the best breakfast. Mrs Bean's cooking left a great deal to be desired, and the only thing that made the unappetising meals she presented at all tolerable was the hope that they might drive Brother Ambrose away. So far this had not happened, though dinner the night before had been a disaster. Sonia had planned what she considered a fool-proof menu – food she thought suitable for grown-ups and the older children too – and Archie had invited his agent, Tim Warner, and his wife Leonie, together with their two teenage sons, to supper.

Sonia had looked forward to an easy evening, with no rush of cooking for herself, and pleasant if not very exciting company. She had allowed herself the luxury of a long bath before dinner, with masses of Floris bath essence in it, and a new life of Madame du Barry, wrapped in clingfilm since she planned to give it to her mother as a present, to read. She always read in the bath. After a relaxing soak she had even bothered to use a hot brush on her hair, and had fluffed a little blusher on her high cheekbones. She might not be conventionally pretty, but Nature had been kind in giving her such thick dark eyelashes and eyebrows in contrast to her heavy fair hair. She had put on a fine wool skirt and a Liberty lawn shirt and looked at her reflection with some satisfaction.

Lady Rosamund, smelling delicious, and Brother Ambrose, not smelling delicious, were already sitting in the library when she came downstairs, and it was clear from the sudden silence when she entered the room that they had been deep in a discussion they did not want her to hear. This had happened rather often lately and Sonia thought she had better get Polly and Tom to do a little eavesdropping.

The library was a lovely cosy room, with big squashy armchairs and sofas, and piles of books lying about, as well as the beautiful leather-bound ones on the shelves. Cassie and Birdie, in their dressing-gowns, came in to say goodnight. Cassie, looking rosy and delicious, immediately pulled a stool close to Brother Ambrose's chair. She had taken an unaccountable fancy to him, the faint odour of old billy goat that hung around him and was so displeasing to everyone else, not seeming to put her off at all. She took hold of the sleeve of his habit and peered down the armhole, as one might look down a telescope.

'What *are* you doing, darling?' Sonia helped herself to a drink and came and perched on the club fender by the log fire that was still necessary in the evenings.

'Brother Ambrose has a secret up his sleeve,' answered Cassie, and she put her hand up his sleeve as though feeling very carefully for something.

Everybody laughed except Birdie.

'I'll bet he does,' said Sonia. 'And your grandmother, no doubt, has some up hers. But I may have a trick or two up mine as well.'

Cassie shook her head vehemently.

'You and Granny don't have proper secrets up your sleeves. I like Brother Ambrose's kind best.' And she gave him a conspiratorial look through her eyelashes.

Brother Ambrose half-closed his eyes and looked maddeningly inscrutable – a cross between Buddha and the Giles baby. Under his monkish white robe he wore a black polonecked sweater, the cuffs of which were very frayed, so that bits of unravelled black wool combined with the abundant black hairs sprouting from his wrists and the backs of his coarse, stubby hands.

Birdie began to look anxious, pleating her blue dressing-gown between her fingers and standing as far away from Brother Ambrose as possible. She had started having nightmares, and either Minnie or Sonia would have to go to her several times during the night, when she insisted on them making thorough searches of her room, peering under the bed and looking behind the curtains, though as she was absolutely unable or unwilling to tell them what it was she feared they might find, it was rather hard to reassure her. Sonia wondered if she had been making the story of the griffins too exciting lately, and made a mental note to check up on what television programmes the children had been watching.

Lady Rosamund wore a long black velvet housecoat of expensive simplicity that set off her wonderful figure and beautiful complexion perfectly. Some people might have thought it looked too like a dressing-gown, and others that it was too smart for the occasion, however Rosamund was one of those fortunate women who always look right themselves, but have an infuriating ability to make other women doubt their own choice of clothes. She had even been known to give Marcia Forsyth doubts over the suitability of wearing her old green Husky as an evening wrap. Black suited Rosamund particularly well. Her skin had the luscious softness of pink and white marshmallows. Marshmallow outside, razor-blade within, thought Sonia. Birdie went to climb on her knee, but her grandmother hated to be rumpled once she had arranged herself, so she pushed her gently off.

'It's my gammy leg, Henrietta darling,' she said. 'It just won't stand any pressure.'

Birdie had watched her grandmother nipping up a ladder in the attics with Brother Ambrose earlier in the day, and the gammy leg had spent a very active afternoon. Her eyes filled with tears and she started to bite her bottom lip.

'Come and sit with me, my love,' said Sonia, holding out her arm, but Birdie pulled proudly away and stood on the edge of the circle. She often had the look of St Sebastian, struck all over with the arrows of other people's unkind or thoughtless words.

The arrival of the Warners, with their two fresh-faced sons, created a diversion, and there was much kissing and greeting and general laughter. Except for Ambrose, everyone knew each other well. Robin and Nigel Warner were both at Eton. Robin was in his last half and about as full of cheerful self-confidence, in an inoffensive way, as it is possible to me, and Nigel was a year or two younger. They were both mesmerised by Martha, who looked at them with mocking indifference and chewed gum in a derisive way that made Robin long to impress her with his manliness and sophistication.

'Where's my Bird?' Archie scooped Birdie up from her self-inflicted isolation and sat on the arm of the sofa with her on his knee. She stopped looking like St Sebastian, and also stopped looking plain. Birdie, who might one day be beautiful, had the kind of looks that are entirely dependent on mood. She was Archie's favourite child. Sonia might consider him insensitive, but for Birdie he kept some extra antennae.

'How lovely to come out to sups,' said Leonie. 'Just what we all felt like tonight.' She was a pretty woman with a talent for wearing shawls and scarves without getting them caught in the door or dipped in the gravy. This evening, she had a plaid rug flung casually round her shoulders that seemed to stay in place no matter what she did. Sonia thought it miraculous. It was not a knack she herself possessed.

'Oh, we're using you as guinea pigs. Guess what? We've got a cook! Don't know what the food'll be like. It's been a bit grim so far, but we're hoping it will improve, and it seemed a lovely excuse to get you over.'

'Anything one hasn't cooked oneself, let alone thought about and shopped for, is always a treat. I'm sure it will be delicious.'

'Well, I don't know. This is her first real test. She's rather a ghastly woman, which is a snag.'

'Minnie says she doesn't wear knickers,' volunteered Birdie.

'She does,' said Cassie.

'How do you know, Cas?'

'I looked,' said Cassie. 'I was under the kitchen table and I saw. She *does* wear knickers. They are *purple*!'

'Put the purple knickers on, put the purple knickers on,' sang Tom, to the tune of 'Polly Put the Kettle on'.

'Put the purple knickers on, Mrs Bean's knickers.'

'You're all very silly,' said Sonia half-heartedly. 'Now come on everyone. Let's go and eat.'

Minnie appeared at that moment to collect Birdie and Cassie for bed.

'How about letting Bird stay up a bit longer?' suggested Archie. He thought it rather unjust of Sonia to make Birdie do everything with Cassie simply because Cassie made herself so unpleasant if she was left behind. Cassie was Sonia's favourite child. It was another point of friction.

Cassie started to look mutinous and opened her mouth ready for a scream. She adored a scene.

'Oh Archie! Don't interfere – it only causes trouble. Why do you always have to start something?' In spite of the presence of the Warners, Sonia could not keep the sharpness out of her voice.

'I have every right to interfere. If I don't think you're being fair I shall say so. Cassie's becoming utterly spoilt.'

Cassie looked smug. Everyone else, except Lady Rosamund and Brother Ambrose, looked embarrassed, and there was a hectic little flurry of conversation, like a sudden breeze blowing.

For Birdie, the dilemma was an agonising one. To have to choose between her parents' wishes was bad enough, but the decision itself was fraught with difficulties. Part of her longed to join the grown-up party, to be counted with Polly and Tom, to be part of the laughter and warmth, not to have to feel she was missing something. On the other hand, to go upstairs now with Minnie and Cassie was safe. All the lights would be on, and she would be able to hear Minnie bustling about tidying up the nursery before she went to sleep. If she stayed downstairs now, she might have to go upstairs by herself later and face the terrors of strange shadows, closed doors and the mysterious night noises that are a part of all old houses. In particular she dreaded the long passage that led to the nursery wing. During the day, the rooms opening off it presented no threat, but at night it was impossible to contemplate the horrors that might lie within. She could only ever manage to get from one end to the other by running flat out and trying to jump across the distance between each door. Accidentally put a foot down opposite a doorway and anything might happen.

'Birdie hates going up later. She's afraid of the passage.' Unforgivably, Sonia exposed Birdie's fears in front of everyone.

'Well, I'll go up with her in half an hour and tuck her up myself.'

Birdie's needs were forgotten while her parents locked horns. As usual, Minnie came to the rescue.

'Tell you what, love, you come up with me and Cassie now, and you shall stay up an extra half-hour with me while I read you a story. And we don't want any of your dramatics either, young lady.' And she gave Cassie a quelling look, and treated Archie and Sonia to her most disapproving sniff.

'I hope you all enjoy your dinner. That's all I can say,' she added darkly.

No one could possibly have enjoyed the food.

The home-made soup, a discouraging shade of grey, tasted as if a few old dishcloths had been boiled in it; the roast lamb was black on the outside and desiccated within, and to the horror of Archie, who fancied his prowess with a carving knife, it had already been hacked up in the kitchen into curious chunks that floated about in a lumpy gravy the colour and consistency of chocolate sauce. The first tender shoots of sprouting broccoli had been converted to a khaki mush, while the roast potatoes presented a serious threat to anyone with dental problems. Finally, the chocolate mousse turned out not to be from Sonia's favourite cookery book, but was instead a particularly nasty variety of instant whip.

As the meal progressed, Archie, to whom food was important, became more and more tight-lipped, so that his constant apologies were delivered in his lesson-reading voice, and just as his words carried admirably through clenched teeth to the back of the church on Sundays, so they were clearly audible to Sonia at the other end of the table, as they were intended to be.

Sonia herself became brighter and more sparkling with each horrid mouthful. Her end of the dining room was alight with laughter. The Warner boys were enslaved by her, and Martha, catching her mood, and perhaps also not unaware that Robin and Nigel were so responsive to Sonia's charm, even if they were only schoolboys, forgot about being sophisticated and aloof and greatly contributed to the general amusement. Tim Warner, a wonderfully engaging man with a slightly manic gleam in his eye, told them hilarious stories about various dramas on the estate in old Lady Duntan's day. He had a talent for believable exaggeration and peppered his stories with dramatic ejaculations: 'So General Panic! Major Catastrophe! General Chaos! Major Drama!' Sonia called these exclamations the officers in Tim's private army. He could make the most mundane tale of plumbing difficulties or local quarrels into wonderfully bizarre confections of story-telling.

Poor Leonie Warner, struggling between a furious Archie on her left, and Brother Ambrose, whom she found totally baffling, on her right, had a heavy conversational struggle, and couldn't help listening enviously to the roars of laughter that good manners prevented her from joining. Lady Rosamund made no attempt to eat anything. She had every intention of making her henchman carry a tray of consommé up to her room later, and was quite unmoved by the cross-currents crackling around her.

'We'll take coffee into the library,' said Sonia when Polly and Tom had removed the plates of instant whip. 'Don't you men be too long, because we're going to play a game.'

'Oh, we're not going to sit in here,' said Archie, who had no intention of being convivial, and even less intention of wasting his vintage port on Brother Ambrose or the Warner boys. 'Tim and I have a lot to discuss and we'll go straight to the Business Room. Tom can bring our coffee in there.' And, picking up the port decanter, he deliberately put two glasses on to the silver salver on the sideboard.

'Oh, aren't the rest of us to be offered anything, then?' Sonia had no intention of letting him get away with this. 'Leonie, darling, have a glass of port before they whisk it away. Roz, I know you'll have brandy, but Robin and Nigel can bring their port through with us if you and Tim are really going to be dreary and talk business, and I know Brother Ambrose would like some too.'

The Warner boys, who had very good manners, did not even need the meaning looks from their parents to make them disclaim any wish for port, though Robin would have liked Martha to see him with a glass. Leonie also refused, but Ambrose accepted with alacrity. Archie opened the cupboard in the sideboard where various liqueurs were kept, and deliberately poured out a glass from the dregs of a bottle of ruby port that had probably been there for years, left over from some shooting lunch. This calculated insult left no mark on Brother Ambrose.

'And I should like some, Archie, please – and not from that bottle either.' Sonia had the light of battle in her eyes. Archie, whose face was much the same shade as his plum-coloured smoking jacket, handed her a glass with ostentatious forbearance. He knew she wouldn't touch it. Vintage port gave Sonia a migraine.

She led her party back into the library.

'What shall we play?' asked Polly when the coffee had been handed round.

'How about the dictionary game?'

'No, let's play round-the-table ping-pong.'

'What about wink murder?'

Eventually a giant racing-demon session was decided on. Sonia went to the walnut tallboy where games were kept and got out nine packs of the battered cards used for this purpose.

Lady Rosamund, who was a dab hand at racing demon, did not seem to find her gammy leg any impediment to crouching on the floor as they all laid out their cards. After much hilarity, Robin's, Martha's and Rosamund's scores were all very even, but Rosamund carried off the final honours, with Robin and Martha sharing second place.

Eventually Archie and Tim joined them, finding everyone much flushed from the excitement of the racing demon and the warmth of the blazing fire. Tim and Archie were much flushed by their lavish consumption of Taylor's '63.

'Come on, darling, we must go. Robin, Nigel, come on, we've stayed far too long. Thank you for a heavenly evening, Sonia.' Leonie, plaid rug still in place despite the strenuous card game, gathered up her menfolk.

'I might give you a ring sometime,' said Robin casually to Martha. 'Might do a film in York if there's anything decent on. I could pick you up in the car.' He had recently passed his driving test and longed to show off his skill to her. He hoped his father, not noted for tact, would not hear and shame him by asking, 'Whose car, I should like to know?' He knew he could get round his mother later.

'Sorry about the filthy food. I shall really have to get rid of the old monster somehow.' Sonia kissed Leonie on both cheeks and escorted the Warners through the hall to wave goodbye.

Three other things happened that night, each in their own way a minor disaster.

Birdie woke up with a nightmare and was sick all over the bed; a piece of the drawing-room ceiling collapsed; and Archie tried to make love to Sonia.

Chapter 9

There was a general feeling of relief after breakfast when Archie, rather late for his train, was seen roaring up the steep drive in his car on the way to the station.

Sonia went into the kitchen. Martha was leaning on the Aga, clutching her stomach and rolling her eyes dramatically.

'Oh I do feel ill – such awful inderjags I've got. That porridge is lying like lead.'

'Serves you right for eating it. You should have known better by now.'

'I know, I know. Don't bang the message home when I'm feeling so frail. You *must* get rid of her, Sonia. That foul poódle came and made a mess in my room last night. I jolly nearly trod in it. One of us will die of food poisoning soon. Bet her hotel was compulsorily closed down.'

Sonia made a shushing face as Mrs Bean lumbered into the kitchen, a cigarette hanging from her cyclamen lips. Tom began to sing 'Put the purple knickers on . . .' none too quietly. Martha made a loud burp.

'What was that?' enquired Mrs Bean.

'That was Martha making a very rude noise.' Sonia was trying to shut Tom up with a look and not laugh at the same time, but wasn't being very successful.

'Ah, well,' said Mrs Bean, 'they say it's either got to coom oop,' she paused, 'or down. It's dangerous to bottle.'

'Look,' said Sonia, trying to distract attention from the children's giggles and pointing to the basket of beautiful pale pink sticks that Knowles, the gardener, had just brought in. 'Look, Mrs Bean, the first young rhubarb from the garden. Such a treat. We shall be able to have rhubarb fool, and rhubarb crumble, and summer pudding is delicious made with really young rhubarb, too.'

Mrs Bean was not impressed.

'She only wants me to cook the boogers three different ways,' she announced to the world at large, or perhaps she was addressing the late Mr Bean. She had told Polly, who was naturally fascinated, that they often 'Communicated'.

Polly and Shirley planned some secret sessions with Mrs Bean's ouija board. Shirley could not at first think of anyone dead whom she might raise, but after much prodding from Polly had eventually come up with a demised great-aunt whom she had hardly known. She was not much good at ideas, and was rather afraid of Polly. She was also well aware that their friendship was entirely due to the interesting revelations of her mother, and was therefore constantly pumping her parent for more information. Luckily Mrs Gillespie responded well to interrogation, and as a rule was a treasure trove of new and astonishing facts. However, Shirley didn't feel confident that her mother would prove helpful as a medium. Mrs Gillespie was an atheist.

Sonia wished that Mrs Bean would leave of her own accord, but, like Brother Ambrose, she seemed impervious to hints. After the fiasco of dinner the night before, she dreaded to think what Mrs Bean might produce for Simon Hadleigh to eat for lunch that day. She was very anxious to make a good impression on her visitor, and would have liked to give him a discreetly gourmet meal – something subtle and surprising in a filo-pastry parcel, perhaps – but the thought of the kind of surprise Mrs Bean might spring was too alarming to contemplate and she decided to play it safe with cold food. Surely even Mrs Bean couldn't do anything very sinister with baked potatoes, and they could have lots of delicious cheese and fruit to follow.

'I know the Aga can be a little tricky if you're not used to it,' she began tactfully, 'but we all thought the lamb was a tiny bit overcooked last night. We have a guest for lunch today, and we'll hope to eat at one o'clock, so I suggest you put the potatoes in the top right at twelve and then move them to the top left as soon as you think they are done.'

'I have baked many a potato in my day,' said Mrs Bean stonily. Sonia didn't doubt it. It was the thought of what they might have been like that was so nerve-racking.

Sonia left the kitchen fearing the worst, and got out the car to go to the delicatessen in Winterbridge, planning to buy as many delicacies to tempt the palate of Mr Hadleigh as were on offer, and also to drop Birdie and Cassie off at the vicarage en route. Millicent had invited them to play with Elizabeth and Ruth. Sonia wondered if she ought to let Birdie go, but she seemed fully recovered after her bad night. She still looked pale, but then she never had much colour anyway. She decided to risk it. Cassie would certainly refuse to go alone, and the Vicarage was so close that someone could easily fetch them back if necessary. She felt a pang of guilt as she remembered Archie's accusations of the night before, but brushed it aside.

When she got back she went into the drawing room with Minnie to inspect the new damage. Luckily the hole in the ceiling had not damaged any of the moulding, but the piece that had come down had fallen on top of a satinwood Pembroke table that was one of the prettiest pieces of furniture in the room. It was badly scratched and wet as well, and she wondered whether, even with expert restoration, it would ever be the same again.

A thick layer of dust and rubble lay on the carpet that had been woven for the room and echoed the design of the lovely plasterwork above.

Sonia's eyes filled with tears.

'Oh Min! Poor old house. I can't bear it. Whatever shall we do?'

'Set about clearing up this mess, that's what. No use crying, that's for sure. I'll get my dustpan and brush and the vac.' Minnie, at her briskest, bustled off, but Sonia mooned uselessly around the room, treading white dust into the carpet and making the mess even worse.

Minnie returned with a full range of cleaning equipment and also with Joe, who had been handyman for as long as anyone could remember. He had officially retired a few years earlier, but had been so bored that he had returned to work after two weeks. He came part-time now, but was never far away, greatly preferring the magic pull of the big house to the emptiness of his own cottage. There was not much Joe couldn't turn his hand to, from plumbing to electricity, fiddling with clocks to mending tricycles. He was Sonia's staunchest ally, but the house was beginning to get the better of him. When he died a wealth of undocumented knowledge would go with him, for he neither wrote things down nor passed anything on to the younger generation of workmen, whom he held in contempt. 'Wouldn't pay that lot in rusty washers,' he was fond of saying.

Now he pushed his cap back and scratched his head. No one ever saw Joe without his cap. The children thought he slept in it.

'Bye! There must 'ave been a fair weight of water to bring that lot down,' he said. 'Have you looked upstairs yet m'lady?' Sonia shook her head. 'We'll go up yon and 'ave a see. There'll be forced to be water in the Red Room too.'

Sure enough, there was a large wet patch on the carpet of the bedroom overhead, and another on the ceiling.

'It'll be them gutters got silted up, or one o' they pesky jackdaws has blocked outlet to fall-pipe. I'll go on roof and 'ave a clear round.' Sonia watched sadly as Joe limped off to the staircase that led into the attics. He had an arthritic hip and moved with difficulty.

In theory, when it snowed, or rained heavily, the water that collected on the flat roof around the dome was conducted through the attics to the outside of the house by a series of lead conduits, but the lead was porous now, and in any case they easily overflowed unless regularly cleared out. In the old days there had been three full-time maintenance men. Now there was only Joe to do everything. Over the years various workmen had scribbled their names on the rafters, and Sonia had added hers, reckoning that in the last six months she had been up there with Joe as often as any plumber or roofer in the past. *Sonia Duntan – 1993*, she had written with love and pride.

Gloomily she went downstairs to get ready for Mr Hadleigh.

Possibly due to Archie's description of lily fingers, she had in her mind a clear picture of what she expected – definitely a 'greenery-yallery Grosvenor Gallery' young man with a long white face, long fair hair and a long silk scarf, probably driving a battered vintage sports car. The reality turned out to be very different.

Sonia knelt in one of the window seats in the morning room. It was a good vantage point from which to watch for arriving visitors as you could see the drive snaking down through the park, giving enough warning for you to be able to hide from the unwelcome or to rush out with loving hugs for the more favoured. Soon a car appeared round the first bend at the top, where it stopped for a few minutes. Casing the joint, thought Sonia, and suddenly felt absurdly excited.

When the car eventually arrived in front of the house, scrunching on the gravel with a confident swirl, it turned out to be a very new-looking dark blue Mercedes in which there were two passengers. Sonia watched, protected by the frayed and faded green damask curtains. The figure from the passenger seat got out first, a dumpy female figure dressed in a baggy denim skirt and a navy blue guernsey sweater that had lost its own shape but clung rather too closely to that of its wearer. A wife? Sonia had not expected two people. When the driver got out she saw a very dark man, older than she had imagined, and even on first sight exuding that indefinable but unmistakable gloss that means style – and probably expensive tastes. She felt her throat constrict. Would he understand about the charm of shabbiness, the importance of atmosphere? She watched him looking at the house, running his eye over it like someone assessing a racehorse. The woman came and rang the bell, setting all the dogs barking as usual. Sonia resisted the impulse to rush to the door. Mustn't appear overeager, she thought, play it cool, and she allowed the clamour to continue for several minutes before going into the hall and opening the front door.

'Lady Duntan? Simon Hadleigh. And this is Bridget Murray, my assistant, to whom you spoke on the telephone.'

His hair was turning grey at the sides and there was a silver streak at the top like a badger. He looked down at her from a considerable height and she had the distinct impression that it was not only the house that was getting the racehorse assessment.

She extended her hand formally, first to Bridget and then to him. Bridget had more than the suspicion of a moustache and a somewhat masculine haircut. Her hand was limp and moist, and shaking it was like trying to clutch at a piece of fog. Simon Hadleigh's handshake was brisk and firm.

'Well, do come in, both of you.' Sonia led the way into the house and through to the inner hall.

'Oh my goodness! Look at that! I knew about it, of course, but this is quite something.'

The staircase at Duntan really was spectacular. Steps jutting out from the wall curved up each side of the circular hall to a half-landing, where the two flights joined and became a single stretch that swept back overhead, completely unsupported, to the top landing, above which rose the dome.

'Yes, it is unusual, isn't it?' Sonia was well pleased with his reaction. 'We're very proud of our flying staircase. Of course no one knows whether it's safe or not, so you'll take your life in your hands when you go up it later. We never allow too many people on at one time, but when the children thunder up and down the whole thing bounces like a trampoline. There are sixteen unsupported treads on that top lot, you know.'

'Remarkable. Quite remarkable. I've been telling Bridget all about the house. Marvellous view of it from the top of the drive. We stopped to have a look.'

'Yes, I know, I saw you,' said Sonia, and then wished she hadn't. Simon Hadleigh looked at her with amusement.

'Ah,' he said, 'a strategic pause. Quite right. How wise.'

She was much put out on entering the library to find her mother-in-law already there. She had wished to have her guest to herself and establish an understanding between them before lunch, when he would meet Lady Rosamund, who was seldom earlier, having managed to commandeer for her own use the delightful little white and gold boudoir on the other side of the house that was one of Duntan's prettiest rooms. Inside, the gilded moulding had murals on the panels – beautiful flowers and birds of great elegance and delicacy which had been painted by Archie's great-great-grandmother in the middle of the last century. Sonia loved the feeling that a previous Lady Duntan had been an artist too; it made yet another emotional link with the house.

In fact, on the whole Rosamund's use of this room really suited everyone because it kept her out of the way, and though Minnie refused to clean it or lay the fire, Brother Ambrose was frequently seen carrying great baskets of the best logs in there. He was not, however, in the library now. Lady Rosamund might deem it prudent to turn the full force of her own charm on the Heritage at Risk representative as soon as possible, but had obviously thought it wiser not to expose him to her odd companion's considerable lack of it a moment before she had to. Sonia was about to make a grudging introduction, but it was not needed.

'Simon! Darling! How lovely to welcome you to Duntan.'

'Rosamund! What an enchanting surprise! I had no idea that you were in this country. Well, this is a bonus.'

Sonia gazed in astonished outrage as her mother-in-law gave the Heritage at Risk representative one of her most lingering scented kisses.

'You know each other! Roz – you never said.'

'You never asked me, darling. You shouldn't be such a secretive little thing yourself, and you might learn a lot of things you don't know.' Lady Rosamund was clearly enjoying herself enormously. 'Simon and I have known each other for a long time – since he was just a schoolboy, in fact. You might almost say I had a hand in his upbringing.' If she had been a cat her purrs would have made the walls vibrate.

'We so badly need your advice, Simon. We have all sorts of ideas about how we can save and finance this darling house, but an expert opinion will be invaluable, especially yours.' Lady Rosamund managed to convey the impression that she was in charge. 'When Sonia has shown you round we must have a little talk, and I will tell you some of the possibilities I have in mind.'

Sonia glared at her.

'I'm afraid there won't be time for that, Roz. Mr Hadleigh has to go back to London and I shall need every moment of the time he can spare us.' She had a nasty suspicion that her visitor was highly entertained by this exchange. 'I had no idea you were a friend of my mother-in-law,' she said to him as she dispensed the drinks, 'and of course she is so sweet in wanting to help us – though not, alas, financially – but my husband and I really have to decide things for ourselves.' She felt she must at all costs regain the initiative.

'Such a pity that Archie isn't here then,' said Lady Rosamund sweetly. 'But if you do have to rush off, Simon, then I'll tell you my scheme – which *would* involve financial help – now, and I know we'll have lots of chances to talk it through another time. I am prepared to put considerable capital into the restoration of the house if it is put to use for a cause of which I approve. We think it could be used as a centre for all religions to teach visualisation and meditation. It would be run by the Brothers of Love – I am a lay member and friend of the Brotherhood. They would make this their main base and organise the running of the house and hold seminars and workshops. I am sure you will agree that we, the family, are just custodians of these treasures and should share them in some worthwhile way?'

Simon Hadleigh roared with laughter.

'Well, I'd bank on you to have some sort of scheme, Roz, and I know how important you think it is to share assets,' he said, and Sonia had a feeling that they were talking about something quite different. She felt uncomfortable and excluded.

'I'm afraid Rosamund's ideas about the Brotherhood are out of the question,' she said. 'My husband and I are not in sympathy with their aims.'

'The Bishop, on the other hand,' said Lady Rosamund at her most sphinx-like, 'is very keen.'

This was news to Sonia, and not good news either. The Bishop of Granby pursued new ideas like a hound running on a burning scent, longing to give new insights to the young and not be shackled by outmoded traditions. He gave the impression of someone ever ready to rip off his mitre and dive into a disco. He had a fresh pink complexion, prematurely silver hair that always looked as if it had just had a blow-dry, and was frequently to be seen jogging round the close in a track suit. Some of his fellow clergy found him hard to keep up with in more ways than one. Sonia could see that it was a master stroke on her mother-in-law's part to get him involved. Archie might pretend that he would be prepared to sell the house to Brother Ambrose's shady cult, but she knew that in reality he distrusted them as much as she did. She was very sure that the Bishop, who was good and sincere, though possibly gullible, knew nothing about what the Brothers were really like, but if he lent his umbrella to Lady Rosamund's schemes, then Archie would have the perfect excuse for closing his eyes to the more sinister side of the proposition.

She decided not to join battle with Rosamund at this moment, but to exert all her efforts into charming Mr Hadleigh. Later she would enlighten him privately as to the impossibility of considering any suggestions from her mother-in-law, but she felt it was vital to find out a great deal more about him first. She was not at all sure that she liked him. He was undoubtedly attractive, but there was something disturbing about him.

Apart from the fact that Mrs Bean had triumphantly managed to undercook the baked potatoes, lunch passed off reasonably well. Brother Ambrose had not appeared; clearly Rosamund was keeping him under his grubby wraps. The food from the delicatessen was excellent and Sonia had chilled a couple of bottles of Archie's best white burgundy, which their guest had much appreciated. She had placed the silent Bridget next to her mother-in-law at the far end of the table and put Simon Hadleigh between herself and Martha. He had proved to be an amusing and easy conversationalist. Over drinks before lunch he had taken just as much trouble to talk to Polly and Tom as to the grown-ups, which sent him up in Sonia's estimation, and he now set out to entertain Martha and herself with highly coloured accounts of the eccentricities of some of the places he had visited in the course of his work.

After coffee he suddenly became very businesslike, and asked to be taken for a complete tour of the house, including the cellars and the roof. Sonia had to work quite hard to keep up with him as he ran lightly down the steps into the cellar, producing a torch from his pocket when none of the light switches worked, sticking his silver penknife into beams and woodwork in the attics, and keeping up a well-informed commentary into a cassette recorder as they whizzed round. Bridget, who despite her Trappist tendency was, he assured Sonia, a very bright girl with a great eye for detail, had been sent to go through some of the documents and old plans that Sonia had laid out on the billiard-room table.

It was as they were scrambling about the attics that led out on to the roof that Sonia said, 'Don't look at the view until I tell you. Please shut your eyes.'

'Not very easy to climb out with your eyes shut, but I'll try.'

Sonia went first and then watched as he folded his long frame through the narrow trapdoor and came to stand beside her. The view from the roof at Duntan was truly amazing; on clear days such as this you could even see the Minster standing up on the plain of York miles away. Just to look at it gave Sonia a sense of timelessness. As they leant against the stone balustrade, Sonia thought that he could hardly have seen it on a more beautiful day, with the sun shining on the great beech trees, the river winding into the distance, and the moors beyond. They were both silent for a few moments.

'I believe this is part of the old house, which was burnt down about 1750,' she said, running her hand along the stone. 'Old Lady D. told me that in the original house, which was even bigger and grander than this one, there was supposed to be a sort of walk up here.'

'Ah,' he said. 'A belvedere. Yes, look, these stones are carved on the inside as well as on the exterior. That would certainly date it as being earlier. I expect they used the same stones when the house was revamped after the fire. No wonder they had a walk up here with a view like this, though.' He smiled at her.

'Mr Hadleigh?' she started.

'Yes, Lady Duntan?' He gave her an amused look, mocking her formality.

'Oh well, Simon, then. How is it that you know my mother-in-law so well?'

'It goes back a long way. I used to spend a lot of time in this part of the world as a boy with the Vanalleyns, and though I never actually came to Duntan, I often met her with them at Ralton before she left your husband's father. I could tell you a lot about your mother-in-law. I vaguely remember Archie as a little boy, though I must be some years older than him. Sybil Vanalleyn is my aunt. I stayed with them last night.'

Sonia had a feeling that there was more to his acquaintance with Rosamund than this, but didn't like to probe.

'Archie's involved over some sort of shooting arrangements with Dukie Vanalleyn at the moment. I think we're supposed to be dining with them sometime quite soon,' she said. 'Let me show you the rest of the house. You haven't seen the drawing room yet. I'm afraid we had a disaster there this morning.'

'This place means a lot to you, doesn't it?' he asked, still gazing down.

'Yes,' she said. 'You can't think how much – probably too much. I suppose you could say it's a love affair.' As she spoke, there was a bleakness in her voice that made him look at her with sudden attention. He had formed an impression of her as being somewhat discontented beneath the charm and flippancy, but what he saw in her face now was real unhappiness.

'Then we'll have to see what we can do for you, won't we?' he said gently. 'I think I've got the feel of the layout. Now show me some of the contents, though I'm not a specialist and we'll need to call in Sotheby's or someone to do a proper valuation.'

All the same, it soon became clear that he was extremely knowledgeable.

'Are these genuine Romneys? Do you know about them? There were so many copies done at the turn of the century. These look a bit dubious to me. But they do look marvellous in here all the same, and they'd be even better if they were cleaned. Ah! A Daniel Delander movement in this clock! What a gem – but the case has been added later. Someone was naughty to let these Russell pastels hang on an outside wall and get damp. Pretty Lawrence head – unfinished, of course. Nice to find a George Lambert landscape. Now I do like that.'

Sonia was left in no doubt that the condition of everything left a great deal to be desired, but also that Simon not only knew what he was talking about with regard to the house and its contents, but was very clued up about the financial side as well.

'Lovely to find an organ. It looks so well in the hall. I see it's a Joseph Walker. Do you play?'

'Yes,' said Sonia, 'though not very well. We always sing carols round it at Christmas, and it sounds wonderful with the sound floating up to the dome. Very flattering – like singing in the bath.'

In the morning room, which Archie's grandmother had used as her special sitting room, he stopped opposite two of Sonia's own watercolours. She held her breath in case he came out with some unfavourable comment, and then, unable to bear the suspense as he looked at them closely, she said lightly, 'You won't be able to place those, I'm afraid.'

'Oh but I can,' he said. 'I can indeed. Of course – it figures. You're Sonia Grey. You see, I have two of your pictures hanging in my house in London. I bought them years ago at what must have been your first exhibition. I fell in love with them.'

They stared at each other.

The telephone ringing broke the moment. It was Millicent ringing to enquire whether anyone was coming to collect Birdie and Cassie. She sounded rather rattled, and Sonia realised with a shock that it was five o'clock and she had forgotten all about them.

Simon took his leave, gathering up Bridget and promising to go away, study his notes, have a good think about everything, and send a report with various ideas and suggestions. But he left her in no doubt that the cost was likely to be formidable, and that any grant would almost certainly have to be matched 'pound for pound' by the owners.

'And of course I will need to meet Archie too,' he said. 'Say goodbye to Rosamund for me, and thank you for a delightful lunch and for the tour of the house. I'll be in touch.'

Sonia watched his car drive back up the park again. She watched till it was out of sight before she pulled herself together and went to collect her abandoned daughters.

Their visit had not been an unqualified success. Birdie, Elizabeth and Ruth all attended the village school under the cosy rule of Mrs Dickinson, a small, birdlike woman who would have looked at home pecking about on a lawn. Every fourth Monday they were used to performing little unscripted plays, mostly of a biblical or historical nature, for the benefit of 'our moomies' monthly assemblies', and so were much given to acting. Cassie was well used to joining in these games. Daniel Miller, aged three, was not, and had not taken kindly to being tightly rolled up in a cot sheet and stuck in the chest in the hall to play the part of Lazarus in the tomb while the girls, doubling up as Martha, Mary, Jesus and the disciples, prepared to raise him from the dead. Luckily, his muffled bellows had been heard by his mother, who arrived in the nick of time to rescue him from suffocation and to save the would-be miracle workers from a rather spectacular failure. Millicent had been badly frightened and none too sure that the children's behaviour might not count as blasphemy.

'Then she was cross all over again when Cassie went to their loo and tried out Benjamin's potty. She said it ought to have been disinfected first,' said an outraged Birdie, 'so I asked if he'd got the scours or something and she thought I was being rude.' The Duntan children, who spent a lot of time playing with the Slaters, were well versed in the complaints of cattle.

'Oh, I shouldn't worry. The middle classes are always obsessed with hygiene,' said Lady Rosamund comfortably. She was not exactly one for pigging it herself, though it would certainly not have occurred to her that hers should be the hand to wield the Dettol or the Harpic.

Altogether it had been a full day, and Sonia was glad when

the younger children had gone to bed and she and her mother-in-law and Martha were sitting in the library before dinner, while Tom and Polly played Cluedo on the floor. There had been a telephone call for Martha from Robin Warner, and though she had said 'Oh, that drip,' in a very bored way when Tom, who had answered the telephone, called her, she was gone a very long time.

'Poor old Tomato,' said Tom provocatively. 'Perhaps you'll be getting some new hair on your Sellotape soon.'

'Shouldn't think Robin Warner's got any hair on his chest. He's just a child.' Martha looked very offhand.

'Talking about hair,' said Polly, 'did you just see that grotty old Bridget's moustache? Surely Mr Hadleigh can't be in love with her? She'd be awfully prickly to kiss.'

'Oh, I don't know,' said Martha. 'Women are always kissing men with moustaches. Min says kissing a man without a moustache is like a ham sandwich without mustard. Why should it be different?'

'Anyway, I thought she looked like a man,' said Polly.

'It's always possible that Bridget *is* a man,' said Lady Rosamund.

'A man! Granny, how could she have been?'

'Oh well, it's all very easy nowadays. They simply have everything lopped off, take a few hormones, and bob's your uncle.'

'Or bob's your aunt,' said the accurate Tom.

Polly rushed off to telephone Shirley Gillespie, pleased that the flow of fascinating facts was no longer one-way traffic.

After a disgusting supper of fish pie, normally a family favourite but this time full of bones and slimy skin, followed by tinned fruit and custard instead of the fresh fruit salad and cream she had ordered, Sonia decided that she must get rid of Mrs Bean the following day, even if the trial period was not yet up.

She went to bed early, feeling drained and exhausted, but at the same time curiously restless. She wondered if Simon Hadleigh was married, and thought that she had discovered very little about him. It was a long time before she went to sleep.

Chapter 10

Next morning Sonia's efforts to dislodge Mrs Bean did not prove very successful. She gave Sonia a wicked look out of her malevolent little ginger eyes and lowered her head as though about to charge. Sonia quite expected her to start pawing the ground with one swollen leg, but instead she muttered darkly about unfair dismissal, not sticking to agreements and tribunals and compensation in a way that made Sonia feel it might be better to wait till Archie returned before they had a showdown. Archie had his uses.

She still hoped the disagreeable meals might help to shift Brother Ambrose, and had been annoyed to discover that her mother-in-law was ordering delicious little food hampers from Fortnum's. None of the delicacies had found their way into Sonia's larder, and she had gone into the morning room to find Lady Rosamund and Ambrose tucking into a pot of caviare, which they were eating out of the jar with silver teaspoons.

If Archie had gone off to London like a snarling dog, he came back looking more like a particularly sleek cat, one whose fur had frequently been smoothed in the right direction, who had been fed on saucerfuls of double cream, and who was by no means sated with this diet.

In the end it was not Mrs Bean who got rid of Brother Ambrose. It was Brother Ambrose who caused the departure of Mrs Bean.

The family were all lunching in the dining room a few days later, Cassie choosing as usual to sit next to Brother Ambrose, and pulling her chair very close to his. Mrs Bean was waddling in from the kitchen with a tepid dish of sodden leeks when she suddenly let out a wild shriek, dropped the dish and fled out of the door with a turn of speed of which no one would have believed her capable.

'What the bloody hell's got into her?' asked Archie, and even as he said it, his eyes came to rest on something small and black that was crawling about on the white damask table-cloth in front of Brother Ambrose.

'Oh my God!' Sonia automatically covered her hair with both hands. 'Oh my God, it's a bat! Catch it someone, quick. Archie, Tom – do something!'

Birdie disappeared under the table, but Cassie, quite unmoved, reached out her hand and to Sonia's disgust and amazement, picked up the little creature.

'You mustn't hurt it,' said Cassie reprovingly. 'It's Brother Ambrose's pet. It's called Dracula.' And she placed it carefully on the back of his hairy hand, from where it slowly crawled on to his black jersey and disappeared up his arm, inside his habit, watched with fascinated horror by everyone else.

The little secret that Brother Ambrose kept up his sleeve was revealed.

In the ensuing pandemonium, Lady Rosamund beat a strategic retreat to her bedroom for one of her little rests. She was not much of a one for standing by friends in moments of crisis, not that Brother Ambrose ever seemed in need of protection. Birdie lay cowering face down under the table, and when Archie attempted to lay a reassuring hand on her leg and pull her out, she thought it was the touch of Dracula and became quite hysterical. It appeared that she, like Cassie, had been well aware of the presence of the bat, but had been sworn to secrecy. She had been terrified of the little creature for days, hence the nightmares and the frantic bedroom searches. Brother Ambrose, it seemed, was given to taking it out at night to have a fly around the house, though for the rest of the time it hung upside down on the curtains of his bedroom, or dozed comfortably up his arm. Polly and Tom were much put out that their younger sisters had not only known of the existence of such a fascinating pet, but had actually managed, though for different reasons, to keep the information to themselves.

By the time Birdie was persuaded to come out, and the leeks and bits of broken china were scooped up off the floor, Sonia decided that she had better go and see what had become of Mrs Bean. She was not in the kitchen, but Minnie, who was, gave a thumbs-up sign.

'She's packing!' said Minnie. 'They say there's good to come out of every trial. Gone straight upstairs to get 'er bags together, and she'll be flitting this afternoon. The ways of the Lord are very mysterious,' she added piously.

'Oh Min,' said Sonia, hugging her. 'How wonderful. I thought she'd never go.'

'Takes one dirty creature to get rid of another seemingly,' and Minnie gave her best cackle. 'But don't you go letting him bring the nasty little thing in here, that's all!'

Joe was called in to drive a palpitating Mrs Bean, together with the smelly Crumpet, into York. Before she left, Mrs Bean gave Sonia a venomous look. 'I am writing my memoirs,' she announced, 'and you're all in them. It will be called *Shits I Have Known*,' and she banged the car door shut. The children ran after the departing car till it was out of sight, singing 'Put the Purple Knickers On' at the top of their voices.

Archie strode purposefully upstairs to see his mother.

Lady Rosamund, covered in a white cashmere rug, was lying on the sofa in her bedroom, a mound of soft pillows piled up behind her head, listening to Wagner while she applied a little fresh blood to her talons. He switched off the music.

'No look here, Mother, this has gone too far. I'm not having the whole household in hysterics because of a bloody bat. That man has got to go.'

'Archie darling,' Lady Rosamund's voice was at its mellowest, 'do stand a little further away. You vibrate so when you're cross, and I don't want to smudge my nails.' She outlined the half-moon on her thumb with great concentration. Archie took a step backwards.

'I am quite serious, Mother. I won't have him in the house another night, and that's final. What do you see in him, anyway? Did you know he kept that disgusting pet?'

'Brother Ambrose is a chiropteraphile,' said Lady Rosamund, as though this were as normal as keeping bees or being a pigeon-fancier. 'He always has to have a bat. Don't be disagreeable, Archie, it doesn't suit you. That high colour may be a sign of blood pressure. I always thought your father's accident was due to heart trouble. You ought to keep a very even keel if you want to live through the mid-life crisis you appear to be having.'

'I am not having a crisis.'

'No? Oh well that is a relief, darling. One would so hate to see you making a fool of yourself, quite apart from any health risk.'

'What are you talking about?'

'I wonder if Sonia minds about your plump little friend? It might be a pity if anyone told her.' Lady Rosamund waved a languid hand in the air to speed the drying of the varnish.

'Told her what?'

'One of the Brothers – Brother François, such a charming man – happened to be having dinner at Le Gavroche the other night. Such delicious food always. I hear you had a very good dinner too.' Lady Rosamund gave her son a brilliant smile. 'Do stop pacing about like that, darling. It reminds me of your father when you get so noisy and restless. No wonder Sonia gets edgy.'

Archie glowered down at his mother.

'You had me followed!' he said furiously. 'What is this organisation, the Mafia or something? Brothers of Love! What have you got yourself mixed up in, Mother? You'll end up in serious trouble.'

'Oh, I don't think so. The Brothers are very useful so long as one makes the position quite clear to them, and they don't think they can pull the wool over one's eyes. I am very realistic, you know. They know just how far they can go. And,' said Rosamund, 'I am not an innocent.'

Archie snorted.

'Well, I won't have it, Mother. That bloody monk does not spend one more night under this roof. He can take his bit of vermin and stuff it up his phoney cassock and get out. And you can tell Sonia what you like. I don't think she'd be all that surprised, and I don't think she'd like you any better for telling her,' said Archie shrewdly.

'Very well, darling.' Lady Rosamund was far too clever to press the point. 'Poor Ambrose shall go. But I have a lot of money since Al died. Martha's independent, which as her trustee you know, and if this house were safely tied up with an organisation, under my direction of course, you could get Sonia away from it and its influence on her. You might find your marriage a great deal better for it. Sonia's very attractive you know, I watched her make quite a conquest the other day, and she won't hold out long if you go on playing away. I know a lot about marriage,' she added disarmingly, 'I've had so much practice. Think about it, darling.'

'Hmm,' said Archie. 'You get rid of that monk and call your sleuths off my trail, and then perhaps I'll think about it.'

On the whole they were neither of them dissatisfied with this conversation.

Chapter 11

With the disappearance of two such sharp thorns in her flesh, Sonia knew she should have experienced a great relief, but instead she felt as edgy and irritable as ever, perhaps even more so. It was as though the combined presence of Brother Ambrose and Mrs Bean had acted on her like a twitch on the nose of a horse that resents being shod, the combined effect of these two lesser irritants to some extent taking her mind off the greater irritations that lay at the root of her discontent. The fact that Archie had said, 'Well, now that we've got rid of those two, perhaps you'll try and be a bit more agreeable for a change,' did nothing to improve matters. The children, except for Birdie, made no secret of the fact that they were greatly disappointed at the departure of the two strange visitors. They had much enjoyed sharing a common enemy, and without this unifying presence the guerrillas turned on each other and old petty rivalries were resumed. The end of a war brings a great deal of quarrelling in its wake. The house was full of disharmony.

Sonia felt a great restlessness, not unconnected with the fact that every time the telephone rang (which was often) she hoped it was going to be Simon Hadleigh. She had secretly expected him to ring the day after his visit, not, of course, with any definite suggestions about the house, there would certainly not have been time for that, but just to keep in touch – possibly to thank her for lunch, or even to discuss her painting. She would have been reassured had she known that this idea had occurred to Simon too, but he was far too experienced an operator to rush his fences.

She had tried to tell Archie about the visit – an edited version, anyway – but all he would say was, 'Well, if they put a definite plan before me, of course I'll consider it, but even if they did offer us a grant, where are you going to find the money we would have to raise to match it?' Sonia would have liked to answer that question too.

'Simon Hadleigh wasn't at all like what you'd imagined, Archie. Your mother has known him for years. He's a nephew of the Vanalleyns. I really liked him.'

'So I gather,' said Archie. Sonia thought she had better change the subject fast.

To make matters worse, the Easter holidays were coming to an end, and the thought of returning to school affected them all. Polly, who was naturally gregarious and had all Archie's energy and need for organised activity, secretly looked forward to the new term with its possibilities for bossing around other less dominant members of the form, for forming élitist groups of which she was the most select member of all, and for terrorising the wretched Shirley to discover further intriguing facts from her factually fertile parent – but she would have died rather than admit it.

Tom, the only one so far to be a boarder, loathed going back to school. It was not that he was always miserable once he was there, but he was not a natural conformer and deeply resented the loss of his liberty. Not one who wished to spare others from sharing his troubles, his gloomy face and lowering presence affected everyone like an impending thunderstorm, and a pall hung over them all.

Now having absolutely refused even to glance at the book the school had set as holiday reading he was anxiouly obsessed about the questions he would inevitably be called upon to answer about it, while still being quite unprepared to waste his last days of freedom studying it. Sonia found herself weakly skimming through the interminable pages of *The Three Musketeers* in order to relay a potted version of the story to him, while he hung gloomily around her, making life as difficult as possible and sucking her emotionally dry, so that much as she adored him, half of her almost longed for the day when he would be back at school and they would all be free of his depressing presence, although she then felt guilty for feeling like this. Until threatened with any activity, such as school or a party in which he did not wish to partake, Tom could be the very best company, but his black moods were a terrible affliction to himself and everyone else. Sonia felt that Archie ought to save her some of the onus and deal with Tom himself, but if he ever attempted to discipline Tom, she always found herself defending him hotly and another row between them would boil up.

Birdie should have returned to school several days earlier, the terms and holidays of the village school being slightly different from those of Polly and Tom, but it had suited Sonia to have Cassie occupied while she concentrated on the older two, so much to Archie's disapproval she had used Birdie's wan face and occasional tummy-aches as an excuse to keep her at home for a few days longer.

'Don't you think you ought to take her to Dr Childs?' asked Archie. 'All this sickness can't be right. She might have a grumbling appendix.'

'Oh, it's just nerves – it's just her make-up. Dr Childs says so himself. Don't fuss, Archie.'

'Well it doesn't seem right to me. Maybe we need another opinion. Maybe we should take her to a specialist or something?'

'Nonsense. She's always been like this. Dr Childs says later it'll probably turn into proper migraines like mine. She gets upset over the least little thing and that brings on these bilious attacks.'

'If she's upset, perhaps you should try to find out what's upsetting her instead of pandering to Cassie and Tom all the time.'

'And perhaps you should make more effort to do things with your son and take him off my hands, and stop fussing over Birdie.'

'I am not fussing. I just don't think she ought to be sick so often.'

'Well, if you'll take Tom fishing this afternoon, maybe I'll take Birdie to the surgery.'

'You know quite well I've got a county-council meeting today.'

'Then perhaps you'll leave it to me? Anyway, you can't be all that concerned if you put some dreary old committee on footpaths above your children.'

Sonia knew she was being unfair. Archie was a good father, loved his children and spent time with all of them. She felt a twinge of guilty anxiety. She did not like to admit that she found Birdie's sensitivity irritating. All the same, she took her to the doctor, who went over her carefully.

'Could it be a grumbling appendix?'

'Well, certainly not at the moment. If she had a fever as well as tummy pains, then you should always take that seriously, but you say she never runs a temperature?'

He asked Sonia some pertinent questions about the state of affairs at home, to which she gave some fairly evasive answers, saying vaguely that there was a good deal of uncertainty going on about decisions over the future and perhaps Birdie had picked up some anxiety about that. She made a resolution to try not to quarrel with Archie in front of Birdie, but didn't feel very confident of her ability to keep to it. She hated herself and felt her own control to be very precarious.

Martha spent a lot of time on the telephone to Robin Warner and had been out with him several times. She professed to find him a bore but it did not stop her accepting his invitations or rushing to answer the telephone when it rang. All the same, Sonia did not think Martha looked particularly happy. She was as flippant and funny as ever, and was often to be found in the kitchen regaling Minnie and the children or Sonia herself with hilarious accounts of her mother's goings-on in New York; she went riding with Archie and Polly, and played endless games of ping-pong with Tom; often she just curled up in one of the wonderfully squashy chairs in the library, deep in a book and apparently oblivious to all that was going on around her. And yet, despite this, there was a tautness about her that showed in heavy shadows under eyes that sometimes looked strangely staring and enormous in her pale, beaky little face, and in the way she twined and tensed her thin fingers. Her moods seemed to swing more suddenly than usual. Sonia supposed it was adolescence, although Martha appeared to have grown up so early. Perhaps the malaise that seemed to be afflicting both the house and its occupants was having its effect on her; perhaps the griffins were casting a spell – Martha's nails were bitten to the quick.

As usual, Lady Rosamund was supremely unmoved by the feelings of anyone except herself. She said she had been invited to lunch with the Bishop.

At last the dreaded day arrived for Tom to go back to school. Jeans were exchanged for grey flannel trousers in which he seemed diminished, somehow smaller and more vulnerable. Sonia's heart turned over for him, and the last morning was spent in letting him drive her round the various tracks and private roads on the estate. Both Polly and Tom had started learning to drive the previous summer when Martha had persuaded Archie to begin teaching her, and they handled Sonia's car with considerable efficiency. Tom had also been allowed to choose his favourite lunch of roast chicken with lashings of bread sauce followed by ice-cream and hot chocolate sauce, but he could hardly do it justice. Polly, who thought he was receiving far too much attention and who would have loved to be going off to boarding school herself, was perfectly poisonous throughout the meal. Birdie, agonising for Tom, toyed with her food too, her eyes brimming with sympathetic tears, until Sonia snapped her head off and made her finish everything on her plate, and then felt deeply ashamed of herself. It was a miserable meal.

At three o'clock, just as Joe was heaving Tom's trunk, cricket bag and all the numerous bits and pieces that would have to be taken loose into Sonia's car, Archie's BMW roared up the drive and jerked to a halt outside the front door.

'Finished my meeting early. Said I had to take Tom back to school and left old Forsyth in the chair. We'd got through the main agenda, so he can't do much damage. Hop in, Tom. I'll take you back.'

Tom flashed Sonia an imploring look. He greatly preferred the prolonged agony of being taken back by his mother, sucking the orange of martyrdom to extract the last drops of miserable juice.

'Oh Archie, don't be ridiculous. Joe's just packed up my car and I'm all organised to go. If you'd told me earlier it would have been different, but you said you couldn't get away.'

'Well I made a special effort. Thought you'd be pleased. Less silly nonsense from Tom, too. Might have a word with old Burrows about cricket coaching.'

Tom climbed quickly into the front seat of Sonia's car. Archie longed for his son to be as keen on cricket as he himself was and couldn't understand his reluctance to spend hours practising bowling, let alone his aversion to the many boys' cricket matches that were organised during the summer holidays. Had Tom been unathletic, Archie would have been very understanding, though he might still have expected him to take a keen interest and make eager little dots in a score book as a spectator, but Tom was very good at games and had a marvellous eye. Tom's opinion that the game was boring struck Archie as being on a par with spitting on the Bible or failing to stand up for the National Anthem. He considered Sonia a subversive influence, and darkly suspected that she encouraged their son's extraordinary attitude. He was, of course, right. Instead of sitting all day in a deck chair, eagerly watching his every stroke like any normal wife, she always made excuses not to attend the various matches in which he himself played. He was sure Rosie Bartlett would have loved to watch him bat. He was, of course, right in this too, though it had very little to do with cricket.

Caught between the wishes of husband and son, Sonia as usual sided with the latter.

'I've got to talk to Matron about Tom's verrucas, and in any case it's too late to change all our plans now. Do stop arguing, Archie – you'll only make us late. If I'd known you were coming home, I wouldn't have had such a ghastly rush, but as it is I might just as well go. You can fetch him in three weeks' time for the first exeat and talk cricket to old Frank to your heart's content then.'

Sonia let in the clutch too quickly and stalled the engine, which spoiled the effect of the speedy departure. Ten minutes later Archie's car was heading in the direction of the Bartletts' house. The weedy little products of Roger's reluctant loins had already returned to school, and Roger himself was still in the Auvergne with various friends of congenial tastes, musical or otherwise.

Upcott House, a vast, castellated pile of red brick not unlike St Pancras Station, looked quite out of place in the Yorkshire Dales, where every other building was of the local grey stone and blended into the windswept landscape. It had been built towards the end of the last century by a millionaire mill owner with ambitions to become a country gentleman, but as he had failed to produce an heir the property had been sold after his death and had been a school ever since. The grounds were beautiful, with spreading trees and large playing fields that at present smelt deliciously of mown grass. Inside the building, the scents were less delicious, the air being heavy with the smell of boys en masse, a combination of sweaty socks, chalk and stale boot polish, which even four weeks of their absence had failed to eradicate. Just to sniff the air would make one expect the place to be rather dirty, but in fact everything gleamed, from the acres of polished green linoleum to the brass rail that ran down the banisters and was supposed to stop small boys from sliding down. Tom's heart sank as he and Sonia entered.

'Don't *smile* at everyone, Mum,' he muttered. He was very possessive of his mother and considered her far too friendly. He glared at all his friends who ran up to greet him, and Sonia sighed. Tom could make life very difficult for himself.

She gave as muted a smile as was compatible with politeness to Flora Burrows, the headmaster's wife, a relentlessly jolly lady of uncertain age with the rough, springy hair of a border terrier and well-developed calves. She had played lacrosse for England. She and her husband were known to the boys as Phallic Frank and Fertile Flora, a particularly witty joke since they had no children of their own. The school was their life.

'Hullo there, Duntan,' she greeted Tom. 'Looking forward to a try for the Second Eleven this term?'

Tom gave her a boot-faced look, and Sonia rushed into the breach with a few gushing irrelevances to hide his lack of team spirit and cooperation. Forgetting about not smiling too much, she beamed nervously. Mrs Burrows made her very uneasy, and she knew that neither she nor Tom measured up to the required standard expected of Upcott House mothers and sons. Archie, on the other hand, was definitely on the approved list.

'Well, you'll be longing to go and see where you're sleeping this term,' said Flora Burrows. 'I think you may just find you're in Upper Dorm Two!' She sounded as though this was the greatest treat in the world, as if she was talking about a suite at Claridges. Tom scowled and Sonia poked him urgently in the back until he muttered 'Thanks' ungraciously.

'Oh darling,' she said as they trailed upstairs, 'I do wish you'd try and look as if you liked people a bit more. Couldn't you just try and be pleasant?'

'I hate her and she hates me.'

'Well it's not surprising if you glower at everyone like that. Just *pretend* to like her and one day you might even find it's true.' Tom gave her an unbelieving look.

They found his bed, with his own tartan rug folded at the foot of it, and unpacked his overnight case. Tom pronounced everyone else in the dormitory to be weeds and grots, though Sonia knew he really quite liked some of them, and would probably be thick as thieves as soon as she had gone. She knew she would have done better to drop him at the front door and not come in with him. Archie was always telling her that she prolonged the agony, but somehow she could never bring herself to do as she should. They would both be relieved when the goodbyes were over, but she felt such a traitor at leaving him that she never made the quick getaway she intended. Tom, wishing to put her and himself through the maximum torment, refused all invitations from other small boys to come and join them, for he was really quite popular, and instead insisted on coming to wave her off, so that she could see him in her driving mirror for as long as possible, a lone figure standing gloomily outside the architectural monstrosity as she drove away, her eyes misted with tears.

There is something very soothing about being alone in a car – a way of suspending one's ordinary life and escaping from one's everyday self and the day-to-day problems that beset us all. Sonia wondered what would happen if she just went on driving indefinitely and simply disappeared. She also wondered if she could think of any good reason why she might ring up Simon Hadleigh on the car telephone, but was unable to come up with any idea that sounded in the least convincing.

The instinct of the homing pigeon is strong, however, and in the end she headed home for Duntan. But she took as long as possible to get there.

Chapter 12

Life settled back into its normal termtime routine. To get to school, Birdie only had to walk through the wicket-gate by the church and down the lane that led to the village, sometimes accompanied by the Slater children, when their mother could rouse herself to send them. Polly had to be driven to South Swale, the next village, and put on a bus to Harrogate, but she quite often spent the night with the Gillespies, who lived in half of one of the big stone houses on the outskirts of the town. She and Shirley had discovered a book on Mrs Gillespie's shelves called *Everything You Ever Wanted to Know About Sex But Didn't Like to Ask*. It was proving a great incentive to putting up with Mrs Gillespie's rather curious cooking, which was going through an ethnic phase. Cassie spent the time till her lady-in-waiting returned from school at three thirty disciplining her dolls, trotting round the house with Minnie, or playing by herself on the swing in the garden. Sonia was free to paint most mornings, and was seriously beginning to get material for her exhibition ready.

She was deeply absorbed in a picture when the telephone rang. Normally she might have let it ring, but she had forgotten to switch on the answering machine and so she picked up the receiver.

'Hullo?'

'Am I interrupting that talented artist at work?'

'Who is it?' she asked, knowing perfectly well. She was afraid the noise of her heartbeat might be audible over the telephone, and could only hope that it was like eating ginger biscuits – not nearly so loud outside as in.

'Sonia – it's Simon Hadleigh here. I did enjoy my tour of Duntan, and thank you for a delicious lunch. I'm afraid I haven't got a report finished for you yet, but there are a few loose ends I want to tie up. All minor things really, but I wondered if you were likely to be up in London at all over the next few weeks? I thought perhaps I could take you out to lunch and discuss it all? Archie too, of course, if he could come.'

'Oh. That's very kind of you,' said Sonia, doing some rapid thinking and deciding to experiment with throwing caution if not to the winds at least to a small breeze. 'I know Archie's very tied up at the moment, and of course I'm busy getting my new exhibition together, but I shall have to come up to London after the bank holiday weekend anyway. Yes, that would be lovely. Of course Archie would need to approve of any scheme about Duntan, but he's rather leaving it to me at this stage.' She felt as if she had most satisfactorily poked Rosie Bartlett in the eye.

'When is the exhibition? I shall want to come to it, you know. Time I added to my collection, perhaps.'

'Oh, not till late July, but this one's not in London. I haven't had one there for ages – not since before Polly was born. I'm trying to find my way back, really. It's at a small gallery up here in Blaydale. I've liked some of the other exhibitions they've put on there, and the *Yorkshire Post* have promised to send their art critic. It's good for American tourists at this time of year too. They come vet-spotting after all those wonderful Herriot books, but they might get trapped into buying a picture. It's all quite small beer, though, and I don't expect my acquaintances to have to come.'

'How about your friends?'

'Well, perhaps some of my friends.'

'I shall stay with my Aunt Sybil and make a special point of being there. Now get your diary out.'

They made a date for the middle of June, though Sonia would really have liked it to be sooner, and chatted on easily for several minutes. Unlike Archie, Simon obviously had a talent for frivolous telephone gossip.

'I shall be seeing your aunt on the twenty-ninth,' said Sonia, hoping she might be sewing a tiny seed. 'We're having dinner at Ralton then. I think I told you we were going over sometime. Shall I gave them your love?'

'Yes,' he said. 'You do that.'

She returned to her painting in a very different mood from any she had been in for a long time.

Sonia was not the only one who had been looking at the post with particular interest. Each morning Martha rushed to the hall when the dogs signalled the arrival of the postman to see if there was a letter with a Windsor postmark from Robin, or one from Venice written in Harry's Bar. She, too, seemed very unsettled, and Sonia thought that she ought to be occupied in some way. Unfortunately, with all her money there was no incentive for her to look for any sort of job, and her mother seemed supremely indifferent about further education, although Martha was very bright.

Lady Rosamund spent a lot of time on her portable telephone, which she only used when she did not want to risk her conversation being overheard. Saving Archie and Sonia's telephone bill did not enter her thinking. She and Archie also made several trips to London, although not together.

Archie had asked his friends Bill and Caroline Bruce to stay for the first bank holiday. He pursued Sonia with his diary and cornered her to make sure that she had entered various social engagements in her diary as well as his so that she could not at a later date pretend to know nothing about them. It was the only way in which he did pursue her. Despite living under the same roof, eating the same meals and sharing the same bed, they were like two strangers. Their only intimacy was the little bursts of irritation that would suddenly flare between them.

The magic week when every tree is a different green had passed, though the complete uniformity of colour that comes with full summer had not yet arrived. The daffodils were over, but 'Pheasant's Eye' narcissi sprinkled stars among the long grass, and bluebells breathed a purple haze through the woods going down to the river. Willow warblers and blackcaps fluted, house martins, newly arrived after their long journey from Africa, seemed to be looking for holiday apartments in the crumbling walls of the stable yard, and swallows gave aerobatic displays above the lawn. Duntan looked its beautiful best. The summer was beginning.

On the appointed evening, the ladies of the parish – the men being conspicuous only by their absence – gathered at the Vicarage for the prayer-group meeting, when there was some jockeying for the leading spiritual position. Piety can be very competitive.

It was a beautiful evening and Sonia would much rather have been taking the dogs for a walk along the overgrown path by the river, breathing in the elusive smell of damp moss and cowslips, and watching the changing patterns on the surface of the water. She thought the presence of God would be far more easily felt there than in the Vicarage, but did not want to let down the Millers. Rosamund, on the other hand, clearly felt that the Almighty was constantly on hand, should she wish to call for him, like ringing for room service.

There had been the usual difficulty of when to eat. Most people at the meeting would have had a meal at six, but neither Archie nor his mother would contemplate dining before eight, so it had been arranged that Minnie would give Archie dinner at the ordinary time and leave soup and chicken salad ready for the pilgrims on their return.

The Vicarage was a small, modern house between the villages of South Swale and Duntan. The dining room also had to do service as Terry's study and the meeting room. The Old Vicarage, a pretty stone house near the church, had been sold for a sum of money that had nearly caused Colonel Forsyth to die of apoplexy once he realised that the Parochial Church Council, of which he was treasurer, would in no way benefit, and that all the money would go into the coffers of the Board of Finance, with whom he was fighting a running battle over the diocesan quota.

Terry had drummed up so much support for this first meeting (doubtless numbers would drop sharply once the novelty wore off) that Millicent had been hard-put to find enough seats, and had had to bring down the cork-topped bathroom stool in which the children's plastic ducks were kept. The top was still very damp. She had set what chairs she could muster round the dining table, which looked set for a gathering of Lenten masochists ready to endure a foodless feast as an exercise in self-denial.

It was clear from the start that both Marcia and Lady Rosamund felt they should be in charge of the proceedings, Marcia in her capacity as president of the WI and, in her own opinion, a natural leader – her wartime years in the Wrens had been a halcyon period in her life – and Rosamund as the one with greater spiritual experience and higher social position. She wore her title like an ancient but becoming garment in which she felt particularly comfortable. The Vicar, who had the more obvious claim to lead the group, was going to have to exert himself to do so. Both ladies had their eye on the armchair at the head of the table, and it looked for a minute as if they were going to skirmish round it like a game of musical chairs. Luckily, old Mrs Porter from the Post Office, not a contender for authority, solved the problem by slipping innocently into it right under their noses. Poor Marcia had to settle for the bathroom stool, her tweed-clad posterior overlapping the sides by several inches.

Finally everyone was seated and Marcia, seeing that she was unlikely to be able to conduct the meeting herself, but determined that her rival should not to do so either, unfairly stole a march by banging loudly on the table, calling for silence, and inviting Terry to take the chair. Mrs Dickinson from the school and Mrs Dawson from one of the farms, who were cosily exchanging knitting patterns, looked rather disappointed. 'But its's really ever so pretty when it's made up,' hissed Mrs Dickinson urgently.

'Welcome, welcome,' began Terry, but Lady Rosamund, not one to be easily upstaged, laid her bejewelled hand gently on his.

'One moment, Vicar. I don't see Millicent with us yet. I feel the least we can do is to wait for our hostess. It's such a struggle getting children off to bed.' Lady Rosamund had never put a child to bed in her life. She smiled sweetly across at Marcia. Fifteen all, thought Sonia.

Millicent, breathlessly apologetic, slipped into the room. She had had difficulty getting the baby, who was teething, settled. Terry gave his wife rather an unchristian look. Though absolutely terrified of Marcia and Rosamund, he felt it important to be master in his own house. He strongly supported the feminist movement, except within the walls of the Vicarage. Millicent sat next to Ailsa Briggs, the community nurse. She might get a chance to have a quick word about Baby after the contemplation was over.

They were a motley crew, attending for a mixture of motives: one or two serious seekers after a better means of communicating with their God, a few staunch church supporters, possibly more at home at coffee mornings or as stallholders at the summer fête, but loyally feeling they should back up the endeavour, and one, Miss Dunn from Chestnut Cottage in The Row, almost certainly bent on sabotage.

Miss Dunn was a disagreeable old lady whose father had been the blacksmith years before. It was said that she had been crossed in love in her youth, jilted at the altar, and this was regarded by the more tolerant members of the community as an excuse for her extreme bad temper. Others, less charitably, considered that the prospective groom had had a narrow escape. She had sung in the church choir for years, but when the dwindling numbers had forced the PCC to abolish it, she had refused to disband, and every Sunday continued to sit, robed in blue, in the choir stalls, following the Vicar through the vestry door like a dumpy, grumpy bridesmaid. She looked like a malevolent old toad and emitted an unpleasant smell. No one wanted to sit next to her, but Ailsa Briggs, who in the nature of her profession was used to smelly old ladies, had nobly taken the windward side of her, and Sonia, feeling it was a hair-shirt occasion, the other.

To these assorted seekers after the Truth, Terry had distributed the week before some leaflets entitled 'Six Simple First Steps to Contemplation', on which he hoped to build the experiment.

'Now, ladies,' said Terry, 'you have all had a chance to read this excellent little book, and I hope found it as useful as we have.' He looked round the room expectantly, but confirmation was not forthcoming.

'Perhaps we could have a short discussion first about these suggestions, share some of our difficulties together, and then spend the last half-hour in what will be for some of us our very first venture into meditation.' He made it sound awfully exciting.

There was a pause.

'I dare say this booklet may be a help to beginners . . .' Lady Rosamund left her sentence in the air, making it clear that though she was well past the L-plate stage herself, she was too modest to say so. Sonia had taken a hurried glance at it in the loo before coming out and had been irritated by its told-to-the-children style, but as she had no intention of siding with her mother-in-law, she avoided this issue.

'I think it's the interruptions at home that make it all so difficult,' she offered. 'It's so hard to find time in the day to set aside for meditation, and if one does, then the telephone will ring or the children will want something, and anyway, it's so dreadfully easy just to drift off and dream about something else.' Several people murmured agreement.

'Thirty minutes a day out of twenty-four hours does not seem very much to set aside for Our Lord,' suggested Terry rather embarrassingly, though he tried to twinkle understandingly at Sonia through his rimless spectacles to soften the reproof.

'Well, speaking personally, I don't find time a difficulty,' said Lady Rosamund, who to Sonia's certain knowledge had not left her bed till noon that day. 'And in any case, I often find it possible to combine it with something else. For instance, if I'm having my hair done, or just waiting for my nail varnish to dry, I just tune in and use every available moment.' She might have been talking about listening to the test match, or *Woman's Hour*, and Sonia had a vision of her twiddling the knobs to get the best possible reception.

'But do you think that really counts?' asked Millicent

doubtfully. 'It seems a bit like, well, sort of cheating to combine prayer with something else.'

Lady Rosamund threw her such a freezing look that she almost shrivelled in her chair.

'I know you'll forgive me, Roz,' said Marcia with quite unjustified optimism, 'but I agree with Millicent. Of course you can't combine it with anything else. But it's all just a question of good organisation really. One thing at a time, that's my motto – and you can't beat a good routine. I brought my girls up that way, and now they both run their houses jolly well, and find plenty of time for other activities too. "Plan your day," I used to say to them. I'm sure God doesn't like muddle. As for daydreaming, Sonia, I can't say I've ever been troubled by that, but I'll tell you what, I did think one tip in Terry's book was jolly good. To make your mind blank, concentrate on a white sheet of nothingness.'

Millicent was too afraid to say that she had tried this helpful hint for the contemplative life, but had only succeeded in visualising a line of nappies drying in the wind.

'When I was a girl,' said saintly little Mrs Porter, much loved by all the village, 'our Rector used to say that whatever you did could be a prayer if you did it for someone else. In those days I used to bicycle to work, five miles there and five miles back, and I used to pedal each mile for a different person. Of course I can't do that now, so I just knit my prayers instead.' And she smiled sweetly at them all. Sonia thought that for the first time someone might have said something worth a bit of thought.

'I do not need these newfangled ways,' said smelly Miss Dunn loudly. 'If like me you have soong in Stainer's *Crucifixion* and Handel's *Messiah*, you don't need fancy methods. I joost speak to the Lord Jesus direct each morning, and He *heeds* my prayer 'imself.' She scowled defiantly at the others. Presumably Jesus had been off duty on her wedding morning.

The Vicar began to look a little rattled and beamed uncertainly round his flock, his teeth glossy as bathroom tiles.

'Well, well,' he said. 'Well, well. What a lot of stimulating ideas have been put before us. Yes, indeed. And now I think we will try out meditation. First I would like you to get really comfortable . Backs straight, hands on knees, eyes closed, and all your muscles relaxed – no tension anywhere.' He shot a doubtful look at Marcia, fearing that if he overdid the instructions she might topple off the bathroom stool, but she looked pretty stable, legs planted like oak trees on the threadbare patterned carpet, her knees well apart. Terry averted his eyes hastily. He had no wish to look up Marcia's skirt. Sonia's skirt would be another matter, but she was wearing jeans.

'We will start with some really deep breathing to help us unwind. In. Out. In. Out,' breathed Terry. He might have been coxing a boat-race crew, rather than steering his group of assorted ladies through the turbulent waters of spiritual discovery. Sonia fought down a rising wave of giggles, thankful that Martha, who had threatened to come along for the laughs, had decided in favour of television.

The Vicar read a few sentences from the Bible to start them off, and an uneasy quiet fell on the room. The clock on the shelf ticked loudly. It was a prized possession, a gift from the parish where he had served as a curate, but he wished he had thought to remove it this evening. Tick, tock, tick, tock, went the clock. Sonia tried not to listen to the volcanic rumblings of Miss Dunn's stomach. Perhaps she would suddenly erupt, cover them all with molten lava and they would be petrified for ever like the people of Pompeii. Sonia's foot started to itch and she wished she hadn't worn boots. A furtive glance at her companions showed Lady Rosamund with a look on her face of such determined ecstasy that Sonia thought she might suddenly float upwards, supported only by heavenly rapture, like the Bernini sculpture in the little church of Santa Maria della Vittoria in Rome of St Teresa of Avila about to have her heart pierced by an angel of the Lord. Marcia's heavy chin sagged a little, though the faintest movement of the muscles in her cheek betrayed the cautious sucking of a Polo mint.

'Be still and *know*,' intoned the Vicar. He took a few stentorian breaths to aid relaxation and encourage the others, before lapsing once more into wheezy silence. Millicent tried not to listen for the baby alarm. Sonia hoped the two Crunchie bars she had consumed before coming were not going to give her hiccoughs.

When the kitchen pinger, set for half an hour, shattered the quiet, Mrs Porter was fast asleep. There was an uneasy stirring. No one wished to be the first to speak and risk being thought irreverent, but after a good deal of shuffling, Terry said, 'Amen, amen,' quite briskly and rose from his chair.

Driving home together through the newly leafy lanes, Sonia felt more in tune with her mother-in-law than she had done for some time. Lady Rosamund, with no gallery to play to, forgot about being a holy lady, and they had a hilarious post-mortem on the evening. Sonia thought she might be sick, they laughed so much.

The evening light had taken some of the brilliance out of the colouring, blurring the outlines of the trees and buildings so that they had the softness of an impressionist painting. Sonia took the turning to the front drive for the pleasure of seeing the house dreaming peacefully below her and the beeches in the park, their winter silhouettes disguised by new crinolines of spring green, swaying faintly in the breeze as if engaged in some stately dance. The griffins brooded threateningly on their pillars, but at this time of day their full malevolence was not so apparent, their battle scars less obvious. It was an untroubled and idyllic scene and might have looked so any time during the last two hundred years, except for the height of the trees. They were both silent as they drove through the park and Sonia pulled up outside the front door. She couldn't be bothered to put the car away.

'What did you pray for this evening, Sonia?' asked Rosamund suddenly, not making any move to get out of the car. Sonia looked surprised.

'Pray for? I didn't pray *for* anything. I thought the whole point of contemplation, or whatever you like to call it, was to leave one's shopping list behind.'

Rosamund, who never left her shopping list behind, brushed

an imaginary speck of dust off the front of her cashmere sweater, and gave her daughter-in-law an amused and pitying look.

'Well I concentrated on the future of Duntan, so that the powers that be' – she did not say God – 'should see it all my way. I so often find that works. I am a great believer in mind magic. If I visualise what I want, I usually get it.'

Sonia felt positively winded with outrage. She felt furious with her mother-in-law for having stolen a march on her in this thoroughly unfair way, and furious with herself for being out-manoeuvred, caught napping on neutral territory without any ammunition.

'Roz! You didn't! How dare you!'

'You are afraid of my powers then? You believe in them too? There is nothing to stop you doing the same after all.' She threw down this gauntlet between them.

Slowly, Sonia picked it up, a *frisson* of apprehension running through her as she did so. The waters on which she was about to embark seemed very murky, and nothing to do with the innocent voyage of spiritual discovery on which she had just been trying, albeit a little mockingly, to set out.

'Very well,' she said. 'As you say, there is nothing to stop me trying too. I shall pray for a miracle.'

'Yes, darling, why don't you?' Lady Rosamund was quite unruffled. 'But if you get your miracle I hope you can cope with it. Miracles can be rather difficult to handle, and you need to be ruthless for that. I, on the other hand, have all the wherewithal at my disposal now. I only need Archie's agreement, and I don't think that requires anything as drastic as a miracle. Such a shame you two are so at odds with each other at the moment.' She gave Sonia her sweetest smile and got out of the car.

They walked in silence towards their soup and cold chicken.

Chapter 13

For once the bank-holiday weekend looked as if it might be fine. A cold wet weekend in May is not the easiest time to entertain energetic sporty friends over a period of three days and Bill and Caroline Bruce were both definitely outdoor types. Bill was Archie's oldest friend. They had messed together at Eton, joined the same regiment, in which Bill still served, played a great deal of cricket together and shared most of the same tastes and interests. He and Caroline were an ideally suited couple and in fact looked not unlike each other, except that Bill was prematurely bald, while Caroline had plenty of hair, the kind, so maddening to other women, that looks just as good windswept or even wet as it does on more formal occasions. They were both very tall, with bright blue eyes, and managed to look permanently bronzed, though they were not given to anything as static as lying on beaches, let alone a sunbed. Sonia could easily imagine Caroline running naked with a spear in pursuit of bison, though Bill's rim of hair, neatly trimmed in military fashion, made such a picture a little more difficult in his case. There may have been bald cavemen, but it's not the image immediately conjured up. At any rate they were both possessed of golden good looks.

They had known each other all their lives, and as far as anyone knew neither had ever seriously looked at anyone else. When Caroline was fourteen, Bill had given her a china frog at the Pony Club dance and they had collected frogs of every shape and size ever since. Their whole house was overrun with frogs. There was a table of china frogs in the hall, toy frogs in soft materials filled an armchair in their bedroom and reclined on their bed, a huge brass frog propped open the door between the kitchen and the dining room, rather better-class frogs filled a cabinet in the drawing room, and little blown-glass frogs, souvenirs of Italian holidays, tended to squat on bathroom shelves. Even the kitchen china was painted with frogs wearing sporting clothes doing all the sporting things that Bill liked best. Caroline had had it specially designed for their tenth wedding anniversary. They even called each other Froggie. To bait Archie, Sonia pretended that she thought the Bruces' three boys looked like frogs too. This was a bit unfair though they certainly did have rather wide mouths. In fact, Sonia was really quite fond of the Bruces, and in their early married days the four of them had had a lot of fun together, but at the moment she felt their extreme devotion to each other was almost more than she could take. She knew that Caroline was just the sort of wife Archie should have married.

'Have you organised tennis for Bill and Caroline?'

'No. Have you?'

'No – you usually do that sort of thing. Try and get a couple for Sunday lunch and tennis, but you've left it a bit late.'

'Terry and Millicent are coming for Sunday lunch.'

Archie looked annoyed.

'Oh really, Sonia! We could have them any Sunday. I meant a proper couple to meet Bill and Caroline.'

'Aren't the Millers a proper couple? You mean they've been living in sin all these years? I wonder if the Bishop knows.'

'Don't be ridiculous, Sonia. You know quite well what I mean.'

'I suppose you want me to ring the Bartletts. You and Rosie could play the Bruces and I could rub up my French with Joli Roger if he's back. What a perfect afternoon that would be.'

'You're just being thoroughly difficult. Can't you put the Millers off? I'm sure they'd come another week.'

'No I can't. What do you want me to say? "My husband doesn't think you're thrilling enough for his sporty friends, so we'd rather you came when we haven't got guests staying"?'

Archie, who was pacing crossly up and down, tripped over Lotus, who was lying doormat-like in his path. It was impossible to tell which end of her was which until Archie kicked her at one end and the other yelped loudly. Archie swore.

'Bloody dogs everywhere!'

Sonia picked Lotus up with exaggerated sympathy. She had no intention of admitting to Archie that she had not as yet actually invited the Millers and had only thought of it on the spur of the moment, though she knew they would almost certainly accept. She felt she had gone a bit far.

'Oh well I'll rustle up someone for tennis in the afternoon. What do you want to do with Bill and Caroline on Saturday?'

'I thought Bill and I might cast a fly down the river.'

'How heavenly. Caroline and I will be able to practise our golf swings on the lawn.' Sonia did not play golf, but Caroline had a handicap of ten and was determined to get it down to single figures. In fact, as Tom had a weekend exeat from school, she had planned to take all the children to Brimham Rocks – a hundred acres of moorland with volcanic rocks in strange and wonderful shapes and sizes, perfect for all ages to scramble over or climb and beloved of generations of Yorkshire children. Caroline, she knew, would be happy to do this or go fishing with the men. She was really a very accommodating guest, though not one to loll about on sofas with a book.

Before the weekend Sonia had a cooking orgy. Archie was a good host, and having behaved in such a provocative way she felt she could at least make amends by producing delicious food, and getting it organised beforehand. She browsed through her collection of cookery books, wasting a good deal of time while feeling busy, and then decided to rely on old favourites for which she needed no receipts anyway.

She made cucumber mousse and cold smoked-haddock soup fairly uneventfully, playing about with the latter by adding prawns and tomato to make it look pretty, and then put a huge brew of mince to cook for lasagne while she started to make paper-thin crêpes for chicken pancakes, but as usual she tried to do too many things at once. The Aga top startd to cool down, so that the pancakes stuck to the pan and settled in a soggy gunge on the end of the pallet knife instead of flicking lightly over, and she forgot about the nuts she had put to roast in the hot oven for a hazelnut meringue. By the time she discovered them they had become sizzling black bullets and had discoloured the tin. To make matters worse, when she tipped them frantically into the washing-up bowl their heat caused it to buckle and there was a dreadful smell of burning plastic.

A batch of chocolate buns for the tennis tea fared no better. Taking them out of the oven, she dropped the first six on the floor where the dogs immediately polished them off. She knew she would have to make more anyway, so it seemed a good idea to sample one of the remaining six. After she had eaten five, there was no point in leaving just one for the tennis tea, so she ate that as well and then felt sick with self-dislike and chocolate. She looked despairingly at the pile of washing-up that filled the sink. She always meant to clear up as she went along, but it seldom happened. She felt herself drowning in domesticity.

The appearance of Minnie, who had gone away for a couple of nights but had returned unexpectedly early, a purple felt hat perched at a jaunty angle on her head, was like the arrival of a rescue squad.

'What sort of fool carry-on is this?' she enquired, and within moments of her taking off her coat and hat and putting on her old flowered overall the kitchen was miraculously transformed from a disaster area into a farmhouse kitchen in a glossy magazine.

'Min! How heavenly. I thought you were going to spend the afternoon with your sister-in-law in York before coming back?'

'Oh, she's such a creaking gate – can't take her moans for long. Just because her fool mother saw fit to name her Edweeena –' Minnie drew the name out like a piece of elastic '– she thinks she's above other mortals. I've no time for her la-di-da ways, so I thought I'd catch the early bus – and a good job, too, by the look of it.'

'Oh I do love you, Min. You're my good angel. I was trying to get ahead with the cooking before Colonel and Mrs Bruce arrive.'

Minnie sniffed. 'And going so fast you'll end up further back than where you started. You get on with your fancy foreign dishes and leave the cakes to me. I'll make one of my lemon sponges that Tom likes. I don't suppose that Mrs Burrows gives those boys proper food. Ready-made cake mix like as not at Upcott House.'

With Minnie's return, the rest of the cooking orgy went off without further drama, and Sonia enjoyed herself cooking to Act 2 of *Rigoletto*, thinking wild, vengeful thoughts about Archie and Rosie Bartlett and passionate ones about Simon Hadleigh. She never painted to music as it was apt to bring colours into her head that had no place in the current picture.

When the Bruces finally arrived on Friday night, Sonia was surprised to find how pleased she was to see them.

'Oh the lovely, lovely smell of Duntan!' cried Caroline, sniffing the indefinable and particular scent of the library as they stood in front of the log fire. 'If you set me down here blindfold, I should know immediately where I was. I couldn't bear it if it had changed. How strange it will seem without old Lady D – she always seemed to be the heart and soul of the house. One almost expected it to have vanished along with her.'

There was an uncomfortable little pause and Archie and Sonia did not look at each other. Caroline was not noted for her tact.

'Yes, well, better make the most of it while you can. That's exactly what will happen.'

Caroline looked at him in dismay.

'Oh no! How awful! Have I said the wrong thing?'

'Good old Froggie,' said Bill, putting his arm round her shoulder. 'Put your foot in it as usual.'

'Not at all.' Archie had his lesson-reading voice on. 'It's better to face up to these things. There's no secret about it. The upkeep of places like Duntan is becoming impossible nowadays. Sad, but inevitable.'

'Sad, but not inevitable,' said Sonia brightly, her voice like diamond chips. 'Come on, Caroline. I'll take you up. We'll leave the chaps to unload the car.'

'Froggie darling, do let Codger have a little run, and give the old boy one of his arthritis pills with his dinns, and don't forget to leave him a drinkie,' instructed Caroline. Codger was the Bruces' very ancient labrador. He dragged his hind legs and sagged in the middle like a badly erected tent; he was also apt to let off the most terrible smells, like overripe Stilton. It was one of the hazards of having them to stay.

'Poor Codgie, he has to sleep in the car now if we're away from home. He can't drag his poor self upstairs anymore,' said Caroline as she followed Sonia into the hall.

'Oh dear. Poor him. How sad.' Sonia tried to sound sorry. There had been occasions when Codger had sprayed the Duntan furniture pretty lavishly. He never seemed to run short of water. The golden rule for guests of never taking dogs into other people's houses was not one the Bruces had mastered.

'I should warn you that Archie's ma is in residence at the moment,' said Sonia. 'She's queening it in the Blue Room, so I've put you and Bill in the Chintz Room. I'm sure you've slept there before.'

'Oh lovely, lovely.' Caroline surveyed the pretty, faded bedroom with delight. 'Duntan's about the only house where we always sleep in a four-poster bed. Four-posters really turn Froggie on.'

'How nice,' said Sonia, but the bleakness in her voice got through even to Caroline, like an icy wind penetrating a Barbour.

'Oh Froggie, darling, I don't think all is very well with Archie and Sonia,' said Caroline later, as she lay drowsily twined in Bill's arms, the four-poster having had the most satisfactory effect.

'D'you know, Froggie, I noticed that too.' Bill sounded enormously proud of his own perception. 'I expect it's the effect of civilian life. Pretty tough leaving the regiment. I wouldn't like to have to cope with that.'

They slept.

Further down the passage, Archie and Sonia lay side by side, also in a four-poster bed. They might have been a million miles apart.

*

Saturday passed pleasantly. Archie left early to collect Tom from Upcott House and got him back home in time for a second breakfast.

'I don't know where you put all that food, I'm sure,' said Minnie fondly. 'You must stuff it down your shins.'

'I've been absolutely starved for the last three weeks. Dreadful slimy, gristly stew, huge great caterpillars swarming all over the lettuce and Fairfax minor found a cigarette stub in his aunt's legs.' Aunt's legs was the Upcott House name for puddings steamed in long circular tins, served two together on long dishes; spotted aunt's legs had currants in them and grazed aunt's legs were topped with jam. 'Tuesday is the only day I can eat a thing because then we have ice-cream for pud.' Tom looked very well on this starvation diet.

It was a beautiful day. Polly and Tom, having enjoyed a little 'space in their togetherness', played tennis and croquet without quarrelling. Archie took Bill round the farm to look at various improvements, and Caroline borrowed Archie's horse and went for a ride while Sonia prepared a picnic tea. After lunch she and Caroline took the children to Brimham Rocks. Bill and Archie decided to try their luck on the river later in the evening. Lady Rosamund was lying out on a chaise longue by the summer-house and Martha joined the Brimham Rocks party. She had intended to gossip with Sonia and Caroline, but once there could not resist the lure of joining the younger ones in the stalking game they always played there, which involved a lot of crawling about in the heather on one's stomach, like a snake, in order to avoid being seen. Birdie, who would greatly have preferred to be seen rather than crawl through the heather, was the only one of the children who did not enjoy the afternoon. She knew there were real snakes – adders – on the moor, and expected to feel the venomous prick of a forked tongue in her leg at any moment.

Neither Tom nor Polly ever wanted Birdie in their team. Cassie, a bold, bad brigand at heart, was a much better bet in spite of her lack of years.

'Birdie's a cowardy custard,' said Cassie scornfully, though in reality Birdie was the only one to be brave since she was the only one with any fears.

'Will you be with me, Bird?' asked Martha, and was amply rewarded for her generosity by the burning gratitude in Birdie's eyes.

'Bags I go alone,' said Tom, the non-conformist.

'OK,' said Polly. 'Come on, Cass – we'll be partners.'

They dispersed quickly in all directions, leaving Sonia and Caroline to walk the dogs. The shih-tzus, not lion dogs for nothing, boldly hunted through the heather and bilberries for prey, but progress was slow because Codger, no longer able to lift his leg properly, squatted shakily to anoint every rock or tussock he passed. The humiliations of old age are great. Once he would have ranged free, putting up grouse and chasing hares and being shouted at fruitlessly by his besotted owners. Keeper and Poacher, two disciplined professionals, had remained with Archie, never leaving his heel or lying motionless but alert wherever he left them on the river bank.

After a bit, Sonia and Caroline climbed to the top of one of the great rocks. It was like sitting on a dinosaur. Curlews bubbled their spring music, and the air was full of the plaintive call of plovers. It was one of those bright blowy days, with clouds racing overhead. They could see for miles.

'You're not really going to have to give up Duntan, are you?' asked Caroline.

'Archie says so.'

'What about you?'

'If I could get my hands on a cool million or so, nothing would make me budge. But I don't see where it's coming from.'

'What about your painting?'

'Oh Caroline, that's peanuts. Pocket money compared with what the house needs. It means a great deal to me and I am trying to get back to it because I shall go mad if I don't, but it's not going to help with Duntan. Archie just thinks it's a nice little hobby for me anyway.'

'I adore your paintings. I think they're perfectly sweet.'

Sonia winced. Caroline, quite unaware that her remark could be construed as anything except complimentary, went on.

'Yes, I think you should keep your hobby up too, but I gather there's another very pretty little house on the estate. Archie was telling me about it last night. You'd be saved so much worry and expense. And warmth! Think how much easier to heat. You must admit that Duntan can be absolutely freezing. Froggie and I came up to shoot a couple of years ago during that very cold spell and I promise there was ice in the glass of water by our bed in the morning. I wore Froggie's shooting stockings in bed to keep my feet from getting frostbite.'

'I know, I know,' said Sonia. 'Really I know all that, but it doesn't make any difference to how I feel. And I hate the Dial House. It's got bad vibes. I should die of unhappiness.'

'But if it made Archie happy . . . ?' Caroline's words trailed away uncertainly. Sonia said nothing for a bit, and they lay and listened to the singing of the wind in which there was no answer.

Then, 'Caroline,' said Sonia, 'do you ever get fed up with Bill? Do you never imagine yourself leaving him, or wishing he was dead – well perhaps not actually dead, but miles away? Don't you ever hate him?'

'Never,' said Caroline simply. 'Absolutely never. I couldn't imagine life without him. I would just die too. I'd be like those Indian women used to be – commit suttee and jump on his funeral pyre.'

'What about the poor boys? I could never leave my children. That's the only bit of me that's nice. Bit grim for the boys if you got barbecued?'

'Oh well, there'd be lots of grannies and things. Of course I love the children, of course I do.' She didn't sound all that convinced. 'They're sweet, and they're part of our marriage, but Bill comes first. Bill's my whole life.'

'Oh you are lucky,' said Sonia. 'You just don't know how lucky you are. I feel awful sometimes. I know I'm so bloody spoilt, know I ought to be grateful for everything, but sometimes I just feel wicked. I want to do something wicked. I try and think about dying people in Calcutta or lonely people isolated in bedsits, and it doesn't make me any nicer. It's like when I was a child and Nannie used to say, "Think of all the starving people," and I still didn't like rice pudding.'

'But you must try, Sonia. Lots of people have rough patches. All right, I'm lucky, I know it, but you simply must try.'

'Yes,' said Sonia 'That's what Sally told me the other day.'

'And Archie adores you so much. He always has. He's always worshipped you.'

'Not any more,' said Sonia. 'Oh, not any more. I've choked him off for too long and now I'm not even sure if I'd want all that devotion again. If I was shut up with him in the Dial House I think I'd go bonkers.'

Caroline gave her a very troubled look.

After dinner that night Martha and the older children watched a video while Rosamund, Archie and the Bruces played bridge. Sonia curled up on the sofa with Lotus on her knee and stitched away at a chair seat in a Bargello pattern. She did not want to play bridge and liked sewing, but all the same she felt like an outsider in her own house, excluded from a charmed circle, and deeply lonely.

'Six no trumps,' said Lady Rosamund.

'Oh for God's sake, Mother!' said Archie, laying out his cards. 'Thank God you're playing the hand, not me. Whatever possessed you to leave us in no trumps?'

'Don't worry, darling. I shan't go down, and I always prefer to play the hand. I shall get my little slam all right,' said his mother, and to the surprise of everyone except herself, she did.

Chapter 14

Archie and the Bruces were the only representatives from the house to attend church on Sunday morning. Sonia, with lunch to cook for twelve people, opted out, whilst Tom said he and old JC saw quite enough of each other at Upcott House with prayers morning and evening and chapel twice on Sundays, so Sonia didn't make the other children go either. She had asked Tim and Leonie for lunch and to stay for tennis afterwards. They were always good value, had often met Bill and Caroline at Duntan before, and as they lived in South Swale knew Terry and Millicent and could be guaranteed to be nice to them.

Minnie lit a fire in the drawing room, more so that it looked cheerful than because the temperature really warranted it. There was still a gaping hole in the ceiling where the water had come through a few weeks earlier, but the carpet had suffered no lasting damage and the beauty of the room could easily carry this temporary blemish. Double mahogany doors led from the library into the drawing room and the same faded blue silk that covered the walls was echoed in the gilt sofas and chairs. The huge chandelier hanging from the central moulding was greatly in need of cleaning, but still looked beautiful; it was lucky that the rain had not brought it crashing down, since it might easily have killed anyone standing beneath it.

The Millers arrived at exactly ten to one, just after the Warners. Millicent had given a good deal of thought to what she should wear, not that the choice was very large. She had not found Sonia's vague instructions of 'Oh, any old thing – wear whatever's comfortable,' at all helpful. Quite the reverse, since it prevented her from wearing her best dress, which would have been her natural choice. What did people who lived in a house like Duntan wear when they had visitors? She was constantly amazed by the curious behaviour of the family – regular church supporters and yet so flippant about everything. Terry called it lacking in reverence. Take the children to tea there, and despite all those other rooms, it might well be in the kitchen; there was unlikely to be a cloth on the table and even the jam and honey would be plonked down in jars instead of being transferred to nice little china pots. The cake, if there was one, would probably be cut straight from the tin, there would be no nicely folded little paper serviettes such as she would have provided, and the children were quite likely to lick their sticky fingers. On the other hand, when they had gone to dinner there ('Only family, not a party') just before Archie's grandmother had died, it had seemed immensely grand, with the men in smoking jackets and the women dressed as though for a wedding. She never knew where she was with them at all. She would have liked to ask Terry's opinion but was afraid of receiving a homily on personal vanity. She did not want her price to be above rubies – she just yearned to look right.

Eventually she had chosen a lacy crochet jersey she had made for herself, worn for decency's sake over a yellow nylon blouse. It had been a complicated pattern and had looked very pretty on the model in the woman's magazine from which she had taken it. 'A Garment For All Occasions' it was headed. "This treasure in your wardrobe will take you anywhere from dawn to dusk', but on entering the drawing room at Duntan the treasure did not feel quite as reassuring as it had done in her bedroom at the Vicarage. No one else was wearing anything like it. To some women this would have been a cause of satisfaction, but Millicent did not possess the sort of social self-confidence that allowed her to feel correctly dressed and different at the same time.

It was true that she would have died rather than look like Martha, whose matchstick legs seemed to be weighed down by huge black surgical boots, and whose extremely short skirt might almost as well have been missing since it barely covered her bottom. With it she wore a skinny-rib sweater so alarmingly tight that not only her ribs but her nipples were all too visible beneath it. Caroline wore very well-cut jeans that showed off her wonderful figure, whilst Sonia's skin-tight flowered leggings worn with a loose silk shirt would not have been Millicent's choice either. It was all very baffling.

There were one or two other things at Duntan that made Millicent feel extremely uncomfortable. The large nude marble figure of a youth in the hall, for instance. One did not wish to look at him. Millicent would have put a little lavender bag in a certain place, or, better still, a pair of bathing trunks. The only things he ever occasionally wore were a pair of sunglasses or someone's riding hat stuck on top of his head. Martha had once Sellotaped hair rollers all over his locks and tied a scarf round like Ena Sharples. Terry had thought the result quite obscene and most disturbing. Neither did they care for the torchère in the form of a turbanned Negro figure with glowing eyes. They didn't feel that sort of thing helped the course of race relations at all.

Archie, a genial host, came to greet them. 'How pretty you look, Millicent,' he said, kissing her. Millicent glowed, morale restored, though all the kissing that went on at Duntan was another thing that Terry thought rather overdone.

'You met Caroline and Bill in church, and everyone else you know. What can I get you to drink? A Bloody Mary, something soft, a glass of sherry, or would you like to risk some house poison?'

'I'll have a sweet sherry, please,' said Millicent, hoping it wouldn't make her neck go red as it sometimes did. Terry boldly asked for the 'house poison'. He sometimes found it difficult to present an image that combined the man of the world with the man of the world to come, but after quaffing the delicious and innocuous-tasting mixture in his glass he felt he might achieve it. He became aware of a faint buzzing in his ears and a curious swaying movement in the room that made him wonder if he might be going to have a rather spiritual experience. However when Bill, circulating with the jug, offered him a 'top-up', which he unwisely accepted, he feared his legs might give way beneath him and was relieved when Sonia, whose practised eye had taken in the situation, suggested they should all sit down. She steered him skilfully to a window seat and left him sitting quietly by himself while she went in search of help.

'For God's sake go and stuff the Vicar up with nuts or something,' she whispered to Martha. 'He looks quite plastered, poor little man. Bill should never have given him any more of Archie's lethal brew.'

Martha giggled. 'That's what comes of mixing drinks. He was probably well topped-up with Communion wine to start with.' But she obligingly went and sat beside him, chatting away so that there was no need to answer, and plying him with cheese biscuits, which he consumed at an alarming rate until he was relieved to find the room gradually becoming more stable.

When Lady Rosamund made her entrance a few minutes later, she was, Millicent thought, dressed far more suitably for Sunday lunch than anyone else so far except Leonie. She wore a pleated wool-crêpe skirt that was obviously very expensive with a perfectly matching silk shirt and a blazer of a slightly deeper shade. A diamond brooch was pinned at her shoulder.

'How lovely you look, Lady Rosamund,' said Millicent shyly, made bolder than usual by the sherry.

'How nice of you. Thank you. Not very dashing, I'm afraid. I read somewhere that skirts and blazers are the routine uniform of the menopausal British woman,' said Rosamund disconcertingly. Millicent went scarlet. What a word to use in mixed company!

'Poor old Ma. You must be mutton dressed as lamb, in that case,' said Martha loudly. She thought it very unkind of her mother to tease such a gentle and unequal sparring partner, but she only succeeded in embarrassing Millicent more than ever.

'Come on everyone,' said Sonia, 'lunch is ready. Mustn't let the Yorkshire puds spoil. Roz, will you lead the way, please?' She shepherded everyone into the dining room and got them all placed around the table, putting Millicent on Archie's right. He was about to pull out her chair for her when Sonia, who had noticed an expectant fluttering on the Vicar's part, managed to catch Archie's eye and stop him.

'Perhaps you would like to say grace for us, Terry?'

Lady Rosamund crossed herself ostentatiously, and the children, who had all sat down, scrambled to their feet looking most surprised. Terry cleared his throat.

'Lord blesh thish food to our ushe, and ush to Thy servish,' he said, swaying slightly and glad to hold on to the comfortingly solid Chippendale chair. Everyone sat down.

'I'll carve today, darling. You look after Millicent,' said Sonia. She knew tht Archie hated her doing the carving and was much better at it than she was. She had intended not to make any declarations of war all day, but stuck the little stiletto in before she could stop herself. It was becoming a habit.

Archie, who was too kind to upset Millicent, for whom he had a soft spot, thinking her underrated by her sanctimonious husband, vented his annoyance by sending Keeper and Poacher to their corner in a fierce voice. They would have gone there anyway.

'I do love your big dogs,' said Millicent. 'Of course I love Sonia's dear little fluffy ones too, but I really like the big ones best and yours are so obedient. My father had an old labby when I was a child and he was a great character. He used to fetch Father's slippers for him.'

'Yes, they're wonderful retrievers,' said Archie. 'Old Poacher's been a fantastic dog in his day – best nose in Yorkshire – and Keeper's coming on well. He likes doing a double retrieve and always brings me two birds at once if he can.'

'Birds? Oh of course, they're shooting dogs.' Millicent was dismayed, but still fortified by the unaccustomed drink before lunch, she went on, 'I expect you'll think me silly, but I'm afraid I just can't approve of shooting for pleasure.'

Archie was saved from having to reply to this by Polly, who was helping to hand round, putting a plate of perfectly underdone beef in front of Millicent.

'Are you a vegetarian then?' she asked.

'Not really,' said Millicent. 'This does look a treat. Thank you, Polly.'

'Well, but think of the awful death of this poor bullock all for your pleasure. Imagine him herded terrified into a lorry like poor old Marie Antoinette off to the guillotine, smelling the terror. Daddy says anyone who objects to shooting and isn't a vegetarian should jolly well spend a whole day in an abattoir. Daddy says –'

'Shut up, Polly. Get on with helping your mother.' Archie cut her short sharply, but too late. Poor Millicent's lunch was ruined. She had been looking forward so much to a meal not cooked by herself, and a large joint of sirloin was not something to which the Vicarage housekeeping money could readily stretch, but her imagination had never before made the leap that joins the succulent slices off the Sunday joint to the beasts in the slaughterhouse. She felt her throat constrict at the thought.

'Tell me about your own dog,' said Archie hastily. 'I see your old fellow round the village sometimes, inspecting the dustbins.'

'Oh yes, he's dreadfully greedy. He's a real old mongrel. We call him Heinz – you know, fifty-seven varieties.'

Archie laughed easily at this not very original joke, making her feel quite amusing, and Millicent thought how nice he always was, in spite of his bloodthirsty tastes.

At the other end of the table the conversation had got on to the topic of saints, in deference to the presence of the Vicar and triggered by his sermon on St Thérèse of Lisieux, the 'Little Flower'.

'I think she sounds awfully wet,' said Tom. 'Now St George is all right. Must have been good fun slaying a dragon.'

'Poor St George, though, such bad luck after all these years. Hasn't he been made redundant?' Caroline made him sound like a stockbroker.

'Perhaps they gave him a sort of heavenly golden handshake before he left the Company of Saints. Turned in his halo and got a golden bowler,' suggested Tim. 'Now come on, Millicent, who's top of the pops of your list of saints?'

Millicent remembered a school trip to Assisi when she was

twelve. She had lost her teddy bear at the *pensione* and had been greatly comforted at the suggestion that St Francis might have claimed him for his own. Ever since, she had nursed a vision of a small, brown-habited figure, surrounded by birds and animals, clutching her bear under his arm. She had often felt that by a concentrated outpouring of love one should be able to draw wild creatures to oneself, but so far her efforts with the rabbits in the fields behind the house had not been too successful, and the birds in her garden seemed more responsive to crumbs.

'I think St Francis is my favourite,' she said. 'Everyone must love him.'

'Oh, I don't know.' Martha rolled a wicked eye at Sonia, forgetting about not teasing Millicent. 'Don't think Archie would like him much. Bet he'd be an "Anti". Can't you just see him lying down in front of the butts – Brother Grouse and all that?'

'Shirley Gillespie's mother says all those saints and martyrs were probably sexually perverted,' announced Polly. 'All that torture and stuff – she says it was probably a turn-on for them.'

Tom snorted derisively.

'Bet Shirley's silly old mother wouldn't like being tortured. Bet she'd soon squeal if you put her on the rack and stretched and stretched her.'

'And think of being burnt.' Birdie's eyes brimmed with horror. In the nursery there was a picture in the old copy of *Our Island Story* that always filled her with a fascinated pity, so that she could not bear to look or to turn the page.

'Which saint do you like, Mum?'

'Well I always think St Paul must have been pretty prosy,' said Sonia. 'Imagine sitting next to him at a dinner party. He'd be a real old travel bore and bang on about all his shipwrecks. "Did I ever tell you about my experiences in Melita?", and one would long to say, "Yes, the last three times we've met", and then he'd bring out all one's most feminist feelings. Now, St Peter would be fun, a real darling – so human. I'm sure he'd have been clumsy like me and knocked over ashtrays and put his foot through the fishing nets. I'd have loved sitting next to him.'

'No, no,' said Bill. 'St Peter wouldn't *be* at a dinner party – that's the whole point. I mean St Paul was, well, a gent and all that. After the Resurrection,' he went on, warming to his theme, 'poor old Jesus must have realised that his team was a bit inadequate, no real organisation or leadership. I mean he'd got all these troops together, volunteers you know, Home Guard types, splendid chaps all of them, don't get me wrong, but a bit *Dad's Army*, all Other Ranks, and he must have realised a bit late that he had to have a first-class chap to get it all together. So what does he do?' Bill jabbed a finger at Terry, who leant back nervously in his chair. 'I'll tell you what he does. He gets hold of Paul – a bit of a shit, but first-class at the admin – and the whole thing gets off the ground. Man management, you see. Organisation. St Peter would never have made it on his own. Bloody good RSM mind you, but needed a proper fellah at the top to start him off.'

'Oh no, Bill. You're forgetting the most important point.' Rosamund was sublimely unaware of the Millers' astonishment at this militaristic assessment of the Apostles. 'I'm sure the Vicar will agree with me. You've forgotten about the power of *grace*. Peter could have done anything if he'd been given grace.'

'Who was Grace?' asked Tom through a mouthful of food, and Sonia had a sudden vision of St Peter accompanied by a beefy WRAC type in uniform, drilling the troops.

After lunch the grown-ups had coffee in the drawing room and the children disappeared. As soon as they had finished their coffee, the Millers left to collect their children from Millicent's mother. Terry's head was beginning to throb, and he was not sorry to have an excuse to hurry home. He felt he had not succeeded in taking charge of the conversation and had allowed some misguided views to be expressed. He lectured Millicent on the way home, as though it had been her fault.

'I hear Robin has asked you to the Fourth of June,' said Leonie to Martha. 'That will be too lovely. If you can find youself a bed in London, we'll take you down with us. We're going to spend the weekend there and we'll all go to a theatre in the evening or something. We'll organise quite a party of young, so it should be fun for you.'

Martha smiled politely but looked non-committal. The idea of a party of young would not be at all to her taste. Sonia, who had heard the conversation and watched Martha's face, gave her a worried look. She did not think Rosamund paid enough attention to her daughter, but fond as she was of her felt she had too many problems of her own to try to organise Martha's life. Nevertheless, she felt uneasy about her. It was not right for someone of Martha's age and considerable intelligence to be allowed to drift along doing nothing. She wasn't using her brain or having a social time, or doing anything for anyone.

The rest of the afternoon was spent playing croquet and tennis and reading the Sunday papers, and all too soon it was time to take Tom back to school. Sonia suddenly felt very tired and this time allowed Archie to drive him back without a protest. He was gone much longer than expected, and looked evasive when Sonia asked him what had happened.

'Oh well, I had a word or two with old Frank. It all took a bit of time.'

'But they have chapel at six. Did you go to that?'

'Er, no. Lot of traffic, though,' said Archie vaguely, and Sonia knew that he must have stopped at the Bartletts' on the way home.

Chapter 15

The Bruces had to leave after lunch on Monday. It was a long drive down to Hampshire and they wanted to avoid the worst of the bank-holiday traffic in the evening. Plans had been made for them to come for a shooting weekend in August or September, depending on which dates Archie would have to let the moor and when he would be able to have a day for his own friends.

'I'll be in touch as soon as I know anything!' he told Bill. 'It all depends what John Brown-Goring's been able to fix up. We're going over to Dukie's soon to discuss the whole thing with him and John and then I'll drop you a line.'

'Fine,' said Bill. 'And you'll come to us in December – and make Sonia come with you this year. Froggie doesn't think she looks too well – thinks you both need a break away from here. Why don't we all try and pop over to Le Touquet for a weekend in July if I can take a bit of leave? You and I could hit a golf ball around and we could all have a flutter at the casino. The girls might enjoy that, and you and Sonia could do with a holiday together.' He hoped in this oblique and masculine way he was letting Archie know that his friends were well aware of his little liaison with the luscious Mrs Bartlett. Caroline had begged him to say something to Archie before he left, but this was as far as he was prepared to go.

'Mind you,' he said to Caroline, 'Archie may be straying off the straight and narrow at the moment, but you can't altogether blame him. Sonia's always given him a bit of a rough ride and she's never been prepared to take much of an interest in his life – all that painting and stuff. Not like you, Froggie, old thing,' and he gave her a hug.

'Yes, you're right, Froggie,' said Caroline. 'I'll try and have a word with Sonia before we leave.'

After lunch Sonia and Caroline took the dogs for a short walk in order that Codger should have a last chance to leave a great many messages behind him before his long incarceration for the journey south. They took the bottom path along by the river. A few fish were rising and willow warblers and blackcaps were fluting rival melodies. A chiff-chaff called persistently. Nag-nag. Nag-nag. Just like me, thought Sonia, and was filled with an aching envy of Caroline, so sure in her marriage, so in tune with her life.

'It's been a heavenly weekend, Sonia darling. Too lovely to see you all again. I do hope things sort of, well, you know, work out a bit better for you both . . .'

'Perhaps I should try and get hold of some imperial Tokay or a little crushed rhino horn.' Sonia threw two sticks into the river and sent Keeper and Poacher after them.

'Why not just try and be a little nicer?'

'I might,' said Sonia. 'I might. Though I think I'll just try praying for my miracle for a bit longer. Anyway, I'm not very good at swallowing my pride.'

'Oh darling. I'm sure he doesn't care two pins for this Rosie really. He's just boosting his morale. One big swallow and your pride would all be gone and things would be lovely again.'

'They never have been very lovely. That's the trouble. We've never been like you and Bill, only Archie's found it out now too. It's taken him nearly fourteen years to work it out. He's not the world's most perceptive person, you know.'

'You haven't got a monopoly on sensitive feelings.' Caroline sounded quite sharp, remembering occasions when she had bled to witness Archie trying so hard to please his clever, attractive, dissatisfied wife and not knowing where he had gone wrong. 'You've seemed pretty dependent on him at times. Are you forgetting how fantastic he was when Birdie was born and you were so down afterwards? And you keep saying you want to stay at Duntan so much, but you can't very well stay without Archie.'

'Yes,' said Sonia. 'That thought had occurred to me too.'

They turned back and walked towards the house. Keeper

and Poacher returned with their sticks and shook what seemed like half the river all over them, so that they arrived at the car thoroughly wet before the drive back.

'What do people wear on the Fourth of June?' asked Martha.

Sonia considered her.

'Are you asking me because you want to wear the acceptable thing, or because you want to know what most people will wear so that you can make yourself look as different as possible?'

Martha gave her a sideways look.

'I just want to *know* what people wear.'

'You're not to embarrass Tim and Leonie, Martha. They're too nice to be teased, and Leonie is very conventional.'

'Robin is dreadfully conventional too,' said Martha. Sonia feared the worst.

'Don't try putting him to the test on the Fourth, Martha. It's not fair. You're not to turn up looking like Minnehaha or something, and for God's sake wash that frightful tint out of your hair.' But even as she spoke she thought it might have been better to keep silent.

Birdie lay in a twilight world between sleeping and waking. She often had difficulty getting off to sleep. Cassie, in the other bed at the far side of the room, was out like a light, sleeping the untroubled sleep of the amoral. Nothing short of an earthquake would wake her till morning. The dreaded, familiar nightmare feeling she found impossible to describe to the grown-ups was creeping over Birdie. She called it feeling 'big'. It started with a curious swelling sensation in her fingers. They felt as large as Cumberland sausages, and her hands seemed to spread. Then her whole body felt as though it was growing rapidly larger, becoming bloated, floating above the bed, and everything in the room was becoming smaller and smaller, speeding away from her, as if she, quite out of control, was whizzing up, not down, a big dipper, away from all the beloved familiar objects in the night nursery. The ottoman at the end of her bed seemed miles away, the rocking chair with her clothes neatly folded upon it was a tiny speck, receding into the distance at an alarming rate, while she herself, huge, grotesque and swelling, was suspended above it all. Just as she felt she was about to burst, she catapulted out of bed with the force of a cork flying out of a champagne bottle, and was running, running down towards the stairs, the terrors of the long nursery passage forgotten in her panic flight. 'I feel big! I feel big!' She wailed, small bare feet skimming along like frightened birds.

Nobody heard. Minnie, after the busy weekend, had gone to her cottage. There was no comforting presence, no stout body sewing in the nursery, only the ominous shadows and half-light falling from the dome. The swelling feeling had gone, her body returned to its normal size, but now a new set of fears assailed her, and she stood at the top of the stairs, her heart hammering against her thin chest as though it might break her ribs. To walk down the great staircase, its flight of suspended steps bouncing so amusingly by day, but creaking and lurching so ominously by night, would be a tremendous ordeal, and yet to return alone down the passage was impossible. From the top of the stairs she could just see a crack of light underneath the library door. As a wounded animal will make for cover, Birdie, keeping close to the banisters, crept towards the comforting light. The stone flags in the hall were cold, but her bare feet were colder.

She could hear the voices of her parents talking in the library, but outside the door she paused. The voices were raised in anger, first one and then the other, in a hideous and all too familiar antiphony. Reassurance was denied. She could not go in. To catch them quarrelling again was to have all her worst fears confirmed, worse even than the darkness. Birdie's stomach muscles tightened into a terrible cramp. Slowly, painfully, she dragged herself upstairs again. Somehow she fought her way down the nightmare tunnel of the nursery passage. Once back in bed, curled tight in a shaking ball of misery, entirely under the bedclothes, Birdie lay for a long, long time before sleep released her.

Chapter 16

Sonia spent a long time getting ready for the Vanalleyns' dinner party. She made her face up with special care and drew her hair into a knot at the back of her head that suited her high cheekbones and rather wide mouth. She spent a long time deciding which dress to wear, and though normally she might have consulted Archie, even if only to disagree with him, she was in no mood now to ask his opinion. In fact, he didn't really like her to put her hair up, saying it made her look too sophisticated, but then it wasn't Archie's approval that she was so anxious to secure this evening. She had a secret hope that there might be another guest at the Vanalleyns', one on whom she very much wanted to make an impact. After a lot of thought she chose a very short sheath of scarlet silk that had been wickedly expensive despite its apparent simplicity, and which showed off her figure to perfection. She knew she looked stunning.

The Vanalleyns lived in a gaunt grey house of perfect but uncompromising proportions high up towards the rolling Yorkshire moors that provided Lord Vanalleyn with so much sport. None of his ancestors had mucked about with the architecture; no one had added little wings or naughtily knocked down pediments to indulge individual whims. They had been far too busy hunting furred or feathered quarry in Yorkshire or political quarry in the Houses of Parliament. The Vanalleyns had a great tradition of service to their country. The family tree was full of viceroys here and cabinet ministers there, with the occasional admiral and bishop (younger sons, of course) thrown in. If their own nests got feathered in the process, so much the better, they were not of the type to turn down honours, and quite a few had come their way.

The house itself did not give one the feeling of being very

lived in, and indeed the family were not often in residence. They came for the grouse – that went without saying – for Christmas and Easter and occasional weekends, but for the greater part of the year Lord Vanalleyn stalked the corridors of power while his wife worked hard for various good causes or knitted in their London house. When she finished her knitting, she rolled it up neatly, stuck the needles, exactly level, into the ball of wool, put it away in a bag, and the bag in a drawer. There was none of the overflowing clutter in either of their houses that lay about at Duntan, no clue as to what anyone might have been doing two minutes before you entered the room. Lord Vanalleyn's shooting dogs lived with the keeper. True, there were two enormous deerhounds who lived in the house, but they seemed more a part of the architectural design than real live dogs. They reclined regally on the stone floor of the hall and never did anything tiresome or intimate like laddering your tights with their paws or slobbering on your evening trousers. You would certainly never find a bone hidden underneath the sofa cushions at Ralton Hall.

Having produced two sons very early in the marriage, one to inherit the title, and the other presumably as a spare, they had not increased their family any further. It would not have interested Lord Vanalleyn to breed daughters, and if his wife might have enjoyed some feminine companionship, it would not have entered into his calculations, and he had done very few uncalculated things in his life. Sonia, who loathed him, thought he was a fatuous old windbag inflated by self-admiration, but Archie could never quite resist his aura of power, though Sonia, a dangerous mimic, could usually force a reluctant laugh out of him with her impersonations of what Lord Vanalleyn actually had said or inventions of what he might have said. Lady Vanalleyn was like a very faded chintz. You could see that the design had originally been charming, the quality of the material excellent, but the colour had been washed out over the years. She would not have looked out of place hanging in any of the bedrooms at Duntan. Sonia liked her very much.

They drove the thirty-odd miles between Duntan and Ralton

in silence, occupied with their own thoughts, but as they approached the house, Archie said, 'This arrangement over the moor could be very important. We need to combine with the Vanalleyns to provide a whole fortnight's let, you know. Do try not to antagonise Dukie – he can be a tricky chap to deal with. Mind you, Johnnie says we're equally necessary to them, but if we do well with the letting it should pay for our own private days and help towards the farm as well.'

'Oh thrillsville.'

'The farm is our livelihood. I do wish I could make you understand that.'

'I'm sure you do. But don't worry, I'll chat him up for you. He's so vain it never occurs to him that we're not all hanging on his every word anyway.'

They were slightly late, having got stuck behind a tractor on the twisty road, and as they drove up to the house Sonia was disappointed to see only one other car there, which she recognised as the Brown-Gorings'. She had half-expected to see a dark blue Mercedes. John and Sally were just getting out of their large Volvo, which bore the unmistakable traces of family life inside. The gravel at Ralton always seemed especially thick and luxurious, a sign of prosperity perhaps, but bad news for those wearing high-heeled shoes. Sally and Sonia trod gingerly over it and they all went up the steps together to ring the bell. You did not wander into the house and shout 'Hello' at Ralton Hall. The Vanalleyns' butler, Blake, a po-faced man who had been with them for years, opened the front door and led the way to the drawing room.

Lady Vanalleyn, wearing an off-white dress that matched her hair and complexion rather too well, greeted them warmly.

'Dukie will be down in a moment. I'm so sorry he's not here to meet you, but he got caught on the telephone. Now, I want you to meet Antonella Venturi who is staying with us and who works at Sotheby's and knows everything about pictures, and this is my nephew Simon, whom I think you know?' Sonia's heart lurched as a tall figure in a dark blue smoking jacket rose from the sofa. But who was the incredibly glamorous woman who had been sitting beside him, looking as sleek and languorous as a black panther, and who unfurled a pair of legs that seemed to go on for ever when she got up? Sonia, who normally never thought about her own perfectly average height, suddenly felt stunted.

'Hi, Simon. Lovely to see you. How's Ellie-May?' To Sonia's surprise Sally gave Simon a kiss and it was obvious that she and John knew him quite well. Somehow she had not expected this. Archie went over and shook hands with him.

'How very good. Just the chap I wanted to meet. Sorry I missed you at Duntan the other day, but Sonia told me all about your visit. We need to have a talk sometime.' He moved on to shake hands with the beautiful Antonella, a gleam of admiration in his eye, and Simon came over to Sonia.

'Well, what a surprise,' she said untruthfully.

'Surely not. You told me the date you were coming. Didn't you think I would be here?'

'Of course not.' Sonia tried to sound casual, and then fatally spoiled the effect by continuing, 'Anyway your car wasn't at the front – ' She stopped abruptly, furious to find herself blushing and unable to meet the laughter in his eyes.

'No, how remiss of me – it's in the garage at the back. How very well you match your beautiful dress. Scarlet is my favourite colour,' said Simon. 'Let me get you a glass of champagne – or would you rather have something else?'

'Champagne would be fine, thank you,' she said coldly, trying to muster her dignity as Simon went to collect her drink, humming 'Lady in Red' to himself. So much for the sophisticated appearance. She felt she had been tricked into being as gauche as a schoolgirl. Luckily, the entrance of Lord Vanalleyn, a tall, thin figure of considerable distinction, especially in his own eyes, gave her a chance to recover.

'A little call from Downing Street. I do apologise.'

He stood with his back to the fire looking as if he was about to address a political meeting, expecting everyone's attention to be centred on him, smoothing the two wings of wavy hair on either side of his silver head with the palms of his hands. Sonia hated his hands, which were long, hairy and flexible and always reminded her of a chimpanzee's.

'Do you use this poison?' he asked, offering her his snuff-box. It was one of his affectations. He knew perfectly well that she didn't take snuff, though she had once been goaded into pretending she did and had sneezed wetly and violently over everyone, to Archie's great embarrassment. Lord Vanalleyn sniffed some expertly up his own hairy nostrils, which did no more than twitch.

'I've had a dreadful day,' he said. 'Antonella here has been trying to convince me that my Rubens drawing isn't by Rubens at all, and Simon wants me to open the house to the public. I ask you! What a good thing you've all come to save me from any more of their nonsense. Fatal to let experts into your house.'

Everyone laughed politely.

Food and drink at Ralton were always excellent, though not in very lavish supply, and soon the dismal butler came to announce that dinner was ready. The dining room was dark and heavy; unsmiling Vanalleyn ancestors of the male sex stared coldly down from the walls. They looked a disagreeable bunch. As the dinner party consisted of such a small number, they sat at the round rosewood breakfast table in one of the windows rather than at the long table in the centre of the room, and conversation was general to start with. An excellent jellied bortsch was followed by escalopes of veal. Lord Vanalleyn took a minute silver pepper mill out of his pocket and rotated the top above his plate with his ape-like fingers.

'Oh how absolutely sweet,' said Sally. 'Do let me see.'

He handed her the little grinder.

'Try a little. I always have my own mixture of white and black peppahcorns. I never go anywhere without it.'

'Even in other people's houses?'

'Especially in other people's houses. You never know what they may produce. I think peppah is so important, don't you?'

'Like high moral tone and regular movements of the bowels?' suggested Sonia, but the shaft went wide. Lord Vanalleyn took himself far too seriously ever to doubt that anyone else might not.

'Well done, Sonia. One up to you, but I'm afraid my Uncle Marmaduke won't notice,' Simon, who was sitting on her other side, said softly. 'Am I forgiven or are you still cross with me? It is unpardonable to tease you, but you looked so beautiful coming in wearing that lovely dress that I knew I was right not to have missed a chance to see you again. Antonella and I have to go and look at a house in Northumberland tomorrow. She's doing a valuation of some pictures and I've been called in to advise on possibilities for their stable block. Of course you couldn't guess that I'd be here.' But he didn't look as if he believed this for a moment.

Sonia decided to overlook it.

'Tell me how your painting's going,' he said, and they talked as easily as if they had known each other for years. It was an effort for Sonia to remember her manners and turn to her host again half-way through dinner.

As soon as dinner was over Lady Vanalleyn got up and caught the eyes of her ladies. 'I know you have business to discuss, Dukie darling,' she said, 'so I'll get Blake to bring your coffee in here, but don't be *too* long, will you?'

'Anyone want to go upstairs?' she asked as she led the way back to the drawing room.

'I think I do,' said Sonia. She didn't really but she was burning to ask Sally some questions.

'Oh well, you both know your way. Go on up to my bedroom, or go with Antonella. I'll just have a word with Blake about taking the men their coffee.' Luckily the gorgeous Antonella did not seem inclined to join them. She did not look the type for girls' gossips, and Sonia thought she would probably be one of those enviable women who are able to last for ages without having to stop for a loo, like a very expensive car with an extra-large petrol tank.

As soon as she and Sally were sitting on Lady Vanalleyn's bed in her huge gloomy bedroom, repairing their lipstick, she said, 'So go on Sal. Do tell. I didn't know you knew Simon. He's just been to us to make an assessment about Duntan.'

'Oh well – no one better. Though I'd have thought you'd

know him too. He's often here. But of course one forgets how little time you spent up here really when Archie was in the army, and then you were always busy with old Lady D. Well, Simon's a dish, as you can see, a real charmer if ever there was one.'

'Umm. Bit smooth,' said Sonia. 'Not really my type. Has he got a family? I never gathered.'

Sally was not deceived.

'Don't you go falling for him, darling. He's very naughty and he's broken lots of hearts. He's got this lovely American wife, Ellie-May, and two boys by his first marriage, which came unstuck. Ellie-May's a decorator and very much a career lady, and she always spends the summer in the States buying and catching up with trends over there. Her family are rolling. It's a funny marriage, but it seems to suit them. Simon always has a bird for the summer and plays around, and then they seem to settle down happily for the winter. I know one or two people who've been badly hurt by Simon. You steer clear, Sonia. He'd be dynamite in your present unsettled state – and anyway, he's very choosy.' Which was not very clever of Sally, all things considered.

'What about Antonella?' asked Sonia as they went downstairs.

'Well, I know they do a lot of work together, and I believe they did have a fling. Whether they're having an affair now, I don't know. On and off perhaps, but nothing too serious I should think. She's been around for ages and she's a great friend of Ellie-May's too.'

There was a tiny fire burning neatly in the enormous grate. It felt as though even the flames would have been drilled to flicker at the same height at Ralton Hall, Lord Vanalleyn's exacting demands for order and subservience permeating to the furthest corners of the house. Antonella was lying on a sofa reading a book. Sonia went and sat down beside her.

'I have so enjoyed sitting next to your delightful husband and talking about the pictures in your house.' She had only the faintest trace of an Italian accent.

'Pictures? Archie? But he doesn't know anything about them.'

Antonella raised her dark eyebrows.

'No? He seemed quite knowledgeable to me. He was telling me you have a Michele di Ridolfo *Madonna and Child*. I'd love to see it. I have just written the notes for one of our preview catalogues about his paintings. You don't often see one.'

'Goodness,' said Sonia, 'I didn't know Archie even knew we had one.'

Antonella looked at her over the top of an enormous pair of dark-rimmed reading glasses.

'Perhaps you underestimate your husband?' she said coolly. 'We had a most interesting talk about all sorts of things. I was impressed by some of his ideas.'

Lady Vanalleyn went over to the coffee tray.

'Dukie tells me that John has landed an Arab prince for us. I must say it sounds most unlikely somehow. How do you like your coffee, Sally?'

'Just black, please. Yes, I gather it's unusual. John says the Arabs don't usually go in for the grouse – it's the French or Americans or Spaniards as a rule – but I think this chap wants to entertain his European friends or clients or whatever, and not fellow Arabians, though I believe he's an absolute crack shot himself, a real old deadeye.'

'I've met him several times in my professional capacity. He is very good to deal with. There would be no problem about payment,' said Antonella.

'I hear you've got Rosamund staying with you, Sonia,' said Lady Vanalleyn, who had settled down in an unyielding chair with some knitting. 'How are you bearing up under that? I haven't seen her for ages, but I don't suppose she's changed much.'

'Oh well, you know what she's like – one moment you could kill her and the next you can't resist her. I'm in a bit of a resisting phase just now, I have to admit. She wants to take over the house from us, and she's got all mixed up in some fishy pseudo-religious sect. She foisted a ghastly member of it on us for a bit, till Archie managed to chuck him out. I don't really know what she's up to, though. I think she's in between lives and looking for a cause or a man – or both. You know how she loves running causes and people so long as she doesn't actually have to do any of the dirty work.'

'She always was impossible. Wild as a hawk as a child and drove her poor parents into the grave. She's a bit younger than me, so I was never all that close to her as a girl, but one of my sisters was an exact contemporary so I always heard the gossip. They shared a governess at one stage and my sister Prudence did lessons with her. Rosamund took against the poor gov and got her sacked by starting a fire in the schoolroom and pretending the woman had been a secret smoker. My sister said Rosamund just dropped a lighted match into the waste-paper basket and strolled away as cool as ice. It was quite a serious fire in their London house – they were lucky the whole place didn't burn down – but Roz was quite unconcerned. And of course the wretched governess was dismissed without a reference. If my mother hadn't heard the truth from Prudence and found her another position, she'd probably have been labelled as a pyromaniac and never got another post.'

'Typical!' said Sonia. 'Do tell us more. I didn't know you knew her so well, Sybil.'

'She was one of my little bridesmaids, and Prue was a bridesmaid to her when she married Douglas. It was a tremendous wedding at St Margaret's, Westminster, and Rosamund looked too beautiful for words, like an angel, but my goodness she did lead Douglas a dance. I don't know how Emily Duntan stood it, really. Most people were rather afraid of Emily, but not Roz! She didn't give a damn what anyone thought. It's lucky Archie looks so exactly like Douglas, otherwise no one of my generation would have believed he'd fathered him for a moment. And then there was that terrible scandal. That was awful for the poor Duntans.'

'You mean when she had the walk-out with the Maharajah?' asked Sonia.

'Oh no, before that. It was before she went off to India to sit at the feet of that guru. I mean the trouble with all the black magic.'

'No!' said Sonia and Sally in unison.

'I've never heard that,' said Sonia. 'Whatever happened?'

'Oh it was very much hushed up and I can't remember all the details, but Rosamund got seriously involved with a coven of witches. I suppose it started because she got bored – she's always had to look for new excitements. But this really got out of hand and there were some quite nasty happenings. People she didn't like started getting ill, or having minor disasters, and someone on the estate who'd had a quarrel with her actually died in rather strange circumstances. I don't suppose she really had anything to do with that – she just liked to hint at it to tease the family – but there were certainly stories about wild orgies. Apparently poor old Douglas came back unexpectedly after some regimental dinner and found these strange women and Roz dancing naked in the moonlight, with all sorts of weird signs and symbols and an altar with an inverted cross, and I don't know what. I think Emily Duntan took a hand then and managed to put a stop to it, but it was a great sensation at the time. Both families had to use their influence to get Douglas posted abroad for a bit, get her out of the way till the fuss had died down. It really was very naughty of Rosamund,' said Lady Vanalleyn mildly, clacking away at her porridge-coloured knitting, two plain two pearl.

'It doesn't suprise me at all to hear she's mixed up in some funny sect,' she continued. 'She's always played about on the fringes of the occult and tried to manipulate religion. You want to get Archie to be very firm with her, Sonia. Think of some sanction that would make her life uncomfortable if she goes on with these people. She's always known which side her bread is buttered and been prepared to compromise, provided it suits her ends.'

The return of the men from the dining room put an end to these interesting reminiscences, but they had given Sonia a great deal to think about. She would also have been interested to hear the conversation Archie and Simon had had together over the port.

'The trouble is', Archie had said, 'that my wife has set her heart on saving the house and I'm afraid she's in for a most terrible disappointment. Of course in a perfect world that's what I'd like too. I'm not as besotted about the house as she is because I'm not such a romantic, but of course I'd like to think of my son living there one day too, after so many generations. But I feel the chances of that are quite remote, and that I ought to save something for him now before the position gets quite impossible and the whole estate has to go. I also feel if we have to part with the house, then the sooner we all bite on the bullet and get it over with the better.'

As it was, Sonia found it hard to concentrate on Lord Vanalleyn's lengthy lecture on the pros and cons of a single European currency whilst he sat, a shade too close to her, on the sofa. She tried not to watch Simon apparently absorbed in talking to Antonella across the room, and wondered what, if anything, was between them.

Soon after this, Sally made a move to go, saying that they had a babysitter and mustn't be too late. Everyone got up. Sonia heard Archie saying, 'Well goodbye, Simon. Sorry I can't make that lunch in a couple of weeks, but I'll hear about your ideas from Sonia. You know my views anyway, but I'll keep an open mind till I've read your report. When we've got all our let days sorted out with this prince of John's, you must come and have a day on Cragside with us if we still have some birds left in October. I gather from Antonella that you do quite a lot of work together. Do bring her over to Duntan with you next time you come and she can look at our Florentine picture she's so interested in. Come along, darling, we must go too.'

Simon came over to her. Sonia hoped he would kiss her goodbye, but he held out his hand instead.

'I'll very much look forward to seeing you again in London for our lunch date, then, Sonia, and we'll have a good discussion about everything. It's been most instructive to have a chance to talk to Archie too. I should have the report finished by then and I'll get Bridget to give you a ring and arrange the time and place.'

Was the masculine Bridget to be there too? Sonia certainly hadn't bargained for that. They said their goodbyes, Lord Vanalleyn squeezing Sally's and Sonia's bare arms with his chimp hands as he kissed them goodnight.

'I hear you talked pictures to the beautiful Italian,' said Sonia as they drove home. 'That's a bit of a turn-up for the books! She seemed most impressed with your knowledge.'

'Not everyone considers me a complete goon,' said Archie.

Sonia decided it would be safer to change the subject. Her own feelings were in a turmoil. There could be no doubting her attraction to Simon, but he seemed to have been sending her contradictory messages. One minute she had been sure he felt the same electricity flowing between them that she did, and the next moment, particularly after what Sally had told her, she wondered if he was just amusing himself at her expense. Also she had not liked the feeling that Antonella Venturi might have found something in Archie that she had overlooked. She had taken him for granted for so long, but though she had not thought she wanted him herself, there was no doubt that she did not at all enjoy seeing him exchange admiration with anyone else, whether it was the voluptuous Rosie Bartlett or someone with Antonella's far more serious charms. The combined advice of Sally and Caroline, coupled with the ominous account of her mother-in-law's dabblings in the occult, made her feel that she must make an effort to re-establish her influence over Archie. Suddenly she longed for him to look at her as he had done so often in the past, for him to tell her that she had taken the shine out of everyone else, and that he felt so proud of her. She felt a frightful urge to cry.

'How did your discussion about the shooting go?' she asked, offering an olive branch.

'It all seems pretty satisfactory,' said Archie. 'Though I must say it sounds a bit of a rum set-up. I'm insisting on meeting the Prince in person before I finally agree to the arrangement. I don't think Dukie was too keen, but John didn't think it was too bad an idea. You've got to show who's boss. I gather arrangements are normally made through the secretary, who's called Fergusson B. Clutter.'

'Don't be funny, Archie – he can't be called that!'

'Yes he is. Really. Anyway, he had the nerve to tell John that the Prince would pay in advance and then if he doesn't want to turn up at the last minute it won't matter! Bloody cheek! Apparently, if he's bought the fortnight he considers it's his to do what he likes with, and if he's not in the mood, or something else crops up, he just won't come. I'm not having that. All my beaters and loaders turning out and then the fellow doesn't show up! What on earth would Thompson think?' Thompson was Archie's keeper, and had taught him to shoot as a boy. They adored each other. 'Anyhow,' Archie went on, cornering violently on the twisty road, his driving made even more exciting than usual by Dukie Vanalleyn's excellent claret, 'Anyhow, I said I must meet the Prince in person or the deal would be off.'

'Well I think you were quite right, darling,' said Sonia, biting back warnings about Breathalysers and clutching at the arm-rest, her feet pressed to imaginary brakes as they hurtled round another bend.

There was a full moon. 'Stop the car, Archie,' said Sonia urgently as they crossed the cattle grid. 'Turn the lights off.'

'Whatever for?' But he put the brakes on and drew to a halt.

The house lay dreaming on its ledge, halfway between the top of the park and the drop to where the river silvered its way along below it. The house itself looked silver, too, and giant shadows cast pools of darkness beneath silver beech trees. Sonia caught her breath.

'It's just so beautiful. Let's look a minute.' It was very still. Unusually for Yorkshire there was no wind and the world seemed enfolded in silence.

'Must do something about the bloody rabbits.' Archie switched the headlights on again, and immediately about a dozen or more could be seen frozen like statues, mesmerised by the lights of the car. Archie started the engine with a roar and suddenly the rabbits were scudding frantically for safety and the spell was broken. Sonia felt tears of disappointment stinging her eyes. Magic moments should be shared in full, or experienced in isolation.

Archie drove round the back. 'I'll put the car away. You go on in.'

'All right. Will you let the dogs out before you lock up?'

She climbed the stairs slowly, not bothering to turn on the lights, loving the feeling that she knew every inch of the house, that she could have found her way round it blindfold, that she knew where she was just by the feel and general atmosphere of each part of it. The moonlight shone down through the dome, casting shadows that would have scared Birdie witless.

Archie was a long time coming up. As she came back from the bathroom that opened off their bedroom, Sonia thought she heard a click from the telephone by the bed, as though someone had replaced the receiver downstairs. She lay in the half-light thinking of all the different pulls in her life, of the children, and how secure they had always been in their family life, of her marriage, of her passionate feelings for Duntan, which had been brought into her life by that very marriage – and she thought about Simon Hadleigh. She tried to will the feeling of sexual desire that thoughts of him stirred up in her to transfer itself to Archie. When at last he came up, he opened the door very quietly and made straight for his dressing room.

'Archie?'

'Oh, you still awake? Thought you'd have been asleep.'

'No, I'm not asleep.' But how often in the past had she pretended to be. 'You've been a long time, darling. Hurry up and come to bed.'

'I had a few things to do. I'll sleep in here tonight and then I won't disturb you in the morning. I've got an early start.'

'Early start? You never said. Where are you going?'

'Something cropped up this evening – to do with the shooting. Got to go to London.'

'Minnie's here all week. I'll come with you. We haven't been to London together for ages.'

'No. No. That's quite pointless – I shall be tied up with

meetings the whole time. I'm taking the car and I'm leaving really early. You'd never be ready in time, and besides, I'm not sure when I'll be back.'

Archie hardly ever took the car when he went to London on business. He always went by train so that he could get back the same day.

'Archie?'

'Yes?'

'Please don't go away, darling. Stay here . . . with me.'

'I have to go to London.' Archie deliberately misunderstood. 'But I shan't disturb you. Goodnight, Sonia.' The dressing-room door closed.

Congreve got it about right: hell has no fury like a woman who drenches herself in Chanel No. 19, leaves a bedside light dimly glowing, slips naked between the sheets – and is scorned.

Sonia wept despairingly into her pillow, in rage, misery, self-dislike and longing. She half-hoped that Archie would hear her, while taking the greatest care that her muffled sobs should be inaudible. The door between them remained firmly closed.

Chapter 17

The failure of the night before left Sonia raw and angry in spirit and unsettled in body, whilst the after-effects of the sleeping pill to which she had eventually resorted in the small hours of the morning now made her feel as though there was a fog between her and the rest of the world, although it had taken a long time to work after she had taken it. Martha was preparing to go down to Eton with the Warners. She was non-committal about what she proposed to wear for the Fourth itself, but was clad for the drive to London in the most surprisingly chaste-looking Laura Ashley dress, which she must have bought specially for the occasion as Sonia knew she had nothing remotely like it in her wardrobe. She looked as though butter would remain chilled in her mouth for a very long time. Sonia didn't trust her an inch.

'Will I do?' asked Martha, glinting at Sonia through lowered lashes. 'Don't I look wild? Just like an English rose?'

'I hardly recognised you. Just keep it up over the weekend, that's all.'

Martha laughed and sat down to wait in the hall on one of the set of six footman's chairs with the griffin crest on the back. Presently a double toot on the horn announced the arrival of Tim and Leonie. Sonia went out to say hello and wave Martha goodbye.

Tim got out of the car and opened the boot for Martha's small suitcase, and Leonie, silk scarf loosely knotted around her neck, but perfectly in place, exchanged a kiss with Sonia through the open window.

'Hop in the back, Martha,' said Tim. 'Let's hope this drizzle clears off before Wednesday. You look very pretty this morning.'

'Thank you,' said Martha, butter pats intact.

'Have a lovely time,' said Sonia. 'Give my love to the boys.

Be good, Martha, and don't eat too many strawberries.' Martha winked.

As Sonia walked back into the house, the telephone was ringing. She answered it in the library. It was John Brown-Goring.

'Sonia? Fun seeing you both last night with Dukie and Sybil. Look, is Archie there? I tried the estate office, but they didn't seem to know where he was.' It was twelve thirty. Archie, who had left the house before six, would have been in London for some time.

'He left really early this morning. Where are you ringing from, John? Are you in London?'

John sounded surprised: 'No, I'm in the York office. I just wanted a quick word with Archie. Will he be in for lunch? I said I'd try and ring him today if I got any further with the Prince.'

'Well, I don't think he'll be back today at all. As a matter of fact he said he'd had to go to London about some shooting arrangements, so I assumed he was meeting you and that you'd suggested it last night,' said Sonia, who didn't see why she should smooth Archie's path for him.

'Oh. Oh. Well I believe there was some mention of it, but I, er, couldn't make it.' John sounded very uncomfortable. 'Look, you can probably answer my question just as well, and get Archie to ring me and confirm when he gets back. I expect he told you that he's determined to meet our Arabian friend in person before agreeing to anything. Frankly I didn't think there was much chance of it, but I've been on to this secretary chap, and the result is that the Prince has asked you and Archie and Sally and me to dine at his London house the week after next. It just happens he's going to be in England for a few days then. He's in the States at the moment but Fergusson Clutter speaks to him twice a day and I rang him as soon as we got home last night, thinking I might just get in before his evening call, and I did. It's fairly unusual to be asked to his house. Sally's absolutely agog. But I don't want to get egg on my face and accept the invitation and then find you two can't make it.'

'Of course we'll make it. I'll be agog too. You fix anything that suits except the Wednesday, and I'll get Archie to ring you as soon as he's back. I have to be in London that week anyway for a meeting with Simon Hadleigh about the Heritage at Risk proposals, and Archie can't make that because he says he's got a council meeting here, but as far as I know any other day would be fine.'

Sonia put the telephone down, then picked it up again and dialled the Bartletts' number. It rang for some time before it was answered by Roger, who presumably was in his workroom at the back of the house, where he worked with three young male assistants whom he was training in the art of stringing lutes and making hautboys, since Sonia could hear strange twangings and hummings in the background.

'Roger? It's Sonia Duntan here. Could I speak to Rosie?'

'Sonia, *quelle plaisir*. I'm afraid Rosie's away. She got a call yesterday to go and see an old aunt of hers who lives in the South and has been taken ill. Can I give her a message?'

'Yes,' said Sonia. 'Yes, you can. Tell her I'm sorry about her aunt. Tell her that by a strange coincidence Archie has got a sick aunt too. I very much hope that they'll both recover soon – the aunts I mean. Tell her I'll be in touch with her when she gets back, and we'll hope to see you soon.'

'*A bientôt*, then,' said Joli Roger politely. '*Au revoir*, Sonia.'

Sonia rang off knowing she had not imagined the little click she had heard on her bedroom telephone the night before. She felt angry with herself for allowing such a situation to blow up so quickly and get so out of hand just at this moment in their lives when they had such a major decision hanging over them. She also felt very, very angry with Archie, but also more deeply hurt than she would have thought possible. She curled up on one of the wide window seats that overlooked the park and tried to do some serious thinking. Lotus, ever responsive to Sonia's moods, came and put her front paws up on her lap and whined, her huge brown eyes peering out anxiously from her chrysanthemum mop of hair. Sonia picked her up.

'Oh Lottie,' she said, 'I think I'm in an awful mess.' And she rocked the little dog in her arms, tears trickling down her cheeks and making a sodden patch on top of Lotus's head. Having failed so humiliatingly in her belated attempt to recapture Archie, she wondered what her next move ought to be. The idea of some sort of liaison for herself was alluring not only on the grounds of restoring her own battered morale, but also as a way of teaching Archie a lesson. She was surprised to find how ambivalent her feelings towards him were.

'I think I'm just a horrible dog in the manger,' she told Lotus miserably. 'Oh Lottie, what shall I do?' She felt very alone, as if her whole world, the one she had taken for granted for so long, was disintegrating, as though she were standing on a crumbling cliff-face that could give way at any minute and any false move on her part might start an avalanche she would be powerless to stop. Thoughts of her impending lunch date with Simon flickered with uncertainties like a video film on fast forward.

She shut herself up in her studio for most of the rest of the day and did some of the best work she had done for ages.

After tea, Archie telephoned from his club to say that he would not be back before Monday night. While he was in the South anyway, he might go down to the Fourth of June, catch up with a few old friends and possibly try and have a word with Tom's prospective housemaster. He might even bump into the Warners and Martha, though it would be no good trying to make a set meeting place in all that crowd. Were it not for the pricking of her thumbs and the newly acquired knowledge of Rosie Bartlett's ailing aunt, it might have seemed a very convincing alibi to Sonia. She told him about the invitation to dine with the Prince.

'Fine, fine,' said Archie. 'Quite right to accept.'

'John sounded surprised that you were in London. He didn't know you'd gone up on business to do with the shooting.'

'Really? No, er, well, I've got a few other lines out that he doesn't know about. I shall have a busy week.'

'I'll bet,' said Sonia.

'Look, I'm playing bridge in a few minutes. I must go. Home on Monday then, but I may be late so don't wait up.' He rang off.

Sonia dialled the number of his club.

'Could I speak to Sir Archibald Duntan? I believe he's staying. I think he'll be playing bridge.'

'Sir Archibald is not at the club at the moment. I don't think we're expecting him this week.'

'Oh, thank you,' said Sonia. 'It doesn't matter.'

'When will Daddy be home?' asked Polly.

'Not till late Monday night.'

'Oh no! He promised he'd help me school Dusty this weekend. He absolutely promised. It's the Pony Club dressage competition next weekend. He knows how important it is. That's gross.'

'Well, it seems that other more important things have blown up in London. You'll just have to do the best you can. I'm sorry, darling. Can I help?'

'Oh Mum, you know you're useless over dressage. It's not fair. That's rotten of him. Shirley's mother says all men are basically selfish and untrustworthy and I think she's absolutely jolly well right.' Polly gave the leg of the kitchen table a terrific welt with her riding switch, and flounced out, bottom wagging angrily. Sonia thought how out of character it was for Archie to let down any of his children. Dependability was normally his strong suit. Birdie came and leant against her mother.

'Have you got a headache, Mum?'

'No, darling. I'm fine.'

'You've got your headache face on. I don't like it when Daddy's not here. I've got a pain. Why is everybody always so cross since we came to live here?' she asked. Sonia felt as if she had been stabbed. The happy atmosphere of Duntan on which so many people commented, of which she was so proud, what was happening to that? She stroked Birdie's fine straight hair and planted a kiss on top of her head.

'Come on, Bird. Buck up. I'll kiss you better.'

But the pain rapidly developed into one of her sick attacks and she had to be put to bed early. Sonia was in two minds as to whether to ring the doctor, but decided to wait a bit and see how things developed. Birdie lay, small and white, with a bowl beside her bed while Sonia read to her. She read aloud very well, and it seemed extraordinary that she could follow the story sufficiently well with one part of her mind to be able to make it sound exciting, even to put on different voices for all the various characters, while another part of her was thinking of quite different things. She felt terribly conscious that the stresses and tensions in the family were taking their toll of Birdie, whose face acted as a sort of barometer to the moods of those about her. At the moment she definitely registered 'Stormy Weather' – possibly 'Change'. It seemed a long time since Birdie's barometer had read 'Set Fair'. Sonia wondered if it ever would again.

While she was still reading, Birdie dropped off to sleep, and Sonia stood for several minutes looking down on this difficult, vulnerable child, so specially loved by Archie. Was the feeling that Duntan was a safe haven, a place filled with love built up over generations, a figment of her imagination? Would Tom live here one day with his children? She looked around her. The wallpaper in the night nursery was of a hunting scene and had been there when Archie's father was a child. Faded ladies in top hats and riding habits soared side-saddle over hedges and walls, and gentlemen with fair moustaches rode lickety-hoop after fox and hounds on horses whose docked tails resembled the tassels on the cord tie-backs round the curtains. One lady had fallen off and lay in a ditch, but she looked very fetching and unrumpled as she gazed up into the eyes of one of the pink-coated men, who was clearly about to spill the beans of his undying love and scoop her into his arms. Perhaps she had fallen off on purpose to bring him up to scratch? Sonia tucked Birdie in and slipped quietly out, leaving the door ajar.

The house seemed very quiet. Lady Rosamund had flown back to the States for a few weeks, on business, or so she had said. She never felt the need to give much explanation about her movements and had been vague about her date of return. A letter addressed to her with the Heritage at Risk stamp on it had arrived, and Sonia had longed to steam it open. Meanwhile, outside the griffins brooded on their pillars, summoning up strength before a great battle, perhaps; a lull before the storm.

On Sunday morning the June weather suddenly decided to

play at summer after all. So often in Yorkshire it likes to perform tantalising tricks, like being cold and grey till about six o'clock in the evening, and then, hey presto!, producing the sun from behind the clouds like a rabbit out of a hat, pretending it has been there all the time. This morning, however, it had dressed up in laburnums and birdsong and smelled of azaleas and lilac; a lark could be heard climbing ladders in the blue sky; and somewhere over the church a cuckoo was calling. It was England in picture-postcard mood. Inside St Stephen's, though, the temperature was rather cooler, and a good deal of ill-will floating about made for a very different climate.

The flowers in the pedestals looked dead. Marcia Forsyth was pleasurably aware that this was entirely due to the fact that Lady Rosamund, who had volunteered to do them this week, had gone away without arranging for a substitute. It was typical. Absolutely typical. Marcia looked forward to tackling Rosamund on her return. Marcia loved tackling people.

Miss Dunn, a lone chorister, bore her customary general grudge against everyone. This was out of both habit and inclination. She would have felt naked without a grudge. The Colonel, Joe in his verger's role, and Mrs Dickinson at the organ were all put out because as usual Terry had at the very last moment altered the hymns Joe had put up on the board. They had been expecting to sing 'Lead us, Heavenly Father, lead us' and instead the Vicar had changed it to one of his own choosing, which was printed on slips of paper in the pews.

> 'Red and Yellow, Black and White
> All are equal in Thy sight,'

sang the congregation crossly.

Polly was having a lovely sulk. The trouble had begun at breakfast when Sonia had said she couldn't read her Barbara Cartland during meals, and had then whisked it away and said she had to help with the washing-up. When Polly had, quite justifiably in her own opinion, muttered 'Silly old bat' under her breath, her mother, usually an easygoing parent, but not one to tangle with in a certain mood, had become unaccountably crabby and said *that was enough*, Polly could jolly well come to church, *no argument*, or she would not be going to the Pony Club next weekend, let alone riding at all today. As Polly had been looking forward to a morning spent schooling Dusty and reading the Kamasutra, which Shirley had managed to filch from her mother's bookshelves and which was currently hidden inside the ottoman in the nursery bathroom, Polly naturally felt very hard-done-by.

She also felt furiously jealous of Martha for going off to Eton with the Warners. Last time Robin and Nigel had been over to Duntan they had not even noticed the fantastic cartwheels Polly had turned for their benefit on the lawn, displaying the maximum amount of stout thigh and knicker. It was all jolly unfair. She had pinched Cassie to equal things up a bit, but Cassie had responded by biting her quite painfully on the hand. It had bled hard enough to need a plaster but Sonia had been very unsympathetic and told her not to make such a fuss because it served her right. Now she was imagining her mother's early demise. Polly was coping brilliantly with this bereavement, and was not at all sad. The only pity was that Sonia, being dead, couldn't see how frightfully well they were all getting on without her.

Next to her in the pew, her mother was thinking equally vengeful thoughts about Rosie Bartlett and Archie. She imagined them sitting outside some expensive riverside inn at Bray, drinking Pimms No. 1 in the June sunshine – Rosie seemed a Thames Valley type. Sonia could hear the clanking of Rosie's charm bracelets as she speared a maraschino cherry with a little red plastic sword. Sonia made it rain so that Rosie's hair would go frizzy, but Rosie just slipped on a leopardskin-print mac and her hair remained as pretty as ever. Sonia turned the rain into acid rain in the hope that Rosie would shrivel up, mac and all, and then made Archie's jaw drop most satisfactorily as she herself purred up to the pub with Simon Hadleigh in a blue Mercedes. She also decided that it was time to outpray her mother-in-law, and do some hard bargaining with God for a fantastic sum of money to drop from the clouds. She half expected to be struck by a thunderbolt for such wickedness, but nothing happened.

So busy was everyone with their own particular brand of Christian charity that Terry's sermon, aimed at Colonel Forsyth, on 'Opening our hearts and minds to *new ways*', was over in a trice and the blessing was on them before they knew it. Terry, white-cassocked arms flailing above his head, whirled round like one of those inverted pyramids for drying washing in small gardens.

'The Peace and Joy of the Lord,' he declaimed excitedly in what was meant to be a thrillingly deep voice, but which came out disappointingly falsetto, 'be with every single one of you for *ever and ever*!'

'And with you too, old cock,' said Jem Slater benevolently, well pleased with the fifty pence he had just nicked from the collection.

'And . . . with . . . thy . . . spirit,' said the Colonel loudly, not to be weaned from the old responses. He dreaded the day, which he felt was approaching fast, when they might be called upon to pray for Sandra, Our Bishop.

'And how is Cassie today?' asked Terry, as the congregation edged past him towards Sunday lunch. He squatted down matily at the church door so as to be on eye level with her. He fancied he had a way with small people (suffer the little children to come unto me), though he found his own brood irritating in the extreme. Cassie looked at him coldly, eyeball to eyeball.

'I have a lot of nasty green gunge up my nose this morning,' she informed him. Terry got up hastily. He had not expected quite such a literal answer. Cassie was a dab hand at non-plussing.

'And how's the painting going on, Sonia?' enquired Marcia.

'Oh dear, not progressing very well, I'm afraid.'

'You must buck up. Don't let the grass grow under your feet. That's what I say.'

It was easy to imagine Marcia leaving a trail of scorched footprints behind her as she walked across a lawn.

Sonia knew that the grass under her own feet was often long and luscious.

*

'Archie away again then?' asked the Colonel, beady-eyed.

'Yes,' said Sonia.

'On business I suppose?' Marcia was digging away like a terrier scenting a bone.

'On business,' said Sonia.

Outside the church the air smelt of honey and wallflowers. The birds sang with heartless ecstasy and Sonia's heart felt as heavy and jagged as scrap iron.

While she was cooking lunch, Sonia ate a whole packet of chocolate biscuits, then, feeling bloated and disgusted with herself, she looked at her reflection to see if they showed. She was as thin as ever.

After lunch the telephone rang. It was Leonie in a frightful state. Robin and Martha had disappeared. Robin had been due back the night before but was not in when she and Tim went to bed. Leonie had decided to let Robin have a good lie-in, but on going to wake him up before lunch, had found that his bed had not been slept in. A telephone call to the friends of Lady Rosamund with whom they thought Robin and Martha were staying had produced the disquieting information that they were not there either, but had been assumed to be with the Warners. Leonie sounded quite distraught, though Sonia would have laid a large bet that she was looking as immaculate as ever.

The Fourth of June had been a ghastly fiasco. Martha had appeared looking an absolute fright. Gone were the suitable Laura Ashley dress and demure demeanour; instead Martha was dressed in chopped-off old jeans with ragged tears in them and a skin-tight black top. Her hair stuck out all over her head in tiny Rastafarian plaits and her face had been painted with butterflies. Had she turned up at their flat Tim said he would have refused to take her, but she had cleverly got a lift down from someone else and had joined them in Robin's room at Eton.

It should all have been such fun, wailed Leonie. It had been a perfect day, and Leonie had provided a wonderful picnic to eat under the chestnut trees on Agar's Plough. Eton had looked its beautiful best, and delicious whiffs of wisteria and Mrs Sinkins' pinks blended with the smells of mown grass, expensive cigars and strawberries. She had felt so proud of Robin in his spongebag trousers and brocade waistcoat, and Emma and Sophie, the two other girls they had invited to join them, had been sweet – so fresh and pretty and well mannered.

But the boys had only had eyes for Martha, who had flirted outrageously. What Robin's housemaster, a bit of an old stick at the best of times, had thought, Leonie trembled to imagine. Then – would you believe it – Martha had put something in Emma's and Sophie's drinks that had made them really very peculiar and dreadfully sick. Robin and Nigel's dame, rigid with disapproval, had had to take them to lie down in the spare room. Leonie was horrified. She could not believe that anyone, let alone someone one actually knew, could behave so badly. She had been very, very cross. The whole day had been ruined and she had had grave doubts about letting them go out in the evening, but Tim had pointed out that Robin was actually eighteen – of age – and it was time she stopped treating him like a little boy. She had felt very hurt, and even more so when Robin had announced that he was going to stay with Martha's friends for a couple of days rather than be with his parents and Nigel, and would not be coming back to the Warners' flat till Saturday night. He had not even wanted to go with his father and brother for a lesson at a Shooting School in Hampshire, and this was quite out of character. It had been so disappointing for them all. She felt he was utterly bewitched by Martha – and now they were missing! Had Sonia any idea where they could be, and was that wicked, irresponsible Rosamund back yet?

'No,' said Sonia. 'She's still away, but that may be just as well. Look Leonie, give me a minute or two to think and I'll ring you back. Will you be in?'

'Yes of course. Either Tim or I will be here all the time in case they suddenly turn up. Robin has important exams coming up which are absolutely vital. He's Captain of his House too, and it would be too awful if he did something disgraceful and ruined all his career chances. Of course I'm worried about Martha as well,' she added hastily, 'but she's led such a different life. I can't believe it of Robin. He's always been so dependable. So easy.'

Sonia could imagine Leonie's state of mind. Her children, somewhat to the irritation of various friends, had never given her a moment's cause for anxiety; which was not, of course, to say that she had not frequently been worried sick about them.

After she put down the telephone, Sonia sat for several minutes wondering what to do and wishing very much that Archie, so practical in a crisis, was there to help. Suddenly an idea struck her, and with it came that instant, illogical certainty that leaves no room for doubt. She went straight to the little boudoir that her mother-in-law had taken over.

All the furniture there was of satinwood, which together with the white and gold walls and ceiling, and the almost translucent white silk curtains hanging in the two south-facing windows, gave the room its special quality of lightness and grace. To be in it on a sunny morning, Sonia thought, was to feel oneself inside a rainbow soap bubble; apart from the delicate murals, the only colour came from the refraction of light through the prisms of the chandelier. Now it was full of Rosamund's possessions. Was it her imagination, or had this charming room become charged with something faintly sinister since Rosamund had started using it, as though someone had puffed a little smoke into the bubble?

She rolled back the top of the satinwood cylinder bureau. Inside were Lady Rosamund's writing things, including the gold fountain pen with the enormously broad italic nib that she had specially made for her.

'Unfortunately I can only write with an absolute spade,' she was fond of explaining, as though this was a positive necessity, like a collar for arthritis or a built-up shoe. Sonia picked out the large green leather address book and opened it at the B section. The pages were filled with her mother-in-law's huge, spiky writing. Sonia ran her eye over several pages until she found what she was looking for.

Brothers, she read, *34 Mongolia Terrace, London SW11*, and there was a telephone number. She dialled the number. She let it ring for ages, but just as she was about to give up a voice with a foreign accent answered.

‘ ’Allo?’

‘Is that the Brothers of Love?’

There was a long pause.

‘What you want?’

‘I’d like to speak to Martha,’ said Sonia, not even bothering to ask if she was there.

‘Nobody called Martha living ’ere. Wrong number.’

‘Oh no it’s not,’ said Sonia, the inner conviction buzzing away in her head. ‘You get Martha on the telephone *at once*, or the police will be round immediately.’

She could hear the intake of breath at the other end of the line.

‘I ask someone. Maybe I see what I can do. You hold on?’

‘I certainly will,’ said Sonia, ‘but you’d better be quick.’ She heard the receiver being put down and then the sound of a door banging. Five minutes, she decided. I’ll give them five minutes.

It seemed a long time before a small voice, but recognisably Martha’s, said, ‘Hullo?’

‘Martha? It’s me – Sonia. Don’t ring off. Are you all right?’

There was a pause.

‘Yes.’ It was a very tiny yes. You could have put it on a pinhead.

‘Can you talk freely? Just say yes or no.’

‘No.’

‘Is Robin with you?’

‘Yes.’ Pinhead voice again.

‘Is he all right?’

Another pause.

‘Sort of,’ said Martha’s voice, very doubtful, very wobbly.

‘Listen, Martha. I know you’ve got yourself in a mess, but you absolutely have to get Robin home no matter what you’ve both been up to. Tim and Leonie are off their heads with worry. I’m going to ring Tim now to tell him where you both are and he’ll come straight round and collect you. Tell your friends that if you’re not there, ready, I shall call the police. I don’t think they'd like that somehow. And Martha, for God's sake don't do anything else silly. Now can you manage that?'

'I think so.'

'Would you like me to come down tonight?'

'Yes. Oh yes.'

'Right,' said Sonia. 'I'll have to organise a few things here and then I'll jump in the car and be with you sometime tonight. I'll go straight to the Warners' flat. Mind you're there. And Martha? Don't worry. It'll be all right. Do you want me to speak to anyone there?'

'No,' said Martha, sounding stronger now. 'No. I'll manage OK. Don't ring the police, though.' There was a click and the line went dead.

Sonia rang the Warners. Tim answered. She gave him the address and told him she was coming down. He sounded hugely relieved. She went to find Minnie.

'You do right, Sonia. You go fetch our Martha home. I always knew that Broother What's-it was a real bad 'un – monk or priest or whatever he calls himself. Common criminal if you ask me, though they do say', said Minnie darkly, 'that you can't get near the fires of hell for parsons warming their backsides. I blame 'er mother. She should never have had the care of the child. You go and bring Martha home tomorrow and don't worry about me and the girls, we'll be fine. But you ought to get hold of Archie. I'll roast that Brother Ambrose if I ever set eyes on him again.'

Minnie looked as though she could take on a whole army of the Brothers of Love with nothing more sinister than the nursery toasting-fork.

It took Sonia longer than she expected to reach the Warners' flat. After such a fine weekend there were a lot more cars on the roads than she had anticipated and by the time she was half-way down the M1 she was caught up with the mass of weekenders returning to London. A hold-up where the south-bound traffic was down to one lane did nothing to improve matters, but at least there were not too many lorries. She listened to Classic FM and tried to stop her automatic pilot from taking over while she became dangerously absorbed in her own thoughts. Ruminating on the new problem of Martha, the ghost of an idea started to form in her head.

The Warners had a flat in a block in the Fulham Road. Sonia left the car on a nearby meter that she could feed first thing the next morning and pressed the buzzer at the main entrance. Tim's voice answered almost immediately, and the latch of the door clicked open. She took the lift to the fourth floor, where Tim was standing in the open doorway of their flat to greet her. He gave a thumbs-up sign.

'Got 'em both safe. Major Panic over. General Catastrophe avoided. What a set-up, though! Come in, Sonia. Wonderful of you to come down. Leonie's done her mother-hen bit and they're both crashed out in bed. Martha looks like a ghost, but Robin was in quite a bad way. Thank God it's Long Leave. He'd been doped up to the eyeballs, but the doctor says he'll be all right by the time he has to go back.'

Leonie, looking white and drawn but with the bandbox aura still intact, came out of one of the bedrooms.

'Sonia darling! Oh the relief! You clever, clever girl to guess where they were. Come in and have a big drink and we'll tell you all about it.'

The sitting room was as neat and pretty as Leonie herself, though rather overfull of knick-knacks that Sonia was afraid of knocking over. Leonie seemed to have a built-in radar system that prevented her from bumping into things, no matter how constricted the space. Sonia, who did not normally drink spirits, accepted a glass of whisky from Tim, collapsed on the sofa, and kicked off her shoes.

'So come on,' she said. 'Tell all.'

Tim had not had any difficulty in finding the house in Mongolia Terrace, a respectable-looking street in a gentrified part of Clapham. The door has been opened by a seedy-looking young man in a grubby track suit, who had several days' growth of stubble covering his pallid face. He had very light blue eyes, one of which disappeared unnervingly into the side of his nose when he looked at you. He spoke with a foreign accent and announced himself as a lay brother.

Tim had demanded, military style, to speak to whoever was in charge, and to have Robin and Martha produced immediately. He was ushered into a room at the back of the house. The white walls were covered with garish paintings, the style of which, to Tim's eyes, looked pure Duntan village school, until he noticed that the subject matter was highly erotic, not to say pornographic. A life-size carving in dark wood of a nude African woman suckling a baby stood by the door. It was so life-like that for an awful moment Tim had thought it was real, and had been about to apologise profusely to it and bolt for the door. He found the room highly disconcerting. The only furniture was an oak chest with lighted candles on each end, giving it the appearance of some sort of altar. There was nowhere to sit. The lay brother shuffled out, moving silently on dirty bare feet.

Just as Tim had been beginning to get extremely restive and was about to go exploring, a door he had not noticed, and which was cleverly concealed in a bookcase, suddenly opened.

'Admiring my collection of Haitian primitives, Mr Warner?' An enormous, dazzlingly good-looking man with silver hair stood in the doorway. He wore the same type of long white robe as Brother Ambrose, only this one was immaculately clean and worn over a silk shirt instead of an old black jersey. Beautifully polished, expensive-looking Italian shoes showed beneath the hem. He smelt of incense.

Tim did not possess a great deal of hair, but said he could feel what little he had rising at the back of his neck at the same time as he broke out in a cold sweat. He had never felt anything like it in his life.

'I am glad that you could come, Mr Warner, and I'm delighted we have been able to be of use to your young people – act as a rescue operation, in fact. Yes, I feel we should have earned your gratitude. How you may wish to express it is up to you. We already know Martha, of course. Her mother is a very dear friend. I am Brother François.' His English was so accentless and perfect that he could not possibly have been an Englishman, but it was difficult to place him.

He extended a well-manicured hand. Tim did not take it.

'Where are my son and Martha? I want them here at once.'

'All in good time, Mr Warner, all in good time. Your son could be in very serious trouble. He appears to have taken large doses of amphetamines and had a bad reaction. So lucky that Martha could bring him straight here where we have some experience of dealing with young drug addicts.'

'If my son was given drugs, I should like to know where they came from.'

'Wouldn't we all? Perhaps, Mr Warner, we should telephone the headmaster of Eton College right now so that he can start to investigate the matter? I should also tell you that we found some powder, which has not yet been analysed, in your son's pockets. I have, of course, several witnesses to this, and we have kept the substance. You may feel, for the sake of the other pupils, that the school should be informed. Or you may prefer, for the sake of your son's future career – and also for Martha's family – as little publicity as possible. I should understand either attitude of course.' The threat was implicit.

'You might not like the Drug Squad here yourself,' said Tim.

'I doubt if they would find anything here, Mr Warner.'

'No,' said Tim. 'You've had twenty minutes' warning. Still, I dare say you might not welcome those forensic chaps sleuthing round your set-up.'

'Any intrusion of privacy is always disturbing to those engaged in the spiritual life. I confess it would be a disruption, but naturally if you feel the police should be informed you are free to use our telephone. Whether your son is in a fit state to be questioned is, of course, a matter of opinion. I will send for the young people. You must judge for yourself.'

Tim Warner was not a small man, but Brother François, blandly smiling, towered over him.

'Damn fellow made my trigger finger itch,' Tim told Sonia. 'It was stalemate, of course. We both knew it.'

When Martha came in, Tim, who could willingly have murdered her the day before, thought she looked so small, so waif-like and so utterly wretched that his anger turned to pity.

'Ah, Martha, my dear. I have been telling Robin's father

how lucky it was that you had the good sense to bring him here, where we know how to deal with young people in trouble. I have tried to give Martha a little fatherly advice, Mr Warner – perhaps under the circumstances I should say brotherly advice. I hope for her sake that she is going to remember everything I have told her.' Brother François' smile did not reach his rain-cold eyes. Martha looked at him stony-faced, but Tim thought she also looked very much afraid.

'Just so,' said Brother François. 'Ah, here comes our young patient . . .'

Robin, supported by the unsavoury foreign youth on one side and Brother Ambrose on the other, was grey in the face and unsteady on his legs. He smelt of vomit.

'We won't hang about,' said Tim. 'Get him into my car. Come along, Martha.'

He had half-expected some last-minute opposition to their departure or further threats or bargaining, but none were forthcoming.

'So here we are, thanks to you,' said Tim to Sonia. 'Quite a little saga. I ought to risk the consequences to Robin and call the cops, but it might be hard to prove they'd produced the dope. It would be Martha's word agains theirs, and she was greatly at fault. They'd be bound to get her into trouble and there'd be a lot of bad publicity, whatever the outcome. I blame Rosamund, of course. I shall never feel the same about her again.'

'Martha told us what she did,' said Leonie. 'First putting "E" or whatever they call it, in the girls' drinks, and then, later, when she and Robin went out to dinner, putting sugar lumps with something else on in his coffee. She said it was only meant to be a joke because he was so pompous and she'd got the drugs from that awful Ambrose – though she says it's quite easy to get them anywhere. What can Rosamund be thinking of? She's only sixteen. Anyway, she says they must have been "dirty", whatever that may mean, and they had a really violent effect on Robin. She panicked and didn't want to bring him home to us in that state and thought those awful Brothers might have an antidote or something, so she took him to Mongolia Terrace in a taxi. Then that awful man said he'd ring up Robin's housemaster and get him sacked if she tried to get in touch with any of us.

'Apparently,' Leonie went on, 'they give young people drugs, then pretend to rescue them, brainwash them not to go back to their families, and try to get their money. Awful. But I really don't understand how she could have done such a wicked, wicked thing. She kept saying she doesn't know who she is and felt that everyone hated her – and we'd tried to give her such a nice time. I really don't understand. She must be very mixed-up. Tim feels sorry for her, but I shall find it hard to forgive.'

Sonia longed to spring to Martha's defence but felt it was not the right moment.

'I just can't tell you both how sorry I am,' she said. 'You really had been kind to her. I expect she'll tell me all about it in the car tomorrow. Long car drives are great for confidences. Tim, will you talk to Archie about it all? He thinks I exaggerate, but he'll have to deal with Rosamund over this. She can't go on with this bogus sect now that we know how sinister it all is. And he is Martha's guardian.'

'Don't worry,' said Tim. 'I'll talk to Archie all right. Meanwhile we've sent Nigel off to friends for the night, so you can have his bed, Sonia. But first I think we all need a really good dinner. It's after nine o'clock. There's this marvellous Italian restaurant round the corner where we go often. Come on both of you, I'll take you out. I'm starving.'

'Oh no, darling,' said Leonie, 'I couldn't possibly go and leave Robin and Martha alone here now.'

'Don't be ridiculous. They can't come to any more harm here. They've had the fright of their lives.'

But Leonie was adamant.

'You take Sonia. She certainly deserves it after that long drive, but I'm too tired and I wouldn't enjoy it. I'd keep fussing. I'll have a boiled egg here and go to bed. I'd rather. Really. Please, Sonia.'

'Well, if you're sure?' said Sonia. 'I must say, it would be heaven. I'm starving too.'

Chapter 18

The restaurant was simple but delightful and the Italian proprietor, who obviously knew Tim well, ushered them to a quiet corner table and hovered attentively while they looked at the menu. There was a choice of three or four dishes for each course, enough to be interesting without being overwhelming or making the decision too complicated. Sonia chose *Fegato alla veneziana* because she adored liver but hated cooking it at home, and Tim had a pasta dish and ordered Chianti for them both. It was a pleasant, easy meal. Tim was always good company and they were both in the mood to relax and laugh after the anxieties of the day.

At the next table a large party of young people were obviously celebrating the birthday of a dark, pretty girl. A marvellous cake, alight with candles, was produced by the proprietor's wife and she and the waiters all clustered round to join in singing 'Happy Birthday'. There was much laughter and clapping and when the girl's health was drunk, Sonia noticed with a pang of envy the long look she exchanged with her husband, both of them gazing into each other's eyes. They were clearly very much in love and wore their happiness for all to see.

By the time Sonia and Tim had reached the coffee stage, the young party was leaving. They were going on somewhere to dance, so there was much discussion about who would go in which car and lots of fond farewells to the owner and his wife, who gave them all smacking kisses. After they had all departed, the absence of their chatter left a slight hush. Sonia, glancing at Tim, saw a frozen expression on his face and followed the direction of his gaze.

At a small table for two, which up to that moment had been blocked from their sight, sat Archie and Rosie Bartlett. They too were gazing into each other's eyes.

'Well, well,' said Sonia lightly. 'What a very small world.'

'Oh hell,' said Tim, looking very concerned. 'God, I'm sorry, Sonia.' He did not pretend that the situation was anything but awkward.

Absurdly, a jingle Birdie had picked up at school, and which she and Cassie had been chanting round the house for days, came into Sonia's mind:

> 'Eh by gum, my mother was a plum,
> My father was a blackbird. He ate my mum.'

Archie, sleek in his dark City suit, was not unlike a hungry blackbird. The plum looked very ripe.

'Would you like to miss out on coffee?' asked Tim. 'We can slip out quietly the back way and I can come back and pay tomorrow. Giovanni won't mind at all.' He looked at her anxiously, and she could tell from his face that though he certainly had not expected to see Archie and Rosie in the restaurant, it was no surprise to him that they should be together. Clearly the affair must be very common knowledge.

Sonia put a hand on his arm and smiled at him.

'No thank you, Tim. This may be rather a good thing in a way. At least it will put an end to all the pretence that's been going on. Come with me – I'm going over.' She got up and went to the table.

'Hullo, Archie, Rosie. What an amazing surprise.'

Archie looked thunderstruck.

'What on earth are you doing here?'

'I might ask you the same question.'

'Sonia! Darling! What a coincidence!' Rosie's long earrings jangled frantically. 'How funny that we should all meet here! Archie and I just bumped into each other and he very sweetly suggested we should have dinns together. Has the same thing happened to you and Tim?'

'Well not quite,' said Sonia. 'You see I happen to be staying with Tim and Leonie, and it was Leonie's suggestion that Tim should take me out to dinner without her because she was very tired. That makes a difference.'

If Archie's face looked strained, Sonia thought the little covered buttons down the front of Rosie's frilly white shirt looked even more so. 'Perhaps we could come and join you for coffee?' she suggested.

'And how is your poor aunt, Rosie?' she asked when their chairs had been moved and the coffee brought over.

'Aunt?' Just for a moment Rosie looked baffled. 'Oh, my aunt. Well she's much better, thank you.'

'Oh good,' said Sonia. 'What a relief. I do hope she recovers completely – or perhaps it would be better if she died? It can be so difficult if these situations linger on. So many people's lives can be affected. So hard on Roger and the boys if you have to keep rushing off – and exhausting for you too, of course. Your life must be very, very tiring at the moment.'

There was an uncomfortable pause. Archie sprang into action with the coffeepot and offered everyone cream and sugar, although he knew, of course, that Sonia always had hers black and unsweetened.

'I should like to know what on earth you're doing down here.' He had himself in hand now and was looking belligerent.

'Poor Tim and Leonie had an awful drama with Martha and Robin, so as you and your ma were both away I had to come down this afternoon. I'll tell you all about it tomorrow. We don't want to bore Rosie with our family affairs. Or perhaps I'll ring you later at the club?'

'I couldn't actually get a bed at the club. They were booked up. I could, er, ring you?' Archie was very red in the face.

'Oh no. Tomorrow then. It'll keep till we get home and it would be a pity to spoil your evening. Tim, I think we should go. We mustn't keep Leonie up and I'm sure Archie will want to run Rosie back to wherever she's staying. Goodbye Rosie. What a bit of luck running into you like this. Goodnight then, darling. See you tomorrow. Don't bother to come out with us.'

She put up her face and Archie pecked her cheek but did not meet her eye. She put her hand through Tim's arm and they left without looking back.

'Well done, Sonia,' said Tim. 'I think you carried off the

honours. Archie's being a bloody fool, but I'm sure it doesn't mean anything serious. We all know he adores you really.'

'So everyone will keep telling me,' said Sonia.

Before she went to bed she looked in on Martha, who lay curled up in a foetal position, her thin arms clutching her skinny body, and her knees almost touching her pointed chin. She looked as if she had been stuck together with superglue and might never be able to unfurl again.

'Why did you do it Martha?' asked Sonia as they drove back north up the motorway the next day. 'I can understand a sudden urge to shock everyone – I often feel like that myself. But you must have planned all this beforehand, taken those awful clothes and got hold of the dope. The Warners have always gone out of their way to be kind to you, and they're great, great friends of ours. We depend on Tim for so many things – he's a marvellous agent to Archie.'

'Don't you ever hate people just because they feel they have to be kind to you? Anyway, I didn't ever mean it to go as far as it did – I just wanted to stir Robin up a bit. He's so conformist it's not true, such a good little Mummy's boy. I wouldn't have used the dope at all if those ghastly Sloaney girls hadn't made me feel such an outsider. Oh they were friendly in a way, but they talked a sort of private language in their ever so blah-blah accents, and always about people I'd never heard of. I'm always the outsider. Always, always. You don't know how ghastly it is never to belong anywhere.'

Sonia cast a quick sideways look at her, glad that having to concentrate on the road prevented her from a face-to-face conversation. She knew this might be a rare chance to discover what was really troubling Martha, and felt as though a wild bird had come to perch on her hand and that a sudden move on her part might put it to flight for ever. The Rastafarian plaits had been undone but had left Martha's hair with a strange, crimped appearance. She looked very defenceless and exhausted, with huge black shadows under her eyes and a large spot forming on her chin, though her skin was usually flawless.

'Don't you even feel you belong at Duntan with all of us?'

'Oh I love it, love it and all of you, more than anything,' said Martha sadly. 'But I don't belong there and Duntan rubs it in. It's the most belonging sort of place I know. That's what makes it so awful. It's all right for Mum – she may be totally bogus in some ways, but she *feels* right anywhere she happens to be, even if she isn't entitled to. She knows who she is. She adores being different and making an impression, but she never for one moment doubts her identity. It wasn't so bad when Daddy was alive. I felt American then, even when Mum dragged me round the world with her because she's so restless, but we always came back to base and Daddy was always the same.' Martha hardly ever talked about her father.

'I always liked Al,' said Sonia. 'He had a great sense of humour and he coped with your mother brilliantly. You're very like him in many ways. Did you know that?'

Martha swallowed. Her voice was very shaky.

'I do miss him dreadfully. In her own way Ma misses him too, you know,' she said. 'He kept her on the straight and narrow more than anyone else has ever done. He used to give me a special sort of wink when Ma was being extra impossible, and even at her worst she made him laugh. Now when we're in the States I feel English and I don't fit in with anyone, and when we're over here I feel American. It's not so bad in Italy because then one can just be a foreigner and that's that, but at Duntan . . .' Her voice trailed away and she made a small despairing gesture with her hands.

'*We* all feel you're part of it and us,' said Sonia. 'The children never feel we're quite a family without you. But go on . . . At Duntan?'

'Now even that's going to change. It's always seemed to me the one place that would stay the same for ever, even if I don't truly belong there.'

'Of course you belong. For God's sake, Martha, you're Archie's sister!'

'Not a Duntan though.'

'No, not a Duntan, but then nor am I by birth, and I feel more joined to the house even than Archie does. You can belong just by loving and being loved. Look, Martha, you and I aren't related by blood, but you've become a vital part of my life – a lovely sort of cross between a sister and a child. Don't you dare say you don't feel part of the family or *I* shall feel rejected by *you*. And don't you dare make me cry either, or we'll have an accident and then we won't either of us be related to anyone! Fish in the shelf and get us some tissues and let's both suck a Polo to pull ourselves together.'

They drove in silence for a bit and then Sonia asked: 'If you had a choice, what would you really like to do? You've lots of brains but you've never been made to use them. If you went to a crammer I'm sure you could make up time. Would you like to go to university over here and make your permanent base with us? Go to the States, too, of course, and keep up with your father's family and flit around with Roz from time to time, but actually live with us?'

'Yes. Oh yes. But I don't want to gatecrash.'

'Martha . . .' The idea that had come into Sonia's head on the way down was beginning to crystallise. 'There might be a way in which far from gatecrashing you might actually help to save Duntan. How much do you know about these awful monks? How involved has your mother really got with them?'

'Well, I do know quite a lot, but Brother François said if I ever split on them she could get into trouble. I think she's got bored with them really, and wouldn't be all that sorry to make a break. After the awfulness of yesterday I'm going to beg her to give them the boot.'

'Your mother has always said she could put money into Duntan provided she controlled everything, which I couldn't bear. But supposing she put money into a Duntan Trust and you became a part of it too? If she was afraid of what might happen if her association with the Brothers came out, she just might put up enough money to help, and might behave herself too.'

'You mean you'd sort of blackmail her?' Martha, who was no one's fool, asked shrewdly.

'I suppose I do. It sounds awful put like that, but yes, in a way. Your mother's not above blackmail herself. I wouldn't be too bothered over that – but you'd have to promise me, absolutely *swear*, there'd be no more drugs. Polly is growing up fast and she admires you enormously and tries to copy all you do. I'd need to be sure about that.'

'Oh I'd promise. I really would. And I *am* sorry about Tim and Leonie. I'll write them a real grovel. I'll absolutely immolate myself. Oh Sonia,' said Martha, 'wouldn't it be just wonderful?'

Then they decided that they both suddenly felt so much better, they would stop at the next service station and make pigs of themselves on chips and ice-cream.

The next few days were difficult for Archie and Sonia. They were extremely polite to each other but constraint hung over them. Archie had been greatly shaken by Tim's account of the weekend's events, and more shaken than he liked to admit, even to himself, by Sonia's appearance in the restaurant. It was not that he had fooled himself into thinking she was unaware of what was going on, in fact, he got a certain satisfaction from it, but suddenly being confronted with her when he was with Rosie had brought him up short and made him ask himself some uncomfortable questions. He tried once or twice to edge near to bringing up the subject, but Sonia made herself very unapproachable, and each time he lost his nerve. At least there was a temporary cease-fire between them. Like the griffins, they sat and brooded on their separate pillars in a sort of armed neutrality, awaiting the next round.

Chapter 19

The following week there was a call for Sonia from the Heritage at Risk office.

'Lady Duntan? It's Bridget Murrary here – Simon Hadleigh's assistant. Simon's asked me to ring you to say we have a preliminary report ready for our meeting with you next Wednesday. He thought it might be best if you came here to the office at twelve o'clock so that we can go over everything and spread all the plans out, and then go on to lunch later. Would you be able to manage that?'

Sonia said she would. It all sounded very formal and businesslike and she still couldn't make out whether Bridget was to be at the lunch or not. Had she misread the signals she thought Simon had sent her? She still wasn't sure. She kept going over their previous meetings in her head, but couldn't come to any conclusion. She knew only that she badly wanted him to like her, and that every time she thought of him her stomach felt as if she was going up and down in a very fast lift. She thought he was the most atractive man she had ever met.

'Oh good,' said Bridget. 'You know where we are in Queen Charlotte's Square? It's very easy from St James's underground – five minutes' walk. We're on the far side of the square. We'll so look forward to seeing you then. Goodbye, Lady Duntan.'

Sonia rang her mother to ask if she could stay with her for a couple of nights, but her mother said she would be away. She was going to France to stay with friends.

'What a disappointment to miss you, darling, but of course you can have a bed if you want one. You know the spare room's always made up, and you've got your key, haven't you? Unless it would be more fun for you to stay with chums?'

Sonia said no, she would be only too pleased to have a quiet night or two and it would be lovely to use the house. 'Shame to miss you, though, but I expect I shall have to come up again soon. Thanks, Mum.'

They gossiped about the children for a bit, and Sonia told her about the meeting next week. 'Keep your fingers crossed that HAR come up with an idea for keeping Duntan. It's so important to me.'

After she had hung up, Sonia, who got on very well with her mother and would normally have been disappointed at not seeing her, was aware that for once she would greatly prefer to have the house to herself.

She presented herself at Queen Charlotte's Square on the dot of twelve. It was a pleasant place, between Birdcage Walk and Victoria Street, convenient for conferences at Whitehall. The houses were of Georgian brick, very classical and plain, and the one belonging to Heritage at Risk had a black front door and window boxes with white dasisies in. Nothing flashy, obviously, though somewhat impersonal. Sonia rang the bell and gave her name. Inside the hall a very pretty girl sat at a reception desk with telephones and a large appointment book. Behind her, a graceful flight of stairs carpeted in dark green curved up alongside one wall, and there were several mahogany doors, all with fine moulded architraves above.

'Lady Duntan? Mr Hadleigh is expecting you. If you'll just come into the waiting room, I'll let him know you've arrived.'

Martha would not have liked her plummy voice, thought Sonia, as she followed her through a door on the right into a room with several sofas and chairs covered in a smart chintz. There were lots of books and magazines about horses and antiques, and Sotheby's and Christie's catalogues and National Trust publications were much in evidence. On the wall were sporting prints and a pleasant small Dutch oil painting of some cows by a river. Sonia checked her appearance in the looking-glass over the fireplace. She looked immaculate.

The door opened almost immediately and Bridget stumped in, wet-lettuce hand extended.

'How nice to see you. Do come upstairs.' She opened a door, behind which a lift was cleverly concealed. 'Simon has his office on the top floor because it's so much lighter and he likes the view, so we'll go up in the lift. The last Director had his office down here, but it was frightfully dark and when Simon took over four years ago he insisted on moving everything round. I must say it's a great improvement.' She seemed much more communicative on her own ground.

Simon's office had obviously once been two rooms, knocked together to make one lovely big one. He was sitting at an enormous leather-topped knee-hole desk in the window. At the other end of the room was a long table on which were spread plans and maps. The whole of one wall was covered by a notice board pinned with photographs of stately houses in various 'before and after' states of renovation.

He got up at once and came over to her. Official smile. Brisk handshake. No kiss. He wore a dark suit and looked slightly forbidding, as though he had not yet turned up the volume on his charm control.

'Good afternoon, Sonia. We have the preliminary report here to show you, together with various schemes. The HAR trustees certainly think Duntan is a wonderful house and worth saving if we can, but it may be difficult. Here's a copy for you and I've sent one off to Archie. I thought we might go through it together and then you can ask me any questions as we go along. Archie faxed the last few years' estate accounts with the costs of running the house and maintenance, etcetera, and has also kindly put me in the picture over the financial situation. I'm sorry about the Lloyd's losses. I'm afraid a lot of people are in the same boat.'

Sonia was surprised to hear that Archie had been in touch with Simon, and felt a twist of quite unjustifiable resentment.

'Simon,' she blurred out, 'I don't know what Archie may have said to you about the house, but I do hope you're on my side?'

He gave her a cool look. 'I'm not on anyone's side, Sonia. I'm not in the business of taking sides. I can put various ideas to you, but finally the decision is for you and Archie to take together – not for anyone else. Now come and sit down. Would you like a cup of coffee?'

'Yes, please.' Sonia's voice was subdued.

'Bridget, could you rustle up three cups?'

He pulled out a chair for her at the long table. There was a pile of clean paper in front of her and a newly sharpened red pencil with Heritage at Risk stamped on it in gold. Sonia picked it up and started making grooves along it with her thumbnail. She felt very unsure of herself. Where were the admiring looks and the irresistible smile?

'We've used the Chorley formula as a guideline to get these figures,' said Simon. 'That's what the National Trust uses for calculating the amount of endowment to cover inflation for the next fifty years. Very helpful. Broadly, I think you have two or three options open to you. You could apply for a straight grant to mend the roof, for instance. That alone would probably cost about six hundred thousand, but you might well get a fifty per cent grant. There would be a few conditions, of course. You'd certainly have to open the house on request, or, more probably, for twenty-eight days a year, but that's not bad, and any other decisions would be entirely up to you so no one could force you to restore or alter anything you didn't want to. You would still be the bosses. However, judging by the state of the house and what Archie's told me of your finances, I doubt if that would really help you much.' Simon paused briefly before continuing.

'Another possibility is that HAR might consider raising a considerable sum, say three million, to start a new charitable trust for the house – a Duntan Trust. There would be trustees, and outsiders would have to outnumber family – say Archie and you and three others. It would need a portfolio of about four million to invest, in order to set the house completely to rights and keep it in good nick for the future. The house would be open all the summer, full-time, but you would live in it, possibly for a peppercorn rent. We greatly prefer it if the original families can still be in residence; it adds enormously to the feel of a house, and the public definitely like it. This would be secure for two more generations, so your Tom could live there one day, and perhaps his children too. After that we can't foresee. The house and most of its major contents would be owned by the Duntan Trust and no longer by you personally. There'd have to be some negotiating over that, but – and I realise it's a big but for you and Archie – you would also have to raise a million pounds yourselves, as well as putting up the house and contents.' Bridget passed Simon a sheet of figures, which he put in front of Sonia.

'Or,' he went on, 'you could of course decide to sell it and keep as much land as possible. You clearly have no hope of raising enough money to hand it to the National Trust, because they would need an endowment of about eleven million. Now,' he said, as Bridget handed round the coffee, 'let's go through everything in detail.'

Sonia, who hated finance, had a panic that she was not going to understand a word of it. She had once had a school report that said 'Figures appear to have no meaning for Sonia,' and had never quite forgiven her father, who thought it a huge joke, for telling Archie. She need not have worried. Some experts manage to wrap their subjects up in so much jargon that they make them quite incomprehensible to the uninitiated, but Simon had a talent for clarity and made everything sound very straightforward. Occasionally Bridget would chip in, and Sonia began to see that whatever she might look like, she was obviously good at her job and really rather nice.

A few weeks earlier, the meeting and its emphasis on the family having to find such a huge sum of money would have filled her with despair, but since her talk with Martha there was certainly food for thought. A small flicker of hope had been kindled. The question was, how much money could be squeezed out of Rosamund, and would Archie be prepared to do it? Meanwhile, there were plans for schemes for the gardens and for turning the stable block into a shop and restaurant.

'Right,' said Simon when they had gone through the whole report, page by page. 'These are our proposals. You'll have to think about it all.'

'So what happens next?' asked Sonia.

Simon suddenly smiled at her properly for the first time. It was like the sun coming out.

'Next,' he said, 'if you've quite finished mangling our pencils, I take you out to lunch.' He pulled some car keys out of his pocket and slid them across the table to Bridget. 'Be an angel and get my car round,' he said. 'I'll just sign those letters for you and I'll bring Sonia down in a minute.'

'There can't be much left to discuss,' said Sonia rather stiffly, still smarting from his earlier snub, as Bridget went out. 'You really don't need to give me lunch. We must have covered everything that needs to be gone through.'

'But of course I'm going to give you lunch. Don't think you'll escape it. This morning was business. Lunch is pleasure. I try never to mix the two. Which is one reason why Bridget suits me so well as an assisant,' he added, glinting at her. 'Climb off your high horse, beautiful Lady-in-Red, and I'll take you to a marvellous place where they do the best quail's egg and mushroom starter I know, but I probably shan't taste it because I'll be looking at you.'

Of course Sonia was lost.

Afterwards she couldn't remember what they had eaten, except that it was the best meal she had ever had. They talked about all sorts of things, discovering a shared passion for opera and a love of Italy, capping quotations and making each other laugh. Sonia told Simon about her childhood following the flag, of how she had adored her father, who had died of cancer a few years earlier, and about her time as an art student, when she had hoped to make a name for herself but had lacked the confidence to go all out for it and had got married instead.

'Not that I regret it,' she said. 'Don't think that. It's given me four wonderful children who are the light of my life – they'll always come first. But children grow up and one mustn't hang on. It seems the right moment to have another go and see if I really am any good, though I find the thought of failure very scary. And now, of course, there's Duntan too. That's very dear to my heart, as you know.' If there was a glaring omission in this catalogue of things important to Sonia, neither of them mentioned it.

'And what about you?' she asked. 'Tell me about you. I think you have two boys?'

'Yes,' said Simon. 'I'm very proud of them. The eldest is an archaeologist and is away grubbing things up in Greece at the moment, and the younger one is up at Cambridge and hopes to be a journalist. They are huge fun.'

'Goodness, how grown-up! I didn't realise they were so old.'

Simon laughed. 'Oh, I'm a greybeard! But I did get married very young – too young. It was a disaster.'

'What went wrong?'

'Well, Helen was eighteen and I was twenty-one. Both our families tried to prevent it, but I was mad about her and very wild and headstrong, so I persuaded her to forget about the big white wedding and come away with me and get married without all the palaver. I thought it was the height of romance but I don't think she ever quite forgave me for doing her out of all the trimmings. We were happy for a bit – she's a very sweet person – but we had absolutely nothing in common, no shared interests, nothing. I was training as an architect in London and Helen hated it. She wanted me to give it up to live in a little cottage with roses round the door and breed pigs or something, and after the boys appeared in rather quick succession she became totally wrapped up in them and never wanted to do anything with me. She was – is – a marvellous mum of the earth-mother type. We rented a small house in the country, but I had to work in London and spent more and more time away.'

'And then you met someone else?' Sonia had a vision of Simon as a huge wild animal prowling round too enclosed a space.

'No,' said Simon. 'No. Not me. She did. Contrary to what you might think, I was rather idealistic in those days. I wasn't happy – things weren't at all good between us – but I loved her and the boys and kept hoping things would work out. I was vain enough to think she wouldn't want anyone else, and that when the boys got bigger she'd stop being quite so wrapped up in them, and then I could teach her to enjoy some of the things I liked – widen her horizons. What an arrogant fool! It was an awful shock when she told me she had found a nice cosy farmer in cords and old brogues and greatly preferred him to me. He sucks a pipe all the time and blows low pheasants to bits.'

'Surely not simultaneously?'

Simon laughed. 'Well, I wouldn't put it past him. I must say he is the dullest man I've ever met. He bores for England. If you ask him how he is, he actually *tells* you. Heaven help you if you said "How are you?" on a day when he'd just developed piles or something. But he's made Helen happy when I couldn't. They have four children of their own now, but he's always been very fair with my two. He's a thoroughly decent chap.' Simon pulled a face. 'Luckily James and Toby find him pretty tedious too, so they've always enjoyed doing things with me and it's all been very civilised. We get on fine so long as we don't have to be with each other. But I swore I'd never, ever let anyone hurt me like that again. And I never have.'

Sonia wondered if she was being given a warning of some kind.

'And your present wife?'

'Ah, that's very different. Ellie-May is a marvellous person, we're real friends. We lead fairly separate lives at times. It was part of the bargain for both of us. We both have jobs we adore, and we give each other plenty of space. It wouldn't suit everyone, but it suits us. We've been married for nearly ten years.'

'And do you love each other?' Sonia persisted.

But Simon had been questioned enough, and just laughed.

'Trust a woman to ask that – they never fail! I think we're going to have to move soon. Look.'

There were no other people left in the restaurant and the waiters were standing around politely.

'Good heavens! How awful, it's after four o'clock. I'd no idea. You'll be terribly late back at the office.'

Simon signed the bill and got up.

'But I'm not going back to the office,' he said. 'I'm going home, and I very much hope you're going to come with me. I have two pictures you won't have seen for a good many years, and I want you to see where they hang.'

Sonia felt her throat tighten and her heart start to thump. She raised an eyebrow. 'Mr Hadleigh,' she said severely, hoping she sounded more composed than she felt, 'you sound very much as if you were asking me to come and look at your etchings!'

'Ah,' he said, smiling at her. 'That too, of course, but only if you want to. No pressure. But really, I do want to show you your own pictures. I think you should take your painting more seriously. Will you trust me and come anyway?'

'Yes,' said Sonia. 'I'll come.'

Simon's house was in Chelsea Square, at the top end. He left the car outside the door, in the private bit of road between the front door and the row of garages, each with a flat over the top, that went with the houses.

'Very useful this,' he said. 'Our friends can park when they come to see us. Come in. Shall we make a cup of tea?'

'Oh yes, please. That would be bliss.'

The kitchen and dining room were on the ground floor, the dining-room windows opening on to the gardens. Sonia thought it all looked extremely grand, and in almost too perfect taste. Compared with the beloved shabbiness of Duntan, it was very, very smart.

'Don't be put off by the décor,' said Simon, reading her thoughts. 'Ellie-May's a professional – she has her own design company both here and in New York. She's forever changing things. I always complain that just when I'm beginning to like something, it's gone. But she's not allowed to alter the furniture or pictures.' He made a pot of tea and put two cups on a tray. 'Come on up. The drawing room's upstairs.'

It was one of the most beautiful rooms Sonia had ever seen.

'Oh,' she said. 'How gorgeous! How clever! Wouldn't I just adore to be able to do this for Duntan!'

'Let's hope you will. But you'd have to be very careful not to spoil it. This is fine for London, but you wouldn't want to take away that special something that would be killed by too much glitz.'

Sonia gave him a grateful look.

'I knew you really understood how I feel about the house,' she said, 'in spite of being so foul and squashing in your office. I don't think I like you there much.' She kicked off her shoes and curled up on the sofa with her cup of tea.

Simon stood with his back to the fireplace looking at her while she drank, though his own cup went untouched. When she had finished, he said: 'Now come over here and have a look.' He took her hand, pulled her up, and then led her over to the far side of the room. There, on the wall, hanging one above the other, were two of her pictures.

She looked at them in silence for a bit, deeply touched. Then she said, 'It's quite extraordinary to see them again after all this time. I remember painting them so well, and being so pleased that they were bought as a pair, but I didn't know who'd got them. I am so glad you like them.'

He stood behind her with his hands on her shoulders. 'Your pictures *are* you, aren't they?' he asked. 'Now, this Sonia I have met.' He reached over and pointed to one of the immaculately painted flowers in the centre of the canvas. 'But the Sonia I want to meet is the one who lives in this strange dream place beyond. Who lives in that wild garden? The truly wild Sonia – where is she? Am I to be allowed to find her?' Very gently he turned her round.

He put his hands on either side of her face, with his thumbs under her chin. Sonia tried to look down, but he tilted her face up so that she was forced to look at him.

'You are very desirable, Lady Duntan,' he said. 'We could have a lovely time together. Did you know that?'

'I don't think I'm very good at lovely times,' said Sonia sadly. 'You might be disappointed.'

'Oh no,' he said. 'I wouldn't be disappointed. And it would be my fault if you were – but I would almost guarantee that you wouldn't be. We have something between us. We both know that.' He started to trace the outline of her face with his finger as though he was making a drawing of her, sketching in her eyebrows, circling her eyes and running his finger along the line of her jaw.

'You sound very sure,' she said.

'Yes,' he said. 'I'm sure. Come and walk down the primrose path with me, darling Sonia. You may surprise yourself.'

Sonia felt like a marionette, as though she had no control over her limbs unless Simon pulled the strings. He moved one hand slowly down to her breast, and slid the other down her back. Then he started to walk her backwards towards the door.

'There are better places to do this,' he said, laughing down at her. 'I like my comforts.'

Later she lay back on the pillows of the huge bed, her hair falling over her naked shoulders, and stretched herself like a cat.

'Well?' he asked. 'Not disappointed?'

'No,' she said. 'Oh no. I think perhaps I've only had nursery tea before, and now I've just been given my first oyster.' And she started to laugh.

'Oysters are my favourite hors-d'oeuvre,' said Simon. 'How about the second course soon? Something a little different but equally delicious?'

'Ummm,' she said. 'Good idea.'

Shirley Gillespie's mother would have had a field day.

Chapter 20

The following night was the date fixed for dinner with the Prince, and Archie was due to come and join Sonia at her mother's house. She had promised to ring and let him know how the meeting with Simon had gone, so, feeling that truth is always safer if at all possible, she telephoned and reported on the morning's business and then airily announced that Simon had kindly asked her out to dinner and that she was going to go as it would give them a chance to discuss things further. She felt that Archie was in no position to object, but did not add that she was at that moment reclining on Simon's bed wearing nothing but his silk dressing-gown.

'I see,' said Archie drily. 'Tit for tat?'

'And why not? Anyway, darling, you'll see Simon yourself tomorrow evening and can fix a time to discuss Duntan with him then if you want to, because guess what? He's going to dinner with the Prince too. It seems Simon advised him about his place in Sussex, so when Dukie heard that we were going with the Brown-Gorings, he wanted to be represented too and asked if Simon could be invited to "look after his interests". I suppose he's terrified you might pull a fast one on him and let more days' shooting than he does or something, suspicious old ape. The beautiful Antonella is also going, you'll be thrilled to hear. She knows the Prince as well and apparently sometimes buys pictures for him.'

Sonia thought that mentioning Antonella together with Simon might well prove a good red herring and put Archie off the real scent, but she had not in fact been pleased with the information that she was to be included in the party. Simon himself was cagey on the subject of Antonella, but she did not want to dig too deeply and look for something she might not wish to find. Archie didn't sound too delighted about the whole arrangement either, but there was nothing he could do about it.

'So, see you at Radnor Walk about six. I'll be there to let you in. 'Bye then, darling. Kisses to the children.'

It was a foregone conclusion that Sonia would spend the night at Chelsea Square, but first she walked the five minutes to her mother's house to change her dress and turn on the answering machine in case there should be any unexpected calls. When she got back Simon was in the kitchen.

'Don't let's go out again,' he said. 'It's getting late and I want you all to myself. I've decided to treat you to one of my famous omelettes. I'm a sensational cook.'

'I think it was your touching modesty that first attracted me to you,' said Sonia. 'It had better be good. I'm ravenous.'

'It will be, and while you were gone I nipped off to the marvellous fruit shop round the corner and got strawberries and a super-smelling melon. Then we'll eat it all to Mozart. How does that sound?'

'Fabulous.' She came and put her arms round him, leaning against him for a moment, then stood on tiptoes to kiss his chin. She thought she had never felt so happy in her life. She felt quite drunk with it.

'You behave yourself,' said Simon. 'You should never distract the chef. Go and perch on that stool over there where you'll be out of the way but I can see you.' And as he whisked the eggs he sang:

> 'I gave my girl an apple – she let me hold her hand.
> I gave her a lemon – she kissed to beat the band.
> I gave her an orange – she loved with all her might,
> So I'm gonna give a watermelon to my girl tonight.'

It had been decided earlier that John and Sally should come and pick up Archie and Sonia so that they could all arrive together. Sonia was relieved that they had made this plan. She did not want to have to spend too much time alone with Archie, and she also looked forward to having a lovely post-mortem on the evening with Sally in the car coming home.

She was very curious about the Prince. Simon had been highly entertained to hear her ideas about what she thought the Prince's house would be like, and refused to describe either it or him. She imagined herself, Sally and Antonella reclining on huge pillows on the floor, dipping their fingers into silver bowls of rose-water after having sheep's eyes popped into their mouths by bearded brigands with tea towels round their heads. She saw them in a tented room with carpets covering the walls and lots of curved swords lying around, and possibly the odd camel saddle hung with bells. Perhaps there would be a cabaret of belly-dancers. She thought an Arabian dancing-girl undulating the diamond in her navel at Archie might take his mind off Rosie Bartlett, though she didn't think she wanted one winking at Simon. She looked forward to watching a dinner-jacketed Archie sitting cross-legged on the floor. Like a lot of men, he was hopeless at picnics, and it wasn't only the music that made him fidgety if she dragged him to Glyndebourne and took a rug instead of deck chairs. Simon, she felt sure, would somehow be reclining gracefully on one elbow in a flowing Arabian robe.

She decided to wear a long black dress that she knew was particularly becoming, and in which, because of the slit up one side, she could sink sexily to the floor in one sinuous movement. She had quite a satisfactory practice session in the bedroom. She wondered what she would look like with a yashmak on, and, covering her mouth with her face flannel, made eyes at an imaginary Simon in the mirror. The result, she thought, was most enticing. Archie, coming in to change, looked at her in surprise.

'You all right?' he asked. 'Got toothache or something? Hope you're going to feel up to coming. Want a couple of Anadin?'

'Of course I'm coming. There's nothing whatever wrong with me,' snapped Sonia, not feeling enticing any more.

The evening turned out to be full of surprises. Not a bearded brigand in sight, just a black-coated Spanish man-servant to open the door and Fergusson B. Clutter, the Prince's American secretary, who was very gushing, to greet them. The second surprise was the house itself; no curved swords, no daggers, only a very elegant but innocuous-looking barley-sugar-twist glass walking-stick propped up against a chair in the hall.

Sonia nudged Archie. 'Do look,' she hissed. 'That's just like one of your ma's. And I thought there'd be lots of wicked weapons!' Archie made a shushing face at her.

There were no cushions on the floor, no tented walls, not a sniff of a camel saddle. Instead of all the expected signs of desert life, there was a stunning collection of French eighteenth-century furniture and porcelain, and wonderful French and Italian pictures. A Fragonard on the staircase of this Arabian household had not been part of her imaginings. Certainly it all spoke of great riches, but the elegance was totally European. The Prince, it turned out, was a notable and exceptionally knowledgeable collector of *objets d'art*.

Another revelation was the quite enormous charm of the Prince himself. But by far the biggest surprise to Sonia and Archie was the presence of Lady Rosamund. The glass stick was explained.

They had no idea that she was even back in England – she had certainly not been in touch with Martha, let alone her son and daughter-in-law – and they were both thunderstruck. What was more, she had clearly arrived at the Prince's house well before them and looked very much at home. How long she had been there – or, indeed, how often in the past – was anybody's guess, but she was clearly enjoying their reaction quite enormously.

'Well darlings, how nice to see you both,' she said. 'I've been telling my old friend all about your little moor, Archie, and how uncertain grouse prospects always are. I hope his cosmopolitan friends are going to enjoy the opportunity to stand out in the wind and rain on the off chance that a few birds may come over and that the day won't be called off at the last moment! It's never been my idea of a great day out.'

From her point of view it was a splendid tease. Archie went

white with fury. He had privately been steeling himself for a major showdown with his mother over her involvement with The Brothers of Love as soon as she got home from the States; to have her pop up so unexpectedly in this particular setting was almost more than he could bear. Sonia had never seen him look so cross, and it suddenly occurred to her that this might prove to be just the spur that was needed to make him get really tough with his mother, and fall in with her own schemes about getting money from Rosamund for the house. She had been biding her time before putting it to him, but now with the Heritage at Risk scheme for a Duntan Trust she felt that all sorts of pieces of a difficult jigsaw puzzle were beginning to fall into place.

Across the room she caught Simon's amused eye. Rosamund was not the only one enjoying the sensation she had made. She suddenly wondered if he might know more about the situation than was apparent. While thinking it extremely funny, she couldn't help feeling very sorry for Archie and admiring his restraint. It said much for his grandmother's training in self-discipline, good manners and the hiding of emotion that he soon had himself well in hand, and after the first blazing look he managed to get through the evening with considerable aplomb.

Rosamund was at her most provocative throughout dinner, and the only sheep's eyes appearing at the table were not popped into anyone's mouth but made by her at the Prince. Simon gave Sonia a very discreet wink, the merest flicker of a lid, but it was enough to reassure her that the current was still flowing between them. She even felt grateful to Antonella, who was clearly doing a marvellous job at smoothing Archie's ruffled feathers.

The Prince himself was delightful, easy to talk to and great fun. Sonia found no difficulty in sparkling away to him, partly, it has to be admitted, for Simon's benefit, but also because she felt she owed it to Archie, having promised to chat up their host for him.

After dinner the Prince took them on a wonderful tour of his treasures, telling them the history of each piece, of how he had come by it and why he had bought it. He spoke of each object with real love. Sonia stood in front of a delightful little Greuze head of a child, which reminded her of Cassie, and Simon came and stood beside her.

'Why didn't you tell me it was going to be like this?' she whispered.

'Because I wanted to watch the surprise on your face. You have the most expressive face I know. Your feelings run over it like a mountain stream. You'd be rotten at poker. By the way, I'm coming to stay with you next week. Archie wants me to go over Duntan with him and have a big discussion with you both.'

'Lovely,' said Sonia. 'I'll take you up into the woods and show you all my favourite places. I can't wait for you to see it all again.' What she really meant was that she couldn't wait to see him again.

'Goodness, what a fantastic dinner!' said Sally as they drove away, Rosamund having accepted a lift from Simon and Antontella, who had come together. 'Have you ever had such scrummy food? And would you have believed there'd be such ravishingly pretty rooms? I gather from Simon that Ellie-May did them up for the Prince, which accounts for it, of course. She's brilliant. She's got marvellous taste. Oh to be able to decorate even one room like that! Far cry from going a bust on material one can't afford and then making a bog of the pelmets. Wait till you see their own house, Sonia. Now that you know Simon, you must go there if they ever ask you. You'd adore it.' Sonia, who was driving, was thankful that no one could see her face. She didn't want the mountain stream running over it now.

Sally prattled on. 'I wonder where he keeps his wives? Do you think they were peeking at us through a hidden grille, or perhaps he keeps this house for his European mistresses? What did you think of him, Sonia?'

'Well, if one stretched him out a bit I think he'd be rather a dish. I really liked him. Once he starts to talk you forget he's so tiny, but you'll have to give him a little tussock of heather to stand on in a butt, Archie, or he won't be able to see over the top.'

'He's supposed to be a real lady-killer, though, for all he's such a midget,' went on Sally. 'What a surprise to see your mother there, Archie! I think he must want to pop her in his harem. Did you notice her flirting with him?'

'Yes,' said Archie. 'I noticed all right.' John gave his wife a sharp dig in the ribs.

'Ow!' said Sally. 'What on earth did you do that for, darling?'

They all laughed and it broke the tension. John and Archie went on to discuss the letting of the shooting. At least that had gone extremely well and they were both well pleased with the arrangements.

Back in the bedroom at Radnor Walk, Archie stood in front of the window looking at a pigeon roosting on the roof of the house opposite. He thrust his hands into his trouser pockets and turned some loose change over and over. It was a habit of his when he had something on his mind.

'Well,' said Sonia, smearing cleansing cream on her face, 'aren't you pleased with me? I chatted your Arab up for all I was worth. If the deal falls through it won't be my fault.'

'No,' said Archie. 'You did very well. Thank you.'

'Then what are you looking so constipated for?'

There was a silence. Jingle. Jingle. Jingle.

'I was wondering what the hell to do about Mother – and Martha, come to that. God, it's a pity Al had to die! They weren't my responsibility then. Any ideas?'

Sonia took a deep breath. 'As a matter of fact, yes,' she said, getting into bed. 'I have got an idea which might solve a lot of things, but I don't know how receptive you'd be. I've been putting off telling you because Duntan comes into it, and, well, we haven't communicated too brilliantly about that lately. I know it's my fault too, but, well, it's difficult. If I tell you, will you promise to hear me out before you get cross and turn it down?'

Archie aimed an imaginary gun at the pigeon.

'Try me.'

He came and sat on the edge of the bed and listened without

interrupting while Sonia told him about her conversation with Martha, about Martha's longing for stability and some sense of belonging, her wish to go to university, and her knowledge of how frighteningly her mother had got embroiled with the sinister sect. Then she told him about Simon's suggestions for a Duntan Trust and the idea that Rosamund might be pushed into putting up the money if Martha could in some way benefit and be guaranteed a home. When she had told him all her ideas, she said rather despairingly, 'But I expect you'll say it's hopeless.'

'No,' said Archie. 'No, on the contrary I think you may have hit on something. I got the report from HAR before I left home this morning and I thought it was very interesting. I just couldn't see how I could possibly raise a million pounds. But my mother could, easily. Normally I wouldn't hear of taking anything from her, but if Martha were to benefit I could probably accept it without too much difficulty. Suppose we gave Ma The Dial House in part exchange? You've never liked it. She'd have a base too then. Anyway, I've asked Simon to come and stay and I'll talk to him about this Trust idea, and when she comes home I'll really tackle Mother. She needs the fear of God putting into her or she'll get herself into trouble one day. I dread to think what she's up to with the Prince. I shall get hold of old Watson too and find out how much hold those blasted monks could have over her and how much we could put the frighteners on them.' Mr Watson was the family solicitor.

Sonia could hardly believe it. Her dream that Duntan could actually be saved might come true! Normally she would have flung her arms round Archie and hugged him, but she didn't feel she could.

'Sonia,' said Archie, jingling in his pockets again, 'there are other things we should talk about too. About us.'

Sonia started to pleat the sheet between her fingers.

'Yes I know,' she said. 'I know, I know, I know. But I just don't feel ready at the moment. I can't. Please don't ask me to talk about us – not yet.'

'All these things are tied together. We have to deal with

everything. It's been me that wouldn't before. I accept that, but now there are things I'd like to say. I know I've hurt you very much. You know I don't find it easy to talk, but I've just listened to you, please will you listen to me?'

Sonia looked at him with tears in her eyes. It was so unlike him to want to bare his heart. It was something she had often longed for him to do, but now she most desperately didn't want to hear. A few weeks ago she would have liked a little accident to befall Rosie Bartlett – nothing too life-threatening, perhaps a sudden attack of acne or halitosis would have done the trick – but now she realised that she would be positively pleased if Rosie hung about for a bit longer. She felt appalled at herself and deeply guilty. The ridiculous thing was that having been in a seething state of irritation with her husband for months, now she suddenly ached with pity for him.

'Archie,' she whispered. 'Darling Archie, you're right, we do need to say things, both of us, but for me it's too soon. I quite simply can't. A step at a time. Let's go home and try and sort Duntan out and get my exhibition over. I've only got just over a month before that and it's very important to me. Then I promise we'll talk about us.'

But she knew she was just playing for time, and she knew, too, that a far more difficult decision than she had ever bargained for might be looming on her horizon.

Sonia was head over heels in love.

Chapter 21

'Oh house! You're going to be saved!' cried Sonia as she and Archie drove through the main gates on arriving home the next day. Archie gave her an inscrutable look and said nothing, but to her it seemed as though Duntan had suddenly been floodlit by a great beam of optimism. She decided that she must make up a new story for Birdie about the griffins making peace. Perhaps they could rub beaks in friendship, Eskimo style, instead of fighting. Perhaps they might fall in love?

On the surface life resumed its normal pattern. Archie threw himself into all his local commitments and the running of the estate and farm with his usual drive and wholeheartedness. The harvest, always a hectic time, would be looming soon, and he watched the weather anxiously. Because of the letting of the shooting, he and Thompson, his keeper, had decided that the butts on the moor needed renovating and draining, and the old stone lunch hut had to be whitewashed and generally revamped and repaired. The Prince might not appreciate a shooting lunch with drips falling on his head if it was wet. Sonia had no idea whether Archie was still seeing Rosie. She had even ceased to wonder. He made no further attempt to discuss their personal lives and to all outward appearances they seemed to be getting on better than they had done for a long time. They were on their best behaviour with each other, not a very natural or intimate state for a marriage, perhaps, but it oiled the wheels of daily life. Several people asked Sonia if she had had a holiday – there was a glow about her and she looked so amazingly well.

She was not the only one. When Lady Rosamund returned she was looking absolutely wonderful and had a completely different hairstyle, usually a sign that she was about to start a new liaison. She was at her most agreeable until Archie announced that he wished to call a meeting of Martha's trustees, had asked Mr Watson to attend, and was collecting him off the train at York the following morning. Rosamund and the elderly solicitor were long-standing adversaries and she had by no means always come off best in their encounters. He was impervious to threats or wiles, and quite unamused by her wilder witticisms. A very tiresome and dreary man.

'I can't think why you want that old bore. If we need to discuss Martha, I would greatly prefer that we keep it in the family – just you and me.'

'I bet you would,' said Archie, 'but I'm afraid he has a legal duty to come. He is my co-trustee.'

'That wouldn't worry me, darling. I've never bothered too much about the law.'

'No,' said Archie, 'but I think you should start.'

He had told Sonia that he would like her to be present.

'But leave it to me. I may have an ace up my sleeve, and I don't think Mother knows that I have it.'

Sonia had made sure Martha spared her mother no detail of her ordeal with the Brothers; nor was she left in any doubt as to Sonia's own knowledge of their goings-on and of Rosamund's association with them. In fact, Rosamund was not a completely uncaring parent; it was simply that she made up her own book of rules to suit herself without considering the consequences to anyone else. She was genuinely surprised at the effect her latest venture had had upon her daughter, but was aware that this time she might have been swimming in treacherous waters. However, she was far too fond of calling the tune to take to the floor and dance to someone else's choice of music without some protest.

They met in the dining room, very formally, like a board meeting. This was a shrewd move on Archie's part. His mother greatly preferred reclining on a sofa while everyone else sat on upright chairs. Her limp was very bad. She could hardly drag herself to her seat and was still in her negligée, an amazing confection of silk ruffles and swansdown.

'Good morning, Mr Watson,' she said, extending a limp hand, though she was capable of a grip like a monkey wrench if it suited her, 'I know you'll forgive me for not dressing, but I should really be in bed, you know.'

'Good morning, Lady Rosamund.' Mr Watson looked quite unmoved. 'I hope we shan't need to detain you long then. Unless you detect any unexpected difficulties and wish to prolong the meeting yourself, I'm sure you will be able to retire again quite shortly.' Sonia caught Archie's eye.

Mr Watson, at his driest, outlined the proposals for the new Duntan Trust, coupled with the suggestions for Martha's future.

'But Archie, I've been offering to help you with money all along – you know I have. I'd be delighted. I shall so enjoy having a hand in decisions about Duntan and being a trustee.' Rosamund gave her son a flashing smile.

'I'm afraid you wouldn't be a trustee, Mother.'

'Then you surely can't expect me to finance you.'

Archie took a bundle of letters out of his briefcase.

'These are your letters to the Brothers of Love. Mr Watson has very cleverly managed to get them back for you. You should be very grateful to him.'

Lady Rosamund stretched out her hand, but Archie handed the bundle to the lawyer.

'No, Mother. Mr Watson will keep these. It will be much safer. Also, I think you should read this copy of another letter. Again, Mr Watson has the original.'

'This is Al's writing.'

'Yes, it's a letter Al wrote to me about six months before he died. I have never felt the need to show it to you before, but I think you probably know what it says.' She read it and they looked at each other across the table for a long moment. Rosamund was the first to drop her eyes.

'My dearest boy,' she said, magnificent in defeat, 'how wonderful it is to have a grown-up son to care for one and manage one's affairs – such a comfort for a widow. And you have got your miracle, Sonia darling, and it's me!'

Archie, who had been dreading the confrontation and wondering whether his veiled threats would carry any weight with his wayward parent, found that he had really been tilting at windmills. It helped, of course, that his mother had already tired of the Brothers of Love, and in any case had a new interest. It suited her book entirely that Sonia and Archie should offer Martha a permanent home with them and make all the arrangements for her further education.

'Though I can't think why you're all so concerned to find something for Martha to do,' she said in genuine puzzlement. 'I've always been able to find my own amusements. I don't think a degree would have helped me in the least.'

She also accepted the offer for the Dial House to be made over to Martha, but granted to her rent-free for her lifetime, with great enthusiasm, though Archie insisted on a clause that Rosamund could not sublet it or allow anyone else to use it for any other purposes during what were bound to be her frequent absences.

'I shall enjoy having a house in England again,' said Rosamund. 'I shall get darling Simon's wife to help me do it up, and it will be so lovely to ask Harry to stay when he comes shooting.'

'Harry who?' asked Archie.

'Why, Prince Haroun, of course,' said Rosamund, opening her wonderful eyes wide and looking at her son as if he was being extraordinarily dim. 'Didn't you even know what his name was, darling?'

Martha later shrieked with laughter when Sonia regaled her with this particular titbit.

'Archie, you were brilliant,' said Sonia afterwards, in genuine admiration. 'What was in that letter from Al, though?'

'The doctors had warned him about his heart – you know how Americans are, always going in to be serviced, like cars – and he was very worried about Martha's future if anything should happen to him. He gave me power of attorney and made me Martha's guardian as you know, but he also gave me some information about Mother that he thought I might find useful if I ever really needed to bring her under control. It's not the first time she's flirted with dubious organisations, but she's very practical. She doesn't give a damn what anyone thinks of her, but she'd never want life to become at all uncomfortable.'

'You never told me.'

'It seems there are quite a few things we don't know about each other,' said Archie.

Martha was like a new girl. A place was booked for her at a crammer in Cambridge for the autumn, and meanwhile Sonia found a retired don from York to give her coaching three days a week. With real generosity, and as the result not only of a very penitent letter but also of a personal visit of apology that took Martha a lot of courage, the Warners invited her to go sailing with them in late August. She exercised Dusty for Polly in the mornings and helped Sonia with arrangements for the coming exhibition, and whilst Sonia was under no illusion that Martha had been transformed overnight into a paragon of virtue, she was at last both motivated and occupied. They discussed the house endlessly. If Martha guessed there might be an added reason for Sonia's almost visible aura of happiness, she kept it to herself.

The next two months were a golden time for Sonia. The signs of dilapidation and decay that had been starting to depress her so much were transformed into exciting challenges. She felt charged with new energy. She returned to her studio with completely fresh enthusiasm, her confidence greatly boosted, and not only worked on and improved several half-finished paintings, but got on with some new ones. She also decided to include some of her drawings in the exhibition along with the oils and watercolours, though not for sale purposes. Simon had reminded her that she had put a few in her first show, and said he had thought them particularly good. She had often sketched her children – hanging in their bedroom were four delightful drawings she had given to Archie – and she dug out one of Minnie podding beans in her old apron, done the year before, and also one of Archie's grandmother reading by the fire, both of which she decided were really much better than she remembered, as is so often the case with work done purely for pleasure. She looked at the drawing of old Lady Duntan for a long time, and hoped that wherever she was now, she would somehow know that there was new hope for this house she had loved so much. Sonia thought she would also have been highly amused if she had known about the plan to get money out of Archie's mother. Perhaps a number of old scores were about to be settled.

She started to get the framing organised. Zara Bennet, who owned the gallery in Blaydale, knew of a young man who had started up locally and of whom she thought highly. Sonia knew that framing could make or mar a picture from a selling point of view. Zara, a colourful lady of ample proportions with a tendency to wear flimsy materials that were intended to float but were more inclined to cling, came over to have a look at what Sonia had done so far, and was delighted.

'We only thought of a week originally,' she said after looking at the pictures, 'but something else has fallen through. How would you like to have a fortnight? These are really marvellous.'

They decided to have a private-view party and Archie said he would provide champagne. Zara said she would take care of all the publicity if Sonia could get someone to organise the party and send out the invitations, and though Sonia knew she would be driven crackers by her, she remembered that bossy Marcia Forsyth had offered to help. Marcia adored knowing more about something than anyone else, and even if her kindness was motivated by one-upmanship, she was extremely efficient. Archie said his secretary at the estate office would type out a list of names and addresses for Marcia, and Sonia suddenly started to feel really excited about it all.

Archie had recently taken on a new farm worker, whose wife wanted a job, so Sonia also managed to get some extra daily help in the house as a reinforcement for the slovenly Mrs Slater, who came in twice a week and sloshed grimy water along the stone passages, making them far dirtier than they had been before, according to Minnie, and waylaying anyone foolhardy enough to cross her path with gripping tales about her stormy relationship with Mr Slater and laments about the shortcomings of Jem, Reg and Marlene, not to mention updates on her gynaecological situation. Polly thought she was nearly as fascinating as Mrs Gillespie, but everyone else ran a mile.

Simon came to stay for three days, bringing Bridget with him for one night. On the first day of his visit, Archie asked Tim Warner, in his capacity as agent, to attend their meeting, and the five of them pored over plans. Sonia was surprised at how well and easily Simon and Archie appeared to get on. It was decided that the Duntan trustees should consist of Archie, Sonia and Tim to represent the family's interest with Simon acting for HAR, plus three other, independent people, one of whom must be a lawyer. Simon promised to start all the arrangements with the board of Heritage at Risk and saw no reason why the vital first step of major roof repairs shouldn't begin in the autumn. Archie, who was due to go off for a landowners' conference in the Borders, decided there was no reason why he should not attend it, and rather to Sonia's surprise departed, as originally planned, on the second day of Simon's visit. Whether he was using it as a ruse to see Rosie, she neither knew nor cared. Bridget set about making an inventory of such chattels as Simon thought should be owned by the new Duntan Trust together with the house itself. Archie was also to keep all the land except the garden in his own possession.

Polly and Cassie were both enchanted by Simon, Cassie flirting with him outrageously and fluttering her indecently long eyelashes, and Polly dogging his footsteps from room to room and pestering him to do things with her in a very tiresome way. Only Birdie held herself aloof, unsmiling, and did not respond to his overtures. Sonia, who was irritated in the extreme by having her eldest daughter clinging to him like a burr, was contrarily annoyed by Birdie's unfriendliness and was sharp with her for being rude.

'Don't be cross with her, Sonia,' said Simon quietly when they were alone together in her studio. 'That little girl of yours has a sixth sense, and she can no more help how she feels about us than we can help what we feel for each other. You should respect her independence of mind. It must come hard.'

Sonia, who was only too aware of Birdie's sixth sense, felt rather abashed and that, yet again, she had handled her badly. Nevertheless, she teased Simon: 'Are you suffering from scruples then?'

'Oh, scruples. Well, I once had a very bad attack of them when I was young, but I've been building up my immunity ever since. Come here and I'll inoculate you against them,' and he took her in his arms and kissed her.

She found his criticism and advice about her painting extremely helpful. He had an unerring eye for weaknesses, and ruthlessly made her discard one or two things she had been proposing to put in the exhibition.

'Better to have less work to show people than have anything second-rate,' he said. 'These few just aren't up to your standard, Sonia. You must chuck them out.' And she knew he was right.

They spent a lot of time going round the house and garden. Nothing had been changed for years, though it was still as well kept as old Knowles, with some help with the mowing and digging, could manage. Simon was full of ideas about what they might do to the two walled gardens to make them attractive but more labour-saving.

'You'll want to keep the nearest one as your private territory,' he said one day. 'There must be somewhere you can all go when the house is open. That would work well as far as access from your end of the house is concerned. I think we should aim to keep the vinery in the far garden and have it repaired, because people don't often get a chance to see muscat grapes growing like that any more, but perhaps the peach and nectarine house should go. The trees are so very labour-intensive with all that constant tying up and daily spraying with water in case of red spider, and all the woodwork there is rotten anyway. It might be brilliant to sell really exotic pot plants from the main glass-house. We'll call in a garden expert to advise in detail. Or you might become a centre for preserving rare species.'

'Oh Simon,' said Sonia, 'you don't know how exciting this is. I feel I could burst with happiness. It's like a marvellous renaissance. It's all my dreams come true. I asked for a miracle and I seem to have got one.'

But she did not stop to ponder on the fact that her new happiness was not tied up with the actual owner of the house. Simon, however, being far more experienced and worldly-wise than she was, despite her sophisticated appearance, was becoming acutely aware of it. He also knew that what had started for him as a delicious summer interlude was rapidly turning into something far more serious. He wondered if he should talk to her about it, but couldn't bear to cloud the sunlight on her face. He made a vow that he would try and see her at Duntan as little as possible and continue their affair on his own ground. There were, after all, plenty of genuine reasons why she should have to come up to London.

That evening, after the children had had their tea, Sonia took Simon along the river path through the woods to her favourite dreaming spot. Here, where the bank had crumbled away, eroded by many years of rushing water when the river was in spate, the roots of an enormous old beech tree jutted out over the river like a gigantic wooden hammock. It made a marvellously comfortable place to sit, stuck out above the water. Behind them a steep bank rose a hundred feet or more to where the upper walk, which was still kept bramble-free, wound through more beeches at the top. But the bottom path was wild and overgrown and this was a secret place. It was not one she shared even with her children.

'There are cowslips growing all up the bank in early May,' said Sonia. 'The best smell in the world. Wonderful bluebells too, but it's the cowslips that are special for me. I wish they were still out for you.'

They sat in companionable silence, watching the changing patterns on the river. Occasionally a trout rose below them with a lazy plop, whilst swallows skimmed daringly low over the river, gorging themselves on a hatch of flies.

'Listen!' Sonia suddenly clutched Simon's hand and held her

breath as they heard an urgent high piping sound, fractionally before two kingfishers flashed past them up-river like a pair of electric-blue darts.

'Oh Simon,' she said. 'That's why I brought you here. They're my special talismans. I don't see them very often, but when I do it marks an illuminated day. I did so want to see one when I was with you – and there were two. She flung her arms around him and kissed him with a passion that surprised them both.

Later that night they made love. 'How funny,' said Sonia afterwards, looking at the cracks on the ceiling of the Bachelor Room, at the heavy brocade curtains that had once been red but which now looked almost brown, and at the arrangement of dark prints hanging on chains all down the walls. She sniffed the faint smell of camphor coming from mothballs that had been kept for years in the big mahogany press. 'How funny, I haven't ever particularly liked this room – it's always seemed a bit gloomy – and I've never slept in here before, but now I shall always love it. I shall never let it be redecorated. Then it will always remind of tonight. Perhaps when Tom's grandchildren live here they'll see my ghost.'

'Better put your nightdress on, then,' said Simon, winding a strand of her hair round his finger, 'or they might get rather a shock. You never seem to hear about naked ghosts.'

They lay talking together for ages.

'Simon, how well do you really know Rosamund?' she asked.

'Do you mean in the biblical sense?'

Sonia giggled.

'Well I didn't actually – but do tell me all if so. I meant, what do you know about her and the Prince? Archie and I were staggered to find her there the other night.'

'Your mother-in-law seduced me when I was a schoolboy. You might say she educated me, so perhaps you should be grateful to her – and it wasn't only me she educated, I may say. I could tell you about several others. I expect she's got her eye on Prince Haroun – she's known him for ages. Al had business dealings with him, you know. But you never know with Roz whether it's all a tease. I wasn't surprised to see her, because she'd rung me up to ask if Antonella and I would be there. Said she wanted to surprise you and Archie. She certainly succeeded, didn't she?'

'And Antonella, Simon? What about her?'

'Jealous?' he teased.

'Well, I would be. Do I need to be?'

'No,' said Simon. 'You don't need to be jealous of anyone, my darling Sonia.'

The next day Simon returned to London, and the day after that Archie came back from his conference.

'Mrs Gillespie says she may come to your exhibition,' announced Polly. 'She wanted to know if your pictures were erotic, but I said they were just frightfully boring flower paintings, so I'm afraid I may have put her off.'

Simon roared with laughter when Sonia told him this on the telephone. 'Tell Polly she's wrong,' he said.

July seemed to go in a flash. Sonia offered Martha pocket money to help with the children and the chores. Not that Martha needed money, but it made her feel responsible, and as Sonia said, 'Then I shan't hesitate to ask for help or feel I'm exploiting you.' It worked well for everyone. School holidays started, so that the house always seemed full of extra children, and friends of the family travelling between Scotland and the South suddenly remembered what a convenient halfway house Duntan was, and what a lovely place to stay in. Lady Rosamund came and went, but mostly went, and Sonia herself made several one-night trips to London. The fact that her mother seemed to be away a lot suited her wonderfully well. The final selection of paintings for the exhibition had been decided on and framed. Acceptances for the preview party were flooding in, and Marcia Forsyth was constantly popping over to 'check a few things out', indulging her passion for detail and for gathering information about Duntan. None of the arrivals and departures there went unmarked by her eagle eyes.

One day Archie said to Sonia, with some hesitation, 'I'd like to look at your pictures before the exhibition. Will you show them to me?'

Sonia was surprised. It was a long time since he'd looked at any of her work.

'Yes, of course. They're all stacked up in the studio. Come up and see.'

She was surprised again when he selected for special comment those pictures she knew to be her best.

'I have picked up a thing or two over the years, you know,' he said sardonically, correctly interpreting the expression on her face. 'But seriously, Sonia, I think these latest ones are really good. Much better than anything you've done for ages. You'll have to keep it up from now on – now that the children are growing up. I think you're going to need it.' The weight of unspoken problems hung silently between them, but neither was ready to examine them.

'Thank you, Archie,' said Sonia. 'Thank you for looking at them.' But she gave a sudden little shiver, as though a chilly wind had got up.

She had not shown him one picture, one she was working on in secret, and which was not destined for the exhibition. Simon had a birthday coming up.

The day before the preview was hectic. Archie and Sonia ferried pictures over from Duntan to Zara Bennet's gallery, which was in a converted mill on the edge of the pretty little town of Blaydale. With its cobbled hilly streets and old stone houses, Blaydale was a considerable tourist attraction in summer. There were two well-known pubs and several small antique shops of some repute, well known to discerning buyers. It was an ideal place for the exhibition, which had cleverly been timed to coincide with a local music festival. Luckily there was ample parking space, and the stream running below the mill had several seats by it, which made it an inviting spot for picnickers, and might draw in a few customers over the next two weeks. Underneath Zara's flamboyant appearance and wild mane of red hair was a very shrewd business brain.

To help with the hanging, Archie had agreed to let his estate carpenter have the day free. Also trying to help, but mostly getting in the way, the children clattered excitedly up and down the narrow wooden stairs. Since Martha and Polly both had clogs on, the noise was deafening.

Hanging pictures is a potential minefield. Archie, carrying up a last pile, found Sonia on the edge of tears and Zara, hands on ample hips, looking hot and mulish. Because they had not changed anything at Duntan, Sonia had forgotten that in their various army married quarters it had often been Archie who had been right in these matters.

'No, no,' said Archie now, not agreeing with either of them. 'It would look much better if you moved this one down a bit, put that little one next to it, and had the drawings together on the other wall as a group. They are lost when you dot them round like that.'

Peace restored, they made themselves mugs of coffee in the little kitchen that opened off the gallery.

On the evening of the party Sonia felt sick with apprehension. What if it was a flop and the critics poured scorn on her? It was like undressing in public. But for once she had no difficulty deciding what she was going to wear: it had to be the red dress she had worn for the Vanalleyns' dinner party.

A caterer was to be in charge of the food, and various friends had volunteered for other jobs. Tim and Leonie had agreed to be in charge of actual sales of paintings, whilst Marcia, in a silk dress originally made for a daughter's wedding several years before and now somewhat tighter, manned the desk at the entrance and thought that if she remained seated no one would notice the old moccasins she was wearing – so much more practical than 'silly shoes' with heels. The Colonel, who was supposed to be helping her sell postcards of Sonia's pictures, had taken his deaf-aid out in self-defence at being in such close proximity to his wife. This was a pity because it meant that

Marcia's asides to him had to be delivered at the full pitch of her very efficient lungs.

'Can't imagine who'll want to buy any of those, dear,' she bellowed confidentially. 'I do think some of Sonia's pictures are getting awfully peculiar.'

Polly and Tom were in charge of handing out catalogues. Cassie, who after much discussion had been allowed to stay up, partly to allow Minnie to come to the party, but also because no one felt strong enough to face the scene she would make if she were left at home, threatened to steal the show. 'Are you going to buy one of my Mummy's pictures?' she asked everyone, to Sonia's acute embarrassment, and then sucked her thumb and gazed at the floor with a totally bogus display of shyness that several people who didn't know her found quite entrancing, but which made Polly and Tom feel absolutely sick.

'Yuk. Yuk. Yuk,' hissed Polly at her smallest sister, who put out her tongue and shot her a self-satisfied look that made Polly want to scream. Birdie remained glued to Archie's side, her hand firmly tucked in his, and as always when she was with her father, looked her very best and happiest.

Zara had organised the publicity brilliantly and as well as being interviewed for Yorkshire Television, Sonia had to pose for photographs for various newspapers and magazines before the guests arrived. Some wanted her pictured alone standing against a particular painting, whilst others wanted her surrounded by her family, which the girls adored, but it caused Tom to look his most boot-faced. Lady Rosamund was in her element, giving little off-the-cuff interviews and then begging not to have her carefully thought-out utterances quoted.

'Of course I am the one who has always tried to encourage her gift,' Sonia heard her say to a journalist. 'Without me I don't think she would ever have kept up with her painting at all, but then I have always had an eye for talent.'

'Specially in trousers,' muttered Martha to Sonia.

To start with the room seemed horribly empty, though at least it was possible to see the pictures, which was, after all, the object of the operation. Soon, however, it was so crammed that it was impossible to stand far enough away to have a proper look.

'Oh dear. This is a disaster. We've asked far too many people,' said Sonia to Zara in a panic.

Zara shook her Medusa locks emphatically. 'Not at all. Anyone who is seriously interested will come back another day anyway. This is marvellous. And just look at how many little red stickers there are already.'

Over the top of the crush of people, Sonia suddenly saw the face she had been looking for. Simon was so tall that his head stuck out above the crowd. He had brought a party of friends to stay at Ralton, including the owner of a very prestigious gallery in Bruton Street that specialised in discovering new artists.

'Oh Sybil, how very sweet of you to come,' Sonia said to Lady Vanalleyn, genuinely touched to see her. 'I know how busy you are and it's a long drive for you.'

'I would have come anyway for you, dear Sonia, but I don't think Simon would have let me miss it for a moment. He thinks so highly of your work. He'd make a very good Chief Whip! Dukie sends his apologies, but he couldn't leave London. How pleased you and Archie must be with this turnout. I must go and congratulate him too. I know your success means so much to him. It's so lovely to have you both back up in Yorkshire. It's such a shame Ellie-May is still in the States and couldn't come with Simon. I'm longing to get you two together.' Sybil Vanalleyn was the least bitchy of women, but Sonia was well aware that she was being given a carefully coded message.

When the evening was over, Sonia and Archie took Zara and various friends and helpers back with them to Duntan, where Sonia had arranged for the caterers to lay on a cold supper. Everyone was very lit up. The preview was pronounced a wonderful success, but Sonia felt curiously flat and very tired, and though she could hear herself talking and laughing, she felt as if she was operating on automatic pilot. She had asked Simon to come back for dinner, but he had refused. 'I don't think that would be right somehow,' he had said. 'We'll celebrate together in London later.' Now she was very conscious that the one person with whom she longed to be was missing.

The next day there were several articles about the preview in the papers. Some were purely social, of the 'Sonia Grey, the beautiful and talented young wife of Sir Archibald Duntan, whose family have lived at Duntan Hall for two hundred years' variety, but there were one or two serious reviews, which on the whole were more complimentary than Sonia had dared to hope. There were also several congratulatory bouquets of flowers, and the van from the little florist in Winterbridge was kept busy. The children, who were riding their bicycles in front of the house, were most impressed. One box arrived by special delivery from London and was filled entirely with gardenias. The smell was fantastic.

'Who are those from?' asked Polly, looking at her mother with new respect. She was sure no one had ever sent Mrs Gillespie a whole box of gardenias.

'I expect they're from Daddy,' said Birdie.

'Don't be soppy, Birdie.' Polly threw her a withering look. 'Of course they're not from Daddy. What does it say, Mum?' she asked as Sonia opened the envelope and took out a card.

'Is it from Daddy?' asked Birdie.

'No,' said Sonia. 'It doesn't say who they're from, but they're not from Daddy.' The card simply read 'To my Lady-in-Red'.

Birdie burst into tears.

'I wanted them to be from Daddy,' she wailed, flinging herself on Minnie, who had come out to gather them in for lunch, and burying her face in Minnie's flowered overall. Minnie sniffed and led her away to the house, her whole walk expressive of extreme disapproval.

Chapter 22

Sonia had promised Zara that for the first few days of the exhibition she would try to spend a few hours at the gallery each day. It wasn't difficult because the girls were only too happy to come with her, and Tom, who would have been very bored, was able to go round the farm or up to the moor with Archie, which he greatly preferred anyway. Meanwhile, Simon's gallery-owning friend had suggested she should take her portfolio down to London one day in the autumn and discuss her work with him.

'You needn't think it's just because of me,' Simon reassured her on the telephone. 'I may have got him to come to the preview, but he would never take it further if he didn't think you had talent. I don't think you really know what you could do if you put your mind to it. But you must sharpen up your act, my beautiful one. Be a bit more dedicated. If you want to succeed, you've got to go for it. Only you can decide where your priorities lie.' The trouble was, she didn't know herself.

It seemed as if everything she could possibly want had suddenly come together at once. She got a surge of pleasure every time she looked at the house and garden, and her feelings for Simon became tangled up with it. It was as though he had galloped up, a white knight on his charger, and rescued her and the house from the dragon of despair.

It had been arranged that the Prince should have his first fortnight's shooting with the Vanalleyns, and then take Cragside, Archie's moor, early in September. Archie planned to take Tom up to Scotland with him for a week's salmon fishing, and Polly had Pony Club camp, so Sonia was able to seize the chance to go down to London for a couple of nights and celebrate Simon's birthday. They had tickets for a much-acclaimed production of Verdi's *La Forza del destino* at the Coliseum. They had discovered that it was the first opera to have infected them both with the opera bug, so it seemed especially fitting that they should go to it together now; afterwards they were going to dine at the restaurant where they had first had lunch together. The forces of destiny seemed to be blowing her way.

Birdie had been extremely difficult before Sonia left. She had cried and clung and begged her mother not to go.

'Darling,' said Sonia, 'I think you're being a little bit silly. If there's anything the matter, do tell me. Don't you feel well?'

But Birdie had just shaken her head and repeated that she just didn't want Sonia to go. She could not explain the sense of dread and foreboding that gripped her; she knew only that she felt overcome by a nameless fear.

'What shall I do with her, Min?' asked Sonia rather desperately. 'Do you think it's just a clinging phase, or do you think she's sickening for something? She hasn't got a temperature.'

'I couldn't say I'm sure,' said Minnie unhelpfully. She was normally the first to reassure Sonia, but she had her own views about the state of Archie and Sonia's marriage and had no intention of making things easy for either of them.

'Well do you think I ought not to go?'

'That's not for me to say.'

'Now look, Birdie darling, I shall be back the day after tomorrow, and Daddy and Tom get back home tomorrow night. You and Cassie are going on a lovely picnic with Mrs Miller, and you've got darling Min and Martha here. You really must stop this silly fuss.'

But Birdie had just stared at her, white-faced, before walking off, a proud, desolate little figure. When Sonia had kissed her and Cassie goodbye, she had turned her face away, which was very unlike her.

Sonia felt uneasy, suddenly remembering old Lady Duntan's death and Simon's comment that Birdie appeared to have 'a sixth sense', something that she herself knew to be true, but the moment she was with Simon she forgot everything except the joy of being with him and the prospect of having two nights together. She did telephone home later that night, deliberately waiting till after the children had gone to bed because the telephone can be such a weepy instrument and she didn't want to talk to Birdie and set her off again. Minnie sounded frosty but said Birdie had been perfectly all right and they'd all had a nice time with Millicent.

The opera was magic, and Sonia wallowed in the outstanding singing and the passionate, stormy music. Dinner was sensational. Afterwards, she gave Simon his birthday present. She had painted just one open flower of a single rose called 'Scarlet Fire'. It was set in a border of twined brambles and beech leaves and at the top a pair of kingfishers skimmed over a river. On a scroll at the bottom of the picture the letters 'SS' were entwined.

'Oh Sonia,' said Simon, greatly moved. 'You've given me yourself.'

'Yes,' she said. 'I know.'

Later that night Simon told Sonia that he loved her. What had started as just another summer affair had become something very different.

'When we first met, I just wanted to sleep with you,' he said as she lay in his arms. 'But now I don't think I could bear to live without you. I love you so much it frightens me.'

They were the words Sonia longed to hear. She had not thought it possible to feel so happy, and was far too lit up to give a thought to the future and its consequences and choices. Simon, however, was all too aware of them.

When Sonia next saw Archie it was at the hospital.

She had caught an earlier train than planned because Simon, who was leaving for a week in Cornwall to stay with a client, but had to inspect a derelict folly in someone's park on the way down, had been able to drive her to King's Cross first.

Archie was not the only one who wanted to ask Sonia some personal questions. Simon had some of his own, but the moment was not right. He kissed her goodbye, very tenderly, and stood waving on the platform till the train pulled out, which was no more in character for him than Birdie's refusal of her mother's kiss had been for her. He promised to telephone her when he could.

After such a lovely time, just the two of them, Sonia had had no inclination to stay in London and see any other friends. Her one thought was to get back to her other great love – Duntan. A roofing expert was coming over to see them that afternoon. She picked up her car at the station and all the way home hummed snatches of *Forza* to herself, going over and over the last two blissful days, and in particular Simon's words of the night before – words she had never dared expect him to utter. As usual she paused after going over the cattle-grid at the top gates for the pleasure of looking down at the house before driving down the hill. She had no presentiment of trouble.

'Hi there!' she called as she went into the hall, dumping down her case in order to take the full onslaught of the shih-tzus' welcome, and to catch an ecstatic Lotus in her arms. 'Hi there! Birdie, Cassie – I'm home!' She knew it was fanciful, but the house always seemed to enfold her in loving arms when she returned. But one look at Minnie's face as she came hurrying with her crab-like walk from the inner hall turned her to stone.

Minnie came straight to Sonia and gathered her into her comfortable embrace. 'Now just keep hold on yourself,' she said, 'but it's our Birdie. She's got an appendix and they fear it may have burst. Archie's with her at the hospital. He says Joe's to drive you straight there. You're on no account to drive yourself, Archie says. There, there, my lamb,' she said, all frost melted, rocking Sonia as if she was one of the children. 'Don't take on. She'll pull through. You couldn't know, we none of us did. Don't take on so.'

Archie was waiting in a little room off the main ward. He was alone.

'Where is she?' asked Sonia, her voice barely audible.

'They've taken her down to the theatre,' said Archie. 'Things don't look too good. May be some time.' He looked awful.

'I must go to her. I must be with her when they give her the anaesthetic. She'll be terrified.' Sonia would have run into the corridor, but Archie held her back.

'I wanted to go with her too. They wouldn't let me. They had to move very fast, said I'd be in the way, and that anyway, she was too ill to know what was going on by the time I got here. She had a roaring temperature. I felt useless, totally useless.'

'Have we got the best man to operate?'

'There was no time for a choice, Dr Childs says he's very good, and has gone down to be present himself. Good of him, but it didn't seem a very encouraging sign somehow. They say we must just wait. They'll keep us informed. They're doing all they can for her. Thank God you're here.'

'How did it happen? Tell me about it.'

'Well, Tom and I got back from the Dee late last night. Min seemed fussed about Bird. Said she'd been all right after you'd gone and when they'd been out with the Millers, and that she'd had a good night, but yesterday she was a bit off it apparently, and went to bed last night complaining of tummy pains. Minnie thought it was her usual trouble because apparently Birdie'd been very upset when you left, and, well, we were both away, and things haven't been very good between us.' Archie looked miserable. 'So she thought that was certainly the cause. I went straight up, but she was asleep, though she seemed a bit restless. Then, about five o'clock this morning, Minnie came for me. It was pretty obvious by then that she was really ill, in awful pain and with a fever, suddenly quite different from her sick attacks. Even I could see that. She kept asking . . .' Archie paused.

'I know,' said Sonia, 'you don't need to tell me. She kept asking for me.'

Archie gave her a sympathetic look but nodded.

'Yes. Well. Anyway, I rang for old Doc Childs. He was very good. Came at once. Didn't like the look of her at all, said we must have a surgeon at once. I rang Radnor Walk but there was only the answering machine on. Did you get the message?'

'No,' whispered Sonia, her face in her hands. 'No. I wasn't there.'

The door opened and a nurse came in. 'We've had a message from Mr Bristow,' she said. 'He thought you ought to know. I'm afraid they will be rather longer than expected. Things aren't proving quite straightforward. Mr Bristow's a wonderful surgeon, though.' Sonia did not feel reassured by the sympathetic glance she gave them.

'I'll send someone in with a cup of tea for you both.'

They settled down to wait.

The ward was in a new wing of the hospital, and the room was painted a lurid mixture of lime green and yellow, doubtless with the laudable intention of brightening everything up. Neither Sonia nor Archie noticed it. They could hear the everyday noises of the ward outside, the clinking of trays, the sounds of busy footsteps and people laughing. It all seemed quite unreal. The sound of laughter in a world where Birdie might die was a mockery.

There was a clock on the wall. It seemed an eternity before the second hand made a full circle. Sonia wondered how long a minute would seem to a prisoner facing a firing squad. Every now and then Archie got up and paced restlessly. At the window was a blind with a plastic knob on the end of its cord. Archie started to knock it against the glass, aiming for a bird's mess on the window's edge. He hit the target about three times out of four. Hit. Hit. Hit. Miss. Normally the noise would have driven Sonia crazy, but now she was quite oblivious to it.

There was a commotion in the passage outside. The doors opened and a bed was wheeled in. Various bottles hung from a stand and were attached to the bed's small occupant. The sheets and pillows looked very clean and white. Birdie looked whiter. She seemed to be surrounded by nurses.

Two green-coated figures came in wearing caps and masks; one was just recognisable as Dr Childs. The other came over to Archie and Sonia.

'Well we've done our best. I'm afraid it's peritonitis and the next forty-eight hours will be critical, but I think she'll do. I've washed out as much poison as I can and we've put a drain in. With antibiotics, it's not the danger it once was. Children can make extraordinarily quick recoveries, but she's a very sick little girl. I'll be in to see her again as soon as I've finished my list.'

Neither Archie nor Sonia could speak. The little figure on the bed seemed to belong to the professionals. They felt superfluous. Sonia groped blindly for Archie's hand. He squeezed hers so hard she thought it might break. His face looked very set, but his cheeks were wet.

Sonia spent four nights at the hospital with Birdie. Archie and Minnie came and took shifts during the day so that she could get the occasional break. To start with, Birdie just lay holding her hand, sleeping fitfully, but later she became very fretful, longing for the drink she was not allowed to have until the drip was removed and wanting the same story to be read to her over and over again. At home Cassie was furiously jealous at getting so little of the limelight and became utterly poisonous, but Polly and Tom both surprised Sonia by being wonderful.

There had been a message to say Mr Hadleigh had telephoned and was very sorry to hear about Birdie. He rang several times to enquire how she was, but got through to Archie's secretary at the office and did not ask to speak to Sonia.

On the fifth night Sonia came home, and Archie made love to her for the first time for ages with a kind of desperation and intensity that left them both exhausted. Afterwards he gave a sigh of thankfulness, turned over and slept like a log. A few months ago Sonia might have found it a thirst-quenching draught, but she had been drinking nectar lately and that is hard to match.

One day when Dr Childs looked in at the hospital and Birdie was asleep, Sonia asked him if he thought Birdie's illness was connected to her usual sick attacks, but he knew she was asking something else as well.

'Well, it's certainly not the same, no. Birdie is an ultra-sensitive child, and it's possible that later her "nervous tummies" may turn into migraines, such as you yourself have, but I don't think you'll find the old problem will just disappear.' He looked at Sonia's troubled and exhausted face. He was very fond of the whole family.

'If you're asking me whether anything you and Archie may or may not have been getting up to has actually caused Birdie's appendix to burst, then I must say no,' he said kindly. 'Stop reproaching yourself, and take off that hair shirt I see you're wearing, Sonia. But if you're asking me whether I think stress can have an affect on health and the ability to withstand illness, then the answer is yes. We are only just beginning to understand the effects the mind can have on the body. It's a fascinating subject.' He patted her on the shoulder. 'Come on, buck up,' he said. 'She's going to be all right, and you're a good mum.'

'Me and Archie,' said Sonia, not looking at the bluff old doctor, 'how did you know about us?'

Dr Childs grinned at her.

'I never discuss my patients,' he said. 'But if as a doctor you happen to have Marcia Forsyth on your list, it's very difficult not to be given an update on everything she thinks you ought to know about life in the village – and nothing passes her by. She'd have been a great spy, except that I fear she'd have got caught pretty quickly! Whenever she has a bit of information she feels impelled to impart, it always seems to coincide with some minor health problem that requires a visit to the surgery!'

On the sixth day after Birdie's operation, Mr Bristow declared himself pleased with his patient, saying that if all went well she should be home in a day or two, and Archie decided to talk to Sonia.

'Oh darling, do we have to talk now? I'm so tired.'

'Yes,' said Archie with great resolution. 'Yes, Sonia, we do. It's not going to go away.' As usual he walked to the window and started jingling in his pockets. Then he turned round.

'Rosie Bartlett,' he said. 'That's all over. Nothing to do with Bird. I finished it after the night you and Tim walked in on us. It brought me to my senses. She wanted us to chuck Roger and you and get married, but there was never a thought of that in my mind, and I know very well she'll find someone else soon. I never felt for her a fraction of what I felt – still feel – for you. I was a bloody fool, but it was like a sort of fever. She's pretty hot stuff, old Rosie, and she made me feel quite hot stuff too. It was a nice change, I can tell you.' Archie made a wry face. 'And, well, I suppose I was just fed up with always coming fourth on your list of priorities.'

'Fourth?' asked Sonia.

'Yes,' said Archie. 'Fourth and now fifth. First the children, though I can accept that, second your painting, and third the house. Increasingly the house. You made me feel like an intruder in my own home after we came here and I gave up the regiment, and I started to feel very angry with you. I know I was bloody and irritable, and a lot of it has been my fault. I know I'm a dull dog,' he went on rather desperately, 'but I do love you, Sonia. Really love you. But now we have a real problem, don't we? Now I come fifth – a long way last.'

'Meaning?' asked Sonia in a small voice, though she knew all too well.

'Meaning that unlike me and Rosie, you're really in love, aren't you? With Simon.'

She knew it was pointless to deny it.

'Yes,' she said bleakly. 'Yes, Archie darling, I'm afraid so. I just can't help it. What are we going to do?'

They were in the library. There was no fire for once – it was a lovely day – but the smell of wood was ingrained in the room, together with the mellow smell of old leather from books and chairs. Outside, a collared dove was making its persistent, repetitive call, and a robin was tuning up for autumnal sessions to come. There was the sound of the mini-tractor mowing the rough grass. Dear, familiar scents and sounds, wonderfully reassuring after the ones in the hospital. Sonia made a complicated plait out of Lotus's topknot of long hair.

'Well,' said Archie, 'we've both had a lot of time to think, sitting all those hours with Birdie. Perhaps it's easy for me because, you see, I know what I want. You've got something now that you wanted very badly too – keeping Duntan. You've got your painting, and I'm thrilled about that; I hope you keep it up. And, thank heaven, we've both got Birdie. Thank God for that. I like Simon, Sonia. He's a nice chap and I can see that for you he's everything I'm not and never can be. But I can tell you one thing. I'm not going to share you with him. So, really it's your decision. I'd never try to part you from our children, but this house is another matter. Are you going to opt for family life at Duntan – and I'm afraid I would be very much part of the package, don't make any mistake about that – or are you going to choose Simon? It's your choice, Sonia, and when you've chosen, let me know.'

And Archie walked out of the library.

When Sonia got back to the hospital, Birdie was restless and uncomfortable. Sonia sponged her face and hands and rearranged her pillows.

'You've been gone ages, Mummy,' she said. 'I've been longing and longing for you.'

The drip had at last come out, but now that she was allowed to drink she didn't really want to, and took a lot of coaxing. Sonia read her, yet again, the same interminable story she had come to dread. Eventually Birdie went to sleep. Sonia looked down at her funny, bony little face. She still looked as if a puff of wind could blow her out of the window. Sonia got out her pen and the writing paper she had brought with her, and started the letter to Simon she knew she had to write. She hoped that never again would she have to write anything that cost her so dear. On the way home she stopped the car at a pillar box and got out. She hesitated for a long moment before suddenly pushing the letter through the slit.

'A libation to the gods,' whispered Sonia. 'For Birdie.' And the tears streamed down her face so that she could hardly see to drive.

Epilogue

On a brilliantly sunny day in late October Sonia climbed up to the top of the park with the dogs. It was half-term and the children were all at home. Polly and Tom were playing tennis with Archie and Martha, who was home for the weekend from the crammer. Their shouts could be heard for miles. The great beeches surrounding the park were all shades of gold, and the fallen nuts made a crackle under her feet as she walked. Strands of cobwebs brushed against her face and the brambles were covered with silver tracery where the sun had not yet caught them. The first real frost, together with a wind the day before, had started to send the leaves fluttering down, and they covered the ground like a carpet. Down below her Birdie and Cassie were making nests of piled-up leaves, in between running wildly about trying to catch lucky wishes before November arrived to take the magic potency from the twirling leaves. Birdie's laughter was music to her ears.

The griffins on their pillars looked very smart. They had already been repaired and cleaned and wore a surprised look, like a pair of old tramps who had suddenly been given a bath by the Salvation Army.

The house lay on its platform of land like a patient on the operating table about to undergo plastic surgery to repair scar tissue. It was covered in scaffolding and the roof had great sheets of temporary weatherproofing draped over it. Sonia felt enormously proud of how the work was progressing, proud, too, of the wonderful efforts everyone was making to try to keep the atmosphere right. Bridget was a tower of strength. Sonia had become quite fond of her. Wherever possible fabrics were being repaired rather than renewed, but she had to admit that doing up the drawing room, where the curtains were quite beyond reclaim, was the most enormous fun. Samples of material and wallpaper were stuck all over the place. The aim was to get the house ready for opening to the public by the following Easter.

She was busy painting too. Simon's gallery-owning friend had not only looked at her portfolio, but had promised her a London exhibition the following year.

She settled herself on a fallen tree stump, the devoted Lotus curled up against her. It was a year since old Lady Duntan had died. A year of growth and change, the realising of some ambitions, and no small amount of heartbreak. Sonia fished in the pocket of her jeans for a letter. It was very dog-eared, and the ink had become smudged in places. She let herself read it only occasionally, but today, the anniversary of the old lady's death, she thought she had earned it.

Darling Sonia, she read, *Thank God Birdie is all right. Don't think I don't understand. You have made the only choice possible for you. I told you once that I vowed never to let anyone get close enough to hurt me again. I don't need to tell you how badly I am hurting now because I think you know, and I believe you feel the same. What I do want to tell you is that for me, no matter how great the anguish of losing you, it has been –* is *– worth it. There is always a price for everything, but for the magic we had together for so short a time (and which no one can ever take away from us)* nothing *would be too high a price. I only wish you didn't have to bear the pain too, but I want you to know that I would choose the same again.*

Perhaps our immunity to 'The Scruples' was not as strong as we thought after all! We are both lucky to have the partners we have to go back to, and somehow life will go on. Please, never lose your gift of laughter.

If I have been able to help make it possible for you to keep your other great love, that wonderful house that means so much to you, then that is my comfort. We shan't be able to avoid seeing each other occasionally, but I am suggesting that Bridget should take my place on the Duntan Trust. She is very clever, and can always consult me.

Thank you for everything, my beautiful, lovable Lady-in-Red. I have your picture – you *– hanging on my wall and I think of you day and night. I do not think you will change your mind, nor would I try to persuade you to do so, but it goes without saying that if you ever did – then I would be waiting. I shall always love you.*

Simon.

Sonia looked down at her beloved house. 'A price for everything,' she said aloud, and the wind that took her words and blew them away like the autumn leaves brought her the sound of the big bell. Once it had rung to summon the head gardener in to see the cook. Now Minnie used it in an effort to gather everyone together for meals. Sonia got up from her log, carefully placed the precious letter back in her pocket, and walked quickly back down across the park to join her family for lunch.